Best Corpse
for the Job

Charlie Cochrane

RIPTIDE
PUBLISHING

Riptide Publishing
PO Box 6652
Hillsborough, NJ 08844
www.riptidepublishing.com

The Best Corpse for the Job

Cover Art by L.C. Chase, lcchase.com/design.htm
Editor: Danielle Poiesz
Layout: L.C. Chase, lcchase.com/design.htm

ISBN: 978-1-62649-192-2

First edition
November, 2014

Also available in ebook:
ISBN: 978-1-62649-157-1

The Best Corpse for the Job

Charlie Cochrane

RIPTIDE
PUBLISHING

To all the school governors who never realise they're giving me plot bunnies.

Table
of Contents

Chapter 1 1

Chapter 2 15

Chapter 3 27

Chapter 4 35

Chapter 5 39

Chapter 6 47

Chapter 7 55

Chapter 8 59

Chapter 9 65

Chapter 10 73

Chapter 11 83

Chapter 12 93

Chapter 13 97

Chapter 14 109

Chapter 15 119

Chapter 16 139

Chapter 17 145

Chapter 18 167

Chapter 19 179

Chapter 20 185

Chapter 21 201

Chapter 22 213

Chapter 23 219

Chapter 24 239

Chapter One

Adam Matthews stifled a yawn, shifted in his seat, and wished he were anywhere else but here.

Outside, the sun was shining. A beautiful late-spring Thursday morning in a beautiful English village. Two blackbirds were having a standoff on a grassy bank dotted with daisies; the world looked bright, exciting, and full of hope. The only sign of schoolchildren was the sound of purposeful activity. Lindenshaw St. Crispin's School was putting on its handsomest face, as if it knew it had to sell itself to the visiting candidates as much as they had to sell themselves to the board of governors. Maybe that handsome face would distract them from learning just how much of a bloody mess the school was and how badly it needed a new headteacher to turn it round.

Simon Ford, one of the applicants for the headteacher post, was droning his way through his presentation on "what makes an outstanding school," sending volleys of jargon and acronyms flying through the air to assault his listeners' ears. The droning was so bad that Adam's head began to nod. Which, in the greater scheme of things, was the least of his worries.

He was one of the poor sods trying to work out whether Ford was right for the job.

Two days of activities, interviews, picking apart everything the candidates said, and this was only bloody day one. He'd been given a particularly important role, or so Victor Reed, the chair of governors, had said. They needed an educational perspective, and Adam's invaluable feedback from the candidates' presentations and his marking of their data-handling exercises would help the rest of the governors—as laypeople—form an opinion. Yet, all Adam could feed back at the moment was the feeling of being bored to death. He knew he should have brought his buzzword bingo sheet.

"Adam? What's your view on that point?"

Oh hell. Victor was talking to him, and he had no idea what it was about. "I'm sorry," Adam busked it, trying to look like he'd been deep in meaningful thought. "I was thinking about the point Mr. Ford made about children in care. Could you repeat the question?"

"Mr. Ford was saying that the key to any school's success is the enthusiasm for learning it produces in its pupils."

"Were I to be headteacher of Lindenshaw St. Crispin's," Ford began again, before Adam could add his twopenn'orth, "I would make it my priority to engender that lifelong love of learning in all the children here."

Bugger. That would have given me full house on my buzzword bingo card.

Still, Ford had hit at the crux of the matter because the previous headteacher had done bugger all to make anybody want to do anything at the school, least of all the teachers to produce good, or even outstanding, lessons. As was typical of too many nice little schools in leafy English villages, St. Crispin's had relied on its reputation for too long. The best thing the previous headteacher had done for the school was leaving it, although the reasons for that lay under a cloud of rumour and secrecy. Why was it proving so hard getting somebody to step into her shoes? They'd tried the previous term and failed.

Adam sneaked a look at the clock. Ten past twelve—not much more torture to endure today. He caught the eye of one of the parent governors, who gave him a wink. Christine Probert was keen, committed, and pretty as a peach. The hemline of the skirt resting at her knees hadn't stopped the blokes present from eyeing up her legs.

"Do we have any questions?" Victor asked, surveying the governors with an expression that seemed to demand they didn't.

"Mr. Ford, what is your view on—" Oliver Narraway, community governor and the bane of much of the community's life, nipped in but not quick enough.

"Simon, I'm a parent governor, so you'll appreciate why I ask this question." Christine had been hotter off the mark than Usain Bolt. "You mentioned parental involvement as being key to children's success. How have you engaged them in your existing role?"

Well done, Christine. Tie down the loose cannon.

Ford beamed. "That's a challenge for every school these days, Mrs. Probert. At Newby Grange Primary . . ." He was off again, leaving Oliver looking furious at having been knocked off his "modern education is rubbish" hobbyhorse and Victor breathing a huge sigh of relief at that fact. Oliver's hit list didn't stop at modern education; it included modern hymns and women in positions of power—apart from Mrs. Thatcher, whom he regarded as a saint. And gay men. Or, as Oliver put it, raving poofs.

Surely they'd break for lunch soon? Adam felt guilty for not being more enthusiastic, but he wouldn't give any of the candidates houseroom on their showings so far. Three years he'd been teaching here, and despite all its failings, despite the lack of leadership and the dinosaurs on the governing body who couldn't be trusted to choose new curtains let alone a new headteacher, he loved the place.

He looked sideways at Oliver, watching him slowly seethe at what Ford was saying. *What would he do if he saw me coming out of that bar in Stanebridge? Bosie's wouldn't be his sort of place.* All right, nobody could sack him for being gay, thank God and employment law, but he wouldn't put it past any of them to make his life intolerable. Subtly, of course. Just like the previous headteacher, had done. Maybe that's why she'd been eased out, or at least one of the reasons, before the wrath of the school inspectors came down like a ton of bricks and even more cow manure hit the fan.

A knock on the door, followed by the appearance round it of Jennifer Shepherd, the school secretary, cut short all talk.

"Sorry to interrupt. The wire's worked loose on the front door release again, and the thing won't open properly."

"I'll sort it." Adam was out of his chair before anyone could stop him. *Freedom ahoy!* Thank goodness the caretaker only worked early mornings and evenings so Adam was the appointed handyman the rest of the time. "Sorry everyone. Class A emergency."

"That's fine," Victor said, sending him on his way with a wave. "Our security system is vitally important," he added, addressing Ford. Vitally important and almost impenetrable. Unless someone was a staff member, and as such, granted knowledge of the entry code for the keypad. Somebody, like Ford himself, couldn't usually get into the school except through the main door. He'd need to buzz the intercom and persuade Jennifer to press the little switch to let him in, after which he'd come into view of her desk, through the hatchway window. Ultimate power for Jennifer, except when the wire had worked loose, then nobody without the code could get in that way short of bulldozing the door down.

Adam followed Jennifer down the corridor.

"Sorry to pull you out," she said. "I didn't have anywhere else to turn."

"I'll give it my best shot," Adam said, stepping into the office and realising that freedom was still a pipe dream. Ian Youngs, another candidate for the headship, was flicking through a book of school photographs. This was part of his free time, intended to let the candidates have a chance to go round the school and get to know it better. Adam could think of better things to do with the time, like talking to the children, rather than lurking in the office.

"Got that screwdriver, Jennifer?"

Jennifer handed over a little box of tools. "I'll leave you to it." She turned her attention to the other invader of her territory. "Are you enjoying those? That's from when St. Crispin's won the local mathematics challenge in 1995."

"Really?" Youngs didn't sound impressed.

"Yes. We used to be one of the top schools in the county."

Adam felt Jennifer bridling, even though he was under the desk, wrestling a handful of wires.

"You seemed to win lots of awards in the 1990s, Mrs. Shepherd," Youngs continued, sounding like he was trying to redeem himself. Adam wanted to warn him not to smile, as that would ruin the effect. He'd weighed the bloke up as soon as he'd seen him, and while Youngs wasn't exactly bad looking, when he opened his mouth, he revealed a set of crooked teeth. Not the most attractive smile, especially in combination with his slightly protruding ears.

"We did." Jennifer didn't sound any happier. She cleared her throat and changed the subject. "Will they be out soon, Adam?"

"Should be." Adam emerged, brushing fluff from his trousers. "All sorted, I think."

Jennifer pressed the button, heard the release catch open, then smiled. "You're so clever. What would I do without you?"

"Have a peaceful life?" Adam winked at Youngs, who just scowled in return.

"It's a shame they can't just change the timetable around and see you straight after lunch, Mr. Youngs, now that we're down to two candidates instead of three. It means you having to kick your heels for ages," Jennifer said. "But our Mr. Narraway insisted we had to keep to what we'd planned, breaks and all."

"It's to do with the timing of assembly," Adam explained. "The vicar has to watch Simon Ford lead an act of worship, like he watched you earlier, before he sits in on your presentation. And we all need a bit of lunch before any of that." Adam kept his eye on Youngs, who was slipping a piece of paper—on which Adam had seen him jot something down—into his pocket.

"I don't mind." Youngs smiled, crooked teeth and all. "It'll be nice to go stretch my legs for a while. This morning's been hard work, what with taking assembly and getting the third degree from the pupil panel."

Jennifer smiled at the mention of the pupils. "You should take a wander around the village while you're at it, Mr. Youngs. You can't say many places have kept their charm and not changed too much over the years, but it's certainly true of Lindenshaw."

Adam choked back a laugh. Parts of Lindenshaw had barely reached the twentieth century, let alone the twenty-first.

"I've got that impression already. I'll see you at about half past one, Mrs. Shepherd." Youngs turned towards the door.

"Good. That'll give you plenty of time to set up your presentation. They're strict about punctuality."

"I'll remember that." Youngs stopped at the office door, and Adam thought he heard the man mutter, "I bet they like being strict about all sorts of things." Youngs pushed against the front door, annoyed that it wouldn't budge, as the rest of the governors came out of the classroom and into the hallway.

"You'll need to use the exit button," Christine piped up, smiling at Youngs.

"Thank you!" he replied, beaming. Every male candidate puffed his chest out when Christine was around, like a gamecock trying to impress a hen.

"It's like bloody Alcatraz getting in and out of here," Oliver said.

Adam gave him a sharp glance; Oliver was watching Youngs with more than a passing interest, as were the vicar and Marjorie Bookham—the only other woman on the governing body—as if there was something about the man that they were trying to fathom out. A hand on Adam's shoulder ushered him along the corridor, and the others following in his wake. The Reverend Neil Musgrave was steering his flock as usual, this time in the direction of the staffroom, where lunch would be waiting.

"The more I see that man, the more I think I might have met him somewhere before," Neil said. "What about you, Marjorie? Does he ring any bells?"

Marjorie bridled. "Of course he doesn't. If I knew him from somewhere, then I'd have already declared it or else I might not be allowed to stay on the selection panel." She stopped, waiting for Victor to catch the others up. "I'm right, aren't I, Victor?"

"Sorry, Marjorie, I missed that." The chair of governors looked preoccupied, his normally neat appearance slightly awry and an untidy pile of papers under his arm.

"I said that if the vicar crossed swords with Ian Youngs in the past, then he should declare it."

"What's all this? Can't have any conflict of interest, Neil," Victor said.

Neil shook his head. "I didn't say that I *knew* him. Marjorie's being mischievous. I just said I had a feeling I'd met him at some point in the past, but even if I have, it's probably something entirely innocuous. I run across an awful lot of people in the diocese, one way or another."

Victor, who had a certain bovine quality, scowled. "Please be careful, Marjorie, even if you're just making a joke. Remember all the trouble we had last time we tried to recruit."

Seconds out, round one?

"I don't think *I'm* responsible for that debacle." Marjorie turned on her heels and headed for the ladies' toilet, sashaying stylishly as she went. Marjorie was a good-looking woman for her age—*early fifties, maybe?*—and was always immaculately dressed in clothes that reeked of class and couldn't have been found even in the poshest of the Stanebridge shops.

Neil watched her go, shrugged theatrically, then led the way to the staffroom and lunch.

Adam flopped into his favourite chair, grabbed a sandwich, and dealt with priority number one. Cheese and pickle would stop the rumbling in his stomach from becoming too audible.

"They both seem to be very nice. Mr. Ford and Mr. Youngs," Christine said.

"Nice?" Oliver snorted from across the room. "I'm not sure nice is what we're looking for in a headmaster."

"Admiral Narraway's looking for a hanging and flogging captain," Neil said under his breath.

Victor grimaced. "We shouldn't make any judgements this early in the process. And it's 'headteacher,' not 'headmaster,' remember? Gender neutral."

"We can decide if we want to send them home." Oliver, ignoring the gender bit, pointed his sandwich crust at Victor as though it were a gun.

"Like we sent them home when we tried last term? Not one of them made it through to the second day and the interviews proper." He fished the tea bag from his mug, flinging it into the bin like a bullet.

"That's because they were all rubbish," Oliver continued, aiming his crust gun at Neil this time. "And I can tell you exactly why. It was because—"

"Sorry, chaps and chapesses. May I remind everyone present about confidentiality?" Victor wagged his finger. "I'm sorry, but what happens in the interview room stays in the interview room. Leave it at the fact that none of them were good enough."

Marjorie, who had returned and was now hovering by the watercooler, nodded. "It's such a shame Lizzie Duncan was taken ill and couldn't be here. Getting a woman's answer to some of the questions would have been enlightening. And yes, I know the last woman wasn't much use, but don't tar all of my sex with the same brush."

"We couldn't have put the process off again, Marjorie," Victor said, tetchily.

"We'll just have to hope these two chaps don't make a mess of things like the last lot did," Oliver said, unable to point his crust gun at anyone as he'd eaten it.

Adam wasn't interested in hearing more if they weren't going to dish the dirt on the last round of recruitment and looked up at the clock. "Blimey, is that the time? I've got a phone call to make."

"Making a date for the weekend?" Christine smiled knowingly.

"Nothing so glamorous. Finding out how Mother's cat got on at the vet. Said I'd ring before one o'clock. Twenty minutes before I get cut out of the will."

Marjorie picked up her handbag. "I think there's time for me to nip home and put my washing out. Shame to waste a good drying day."

"Just make sure you're back in time." Victor kept looking at his phone. "Ian Youngs is giving his presentation at one fifty-five."

Marjorie headed out of the room as Oliver got to his feet. "I'm going to find somewhere to have a cigar. Don't worry, I'll make sure I'm far enough away from the school not to pollute the air the little ones are going to breathe." He slammed the door behind him.

Neil, hovering over his seventh sandwich, shook his head. "He's always been a bit of a loose cannon, and I fear he's getting looser by the day."

"Then tie him down," Jeremy Tunstall said, looking up from the huge pile of papers he'd been flicking through. Lead Learning Partners, or whatever it was they were calling the people from the county education department this week, seemed to go through a lot of trees. "You don't want a repeat of the mess you got into when you tried to recruit before. Now, I've got calls to make, assuming I can get a bloody signal. I'll be back about half past one."

Adam watched him go. "I should have told him about the ladies' loo. You're supposed to be able to get a signal in there."

"How do you know?" Neil asked, grinning.

"Jennifer told us, of course." Adam eased out of his chair. If he went out into the lane by the school field and faced south, he could generally get a decent fix on the network. Maybe it would be easier just to see Jennifer and ask to use the landline?

He was halfway through the office door when Jennifer's voice—in conversation with Marjorie about sandwiches or some such nonsense—stopped him. He didn't want to be nabbed by these two formidable females, who, for all their superficial spikiness with each other, had always been thick as thieves.

"Neither Simon nor Ian joined us for lunch, even though there was an open invitation. Are they in the candidates' hidey-hole?"

"Hidey-hole? Oh, you mean the children's kitchen? Not as far as I know." Jennifer waved her hand airily.

Marjorie sniffed. "Good. We were hoping they might spend their spare time looking around the school and talking to the children rather than hiding away."

"Oh, that nice Mr. Ford was certainly keen to do that. Last time I saw him, he was being led off by a group of children to eat his sandwiches with them on the field." Jennifer smiled; it was clear which candidate she had her eye on. "It's such a lovely day, we let the children have a bit of a picnic out there. Much healthier."

"I wish I'd joined them. I feel the need of some fresh air, especially having been cooped up with Oliver most of the morning." Marjorie eased past Adam, who was still hovering in the doorway, leaving a trail of good-quality perfume behind her.

"Maybe you could rescue Mr. Ford if he's still out there," Jennifer shouted after her. "I wouldn't put it past some of the year-six children to have tied him to a tree by now, pretending he's a human sacrifice."

The ringing of the bell signalled the end of the children's lunchtime but not quite the end of Adam's phone call. They'd established that the cat was fine and the vet hadn't charged an arm and a leg, and were just getting onto the "when are you next coming to dinner?" bit.

"Let me get through these next few days, and I'll organise something. Bell's going. Got to go. Love you."

The vicar was coming up the field, weaving his way between children as they dawdled over getting into line. He looked distracted.

"Penny for your thoughts?" Adam asked as Neil approached.

"Eh?" He took a deep breath. "Oh, they're not even worth a farthing. Come on, better not be late or Victor will have my guts for garters."

"I think you've got the short straw. Watching Ford lead assembly and then back in to listen to another presentation."

"Collective worship, not assembly. The bishop insists on the right name as we're a church school." Neil winked. "Only the second collective worship of the day. I'll survive." Neil steered them towards the side of the school. "I'll take the shortcut and see if anyone will let me into the hall direct."

"I'll sign you in, then, or Jennifer will have your guts for garters too."

"Don't bother. I forgot to sign out."

Adam wished he were going with the man. Watching assembly had to be better than going through Ian Youngs's data analysis—another one of the many hoops they'd made the candidates jump through. He'd take the file into Jennifer's office and plonk himself at the spare desk, which was about the only bit of free space available today, then plug in his iPod so the background noise wouldn't disturb his concentration.

He was a third of the way through the task when a quiet passage in his music coincided with a harsh buzz from the front door intercom.

"Who is it?" Jennifer spoke into a little grey box, out of which a tinny version of Marjorie's voice emerged in answer. She flicked a switch under her desk. "It's open, come in."

Marjorie soon appeared at the hatch. "Does someone eat all of the pens here?"

Jennifer looked up. "What? Oh, sorry, Marjorie, I've been fighting with the computer all lunchtime. It's got a mind of its own. Here you are." She eased herself out of her chair and passed a Biro through the hatchway.

"I'm not late, am I? Oliver would tear me off a strip if I was." Marjorie didn't seem overly concerned about the fact.

"More likely give you six from the cane." Jennifer appeared pleased with herself for making a slightly saucy joke, even though Marjorie didn't seem at all amused. "No, you're fine."

Adam gave up trying to sort out the data. "The presentation's not due to start until one fifty-five, so you've even got the chance to grab a cup of tea."

"Anyway, Mr. Youngs went for a bit of fresh air earlier on and isn't back yet, so he'll be the one getting the wigging." Jennifer shook her head.

Marjorie sniffed. "How was the cat, Adam?"

"Cat? Oh, yes, fine, thank you."

"Adam had to ring his mother about her cat," Marjorie explained, showing no sign of going to get some tea, or even of going anywhere.

"Are you sure he wasn't ringing his girlfriend?" Jennifer said, archly.

Oh, joy.

"If I was, I wouldn't tell *you*. You'd be working out how to get in touch with her and snitch about all my bad habits." Adam cringed. Why did he always feel as if he had to hide? Why couldn't he bring a partner to the summer social without risking somebody like Oliver having palpitations? Might help to have a partner to bring, of course.

"I can't believe you have *any* bad habits, Adam." Marjorie smiled.

Better ask the ex about that, Marjorie. He'd make your eyes stand out like organ stops.

"It's nearly ten to two. I'll give Mr. Youngs another couple of minutes, and then I'll ring his mobile." Jennifer was back at her desk, scowling at the computer, which seemed to be misbehaving still.

"If he's got his phone turned on. We do ask candidates to switch them off during the activities." Marjorie sniffed again. "I think I *will* get myself a cup of tea. It's been a bit more hectic today than I thought it would be."

"You shouldn't have rushed home; you should have put your feet up," Jennifer said, still making faces at the screen. "Your husband could have put the washing out, couldn't he?"

"Could he? That would be an unexpected case of taking initiative." Marjorie turned on her heel and headed for the staffroom.

"She leads a dog's life." Jennifer kept her voice low, even though Marjorie had gone around the corner. "When you get wed, don't you expect your wife to wait on you hand and foot."

"I promise I won't," Adam replied. That was a cast-iron guarantee.

Back again. Same classroom, same panel, same anticipation of death by PowerPoint.

Same Oliver, glancing at the clock and looking like he was about to explode.

"I say we should just scratch Youngs's presentation and count it as a definitive black mark against him." Oliver clenched and unclenched his hands. "We don't want a headmaster who can't keep his appointments."

Christine, inevitably, was the voice of reason. "We should give him another few minutes. Maybe he got lost."

"Got lost?" Oliver glowered. "Then he shouldn't have been wandering around, should he? What's that chappie Ford doing now?"

"It's all on the timetable, of which you have a copy, although I don't suppose you've bothered with it." Victor rummaged in his inside pocket, producing a folded sheet of A4 paper. "He's into his second session of free time. You've just been watching him lead an assembly, haven't you, Neil?"

Neil rubbed his hands together. "Yes. And very good it was. The children loved singing 'Our God is a great—'"

"This is ridiculous." Tunstall got up, prowled over to the window, and peered out. "Can't see him."

Marjorie turned in her seat to address Adam. "He *did* go out for a walk?"

"Yes. He made his escape just when I'd finished sorting that buzzer out."

Tunstall shook his head. "I was hoping he'd show a bit more gumption. Simon Ford certainly seems to be on the children's wavelength."

Adam waited for the inevitable comment from Oliver. It came.

"Do we want someone on their wavelength? When I was young, I was scared stiff of my teachers, and when I was a headmaster, the children would never have wanted to play skipping with me. Fear and respect—that's what's lacking these days."

Oliversaurus archaicus.

Tunstall swivelled in his chair. "We want someone who can take the school into the twenty-first century. You seem to want to drag it back to the nineteenth."

Oliver stood up. "Now, you just—"

Any likelihood of fisticuffs was put on hold by a knock on the door. Shame. Adam had been looking forward to Tunstall versus Narraway, heavyweight knockout.

"Come in!" Victor said.

Jennifer stuck her head around the door. "I've tried ringing Mr. Youngs, but he's not picking up his mobile. Do you think he's all right?"

"Good lord, you don't think he's had an accident or something, do you?" Christine grabbed Adam's arm.

"What on earth makes you think that, Christine?" Victor asked. "Would you try ringing again, please, Jennifer? If there is some genuine problem, we should allow him a bit of leeway."

Tunstall forestalled any dissent. "Ian Youngs is a good candidate, and you can't afford to turn your noses up at him if he's been delayed by something out of his control."

The increasingly awkward silence just continued. Apart from a faint noise . . .

"Is it me, or does that sound like a mobile phone?" Adam jerked his thumb towards the wall dividing the classroom from the children's kitchen, where space had been set aside for the candidates to take refuge.

Victor leaped out of his chair. "I bet Youngs got the timetable buggered up—sorry, vicar—and he's sitting there waiting."

"Or he's gone off and left his phone, and that's why Jennifer can't get him to answer. Although, how he's got signal when most of us struggle . . ." Marjorie stared out of the window, as though she was trying to spot him.

Victor rose and headed for the door, raising his voice as he went out. "Don't bother trying to ring Youngs, Mrs. Shepherd. He's left his phone in the kitchen. We can hear the bloody thing ringing, and I'm going to go and find out what's going on."

"Language, Victor. There are children around, you know," Neil said as Victor left. He grinned at Adam. "He must be rattled to have sworn twice in as many minutes."

"How rattled do *you* have to be to turn the air blue?"

"You should hear me in the shed if I hit my thumb with a hammer! There was once . . ." Neil stopped, as the chair of governors reappeared at the door. "Are you all right, Victor?"

"Um, got a bit of a problem. Neil, could you and Adam give me a hand?" Victor's face was as pale as if he'd met the school ghost in the corridor.

"Of course." Neil, unhesitating, followed Victor out the door, and Adam slipped into their wake, intrigued.

The children's kitchen was barely bigger than a generous broom cupboard, with a door to the corridor and a fire door leading to the field in case the little horrors set their fairy cakes ablaze. The table where the ingredients usually got slaughtered was tucked in an alcove with a bench on either side of it. Only, this time, something else had come to a sticky end there.

Ian Youngs.

Even though there wasn't any TV-forensic-show-type bloodbath, the man was obviously dead, eyes wide-open and unseeing, body slumped and unmoving. Adam, who'd never been in the presence of sudden death, wasn't sure if he was going to faint or throw up.

"Should I get Jennifer to call an ambulance?" Victor, transfixed by the corpse, seemed like he might beat Adam to the fainting bit.

"Get Adam to do that." Neil exuded professional competence, leaning over the body. He gently shook Youngs, got no response, felt for a pulse in his neck, and shook his head.

"He's not just been taken ill?" Victor asked.

Why did that voice sound so faint? And why had the room started to swim in and out of Adam's vision?

"Gone, I'm afraid. But I don't like the appearance of his face, nor the bruising on his neck." Neil looked up, face ashen. "Be a good chap, Adam, and ask Jennifer to get the police to come, as well. I don't think this was from natural causes."

Adam, who'd made the mistake of getting a glimpse of that contorted face, managed to pass the message on before heading for the men's toilet and losing all his Waitrose sandwiches.

Chapter Two

Inspector Robin Bright peered out his office window at the magnificent view of assembled glories the Stanebridge Police Headquarters car park could boast. Two traffic-division bobbies were chatting beside a police motorbike, one of the handlers was lugging a hot and bothered dog into a van, and somebody else was shaking his head over some scraped bodywork. Another typical day in Rozzerland.

Bloody hell, the day had turned hot. No wonder that Alsatian looked as if it wanted to take a chunk out of someone's leg.

He turned away from the window. His sergeant was at his desk. How did the bloke always seem so cool? And so young? Granted, Robin wasn't exactly long in the tooth, having gone straight on the promotion fast track, but Sergeant Anderson had the face of someone barely out of nappies.

"This weather makes no sense." Robin ran his fingers round his collar then eyed a pile of paperwork that needed to be dealt with. It could wait. "I was so cold last night I ended up putting the heating back on."

"You want to be living with my Helen, sir. I'm always last in the pecking order." Anderson grinned. "She nabbed the fan heater. She almost sits on top of it when she's marking essays. And the dog was parked by the radiator."

"You should have got the dog to lie on her feet and killed two birds with one stone." Robin tried to keep his voice free of envy at the cosy domestic setup. There were times when having a lecturer—or anybody—to come home to would be the summit of all desire.

Anderson groaned. "If I'd suggested that, my life wouldn't have been worth living. And we forgot to turn the bloody heating off this morning too. The house will be sweltering when we get back."

The phone rang, cutting off any further meteorological discussion.

"Inspector Bright's office," Anderson said in his best telephone voice.

Who is it? Robin mouthed.

Anderson mouthed, *Some school*, in return, which left his boss none the wiser.

"Yes . . . Got that . . . Right," he continued. "Have they rung for an ambulance? Good. I hope they have the sense to keep people away. The less tramping around the better. Thank you."

"There's nothing more frustrating than only hearing half a phone call. I take it we're wanted?" Robin was already out of his chair and heading for the door.

"Lindenshaw St. Crispin's School, sir," Anderson replied, joining him. "The emergency services had a call that they'd been recruiting for a new headteacher today and one of their candidates has come a bit of a cropper."

Robin had a cold feeling in his stomach on hearing the location. "Do you mean they've had an accident?" Maybe they wouldn't need to go there.

"Doesn't sound like it. He was found dead in the kitchen the children use for doing their cookery lessons. The people at the school think there may be suspicious circumstances."

"Right." Robin felt in his pocket for his car keys. *Keep to the professional and objective.* "I guess it won't be anything as simple as him having choked on a fairy cake. Police surgeon been notified?"

"I was just about to make sure, sir." Anderson waggled his mobile phone. "The school secretary apparently rang for an ambulance, but she said that's a case of shutting the stable door after the horse has bolted."

"Isn't it always?" Robin headed down the stairs, his sergeant on the phone and hot at his heels. Murder, if this was what they had on their hands, wasn't a quantity they came across a lot in Stanebridge, despite the depiction of murderous middle England in television crime dramas. And most of the violent deaths he'd had to deal with had been easily solved, the culprit close at hand among relatives or friends. What was it about families that drove people to such extremes?

I was tempted to bash Patrick over the head with a blunt instrument. More than once.

Oh yes, he'd loved Patrick with a fiery ardour, and it had blazed away to leave nothing but ashes. And a bitter taste in his mouth that the best part of a year hadn't yet washed away. Maybe this poor bloke had rubbed their nearest and dearest the wrong way, and they'd chosen to do the deed away from home.

"Jigsaw time," Anderson said, slipping his phone back into his pocket. That was Robin Bright's line, his description of putting together the evidence surrounding any suspicious death, seeing how the pieces fitted together.

Even though he had no idea what the picture on the box lid was supposed to be.

Lindenshaw was only a fifteen-minute drive away, the first village out of Stanebridge, just off the same main road the police station stood on. Robin parked in the staff car park, next to the ambulance, blocking all the other cars in; it didn't matter, because nobody was going to be allowed to go anywhere for the moment.

The playground was empty, although sounds of children playing games filtered round the building. Robin pulled the front door handle, then pushed it, then pulled the bloody thing again.

"Is it me or is this sodding thing fighting back?" He couldn't remember it being this hard to get into the place, but then school security had gone mad since then.

"You need to press the bell, sir." Anderson reached across to press the intercom button, clearly fighting a grin.

"Must be easier to get into Parkhurst prison." Robin's mutterings were interrupted by a sharp, efficient-sounding female voice. One he recognised all too well.

"Yes?"

"This is Inspector Bright, Stanebridge police." Robin hated talking into intercoms with his sergeant standing by. It felt so idiotic. "I . . ." A sharp *click* and the door yielded to his shove. The entrance hall and corridors appeared much the same as they had when he'd been a boy, except they'd been brightened up by pieces of the children's work and pot plants with decorative stones round their stems.

But there was the perennial Mrs. Shepherd, leaning through the hatchway window, looking no older than she had twenty years previously, and pointing to a book on the ledge. The door, the little window, and the book might be new, but nothing much else seemed to have changed.

"Could you please pop your names in our signing-in book? Everyone who visits the school is supposed to do it. You'll need a visitor's badge too."

"Must we? We're supposed to be dealing with a dead body." Why did they have to go through such a rigmarole?

"You must. Even police inspectors have to obey the rules." She fixed him with a gimlet glance, just as she'd done when he'd been rising eleven. Maybe she remembered him as clearly as he remembered her. Back then, the height of Robin's ambition had been to win an argument with her, but this wasn't the time he'd at last be successful. He took the pen, signed in with a touch of theatricality, then gave it to Anderson, who was still grinning. By God, if he didn't stop it, Robin was going to have to whack that smile off his face.

"Put these on, please." She gave them each a brightly coloured adhesive badge, which they dutifully stuck on their lapels.

"Now, will any more of you be coming through this way? It's bedlam, what with the crime scene people and the ambulance crew and who knows what." An unexpected crack appeared in her façade as her voice faltered. "I'm sorry. It's been a trying day. I just wanted to make sure I was on the alert to let them in."

Time to be magnanimous. "Very wise. So the CSIs are here." Would he ever get used to the change from scenes of crime officers, which rolled off the tongue, to crime scene investigators, which just smacked of American TV? "What about the police surgeon?"

Mrs. Shepherd nodded. "I sent him through the school, after the ambulance men. The children are out on the field, so they won't get wind of what's going on."

Robin fought to control his voice. "On the field? There could be vital stuff out there being ground to pieces under a hundred pairs of plimsolls."

"It'll be trainers, sir. No one wears plimsolls anymore," Anderson cut in, although it wasn't helpful.

"It was already too late, according to the CSI woman." Mrs. Shepherd sounded on the verge of tears. "She had the same concern. I told her the children were out on the field all over lunchtime and most of the younger children were out there for their first afternoon lesson, practicing for sports day. She said anything would likely be long gone."

"If it was there at all. I doubt the killer risked wandering past all those prying little eyes if they've been out there most of the day," Anderson continued, soothingly.

"I suppose you did the right thing," Robin said at last. He didn't feel like scoring points anymore. Murder wasn't a matter for one-upmanship, no matter how much satisfaction it would have given his inner schoolboy. "Right. Nobody should leave the school until we give our say-so. I'll rely on you to help us with that."

"You can rely on me entirely, Inspector. I'll watch that front door like a hawk." Mrs. Shepherd paused, biting her lip. "What are we to do with the children? They're due to be picked up at three fifteen."

"There's no reason they can't go home. So long as all the adults stay here until we've taken their statements. "What have you told them? The children, I mean."

"That they've all been so good they can have extra games out on the field for the rest of the afternoon." Mrs. Shepherd smiled. "Mrs. Barnes's idea—she's our acting head—to keep them busy and away from what's going on in here. They can't really see the children's kitchen windows from the field, so hopefully they'll be none the wiser."

Robin nodded. There was a convenient shrubbery dating back to his time at the school that would have hidden everything from view. Which was just as well for the murderer, come to think of it. "Your acting headteacher sounds very sensible."

"She is. Mind you, we won't be able to stop everyone seeing the ambulance. They'll come in here asking things." The secretary seemed as though she was fighting a losing battle with a bucketful of tears. "Mrs. Barnes has been back at her own school for the day, and even though she's on her way, she may not make it in time to fend off the parents."

"Then don't let them through the door," Robin said. "You stand guard and keep anyone outside from nosing about too much. That would be really helpful." Fat chance of that happening, though.

These small communities were all the same, and the parents would be thinking up excuses to come in and find out what was going on.

Still, Mrs. Shepherd appeared relieved to have something proactive to do. "I'll get on it straightaway, then."

"Can you show us the way to the kitchen?" Anderson was champing at the bit.

"Along the corridor, past the classroom, and around the corner. You won't miss it. Inspector Bright will remember it as the old kiln room."

Anderson gave his boss a sideways glance and mouthed, *Remember?*

"Keep walking." Robin led the way.

"Can I help you?"

Robin swung round to see a grey-haired, harassed-looking man coming out of one of the classroom doors. *His* old classroom, scene of many a murder, although only of the English language and that was usually in one of Robin's stories.

"Ah, the police." The man held out a hand for Robin to shake. "Victor Reed, chair of governors."

Robin shook his hand, introduced himself and his sergeant, and tried to edge towards the kitchen. Were they never going to get to the corpse?

"Thank you for being so prompt. Such a terrible thing to have happened to the school." Reed rubbed his temples.

"Pretty terrible thing to have happened to Mr. Youngs," Robin muttered, although not quietly enough for Reed not to have heard.

"Of course. Yes." He appeared even more distressed. "I found the body. Shall I show you . . .?"

"No, thank you," Robin said, trying not to be too officious. "We can find our way there."

"If you're sure." Reed seemed relieved. He pointed to the door, carefully closed behind him. "I have the rest of the panel and governors in there."

"The interview panel? Would you warn them we'll have to take statements from them all before they can go home? And I'd like the school shut tomorrow, so we can go over everything unimpeded. Could you arrange that too?" There was a time when Robin would have been grateful for a murder coming to St. Crispin's—anything to get an extra day off school.

"Luckily we'd already booked tomorrow as a teacher-training day so the children wouldn't be around when we conducted the interviews themselves. So at least we won't have hordes of parents complaining they can't get childcare on short notice." Reed looked as if that was a much worse prospect than even *fifty* unexplained deaths would be. "I'll just tell everybody about their statements."

"Yes, you do that. We have to get into our gear." Robin escaped along the corridor, hauling Anderson with him. The memories the building evoked didn't make him want to hang around. He concentrated on getting into his protective clothing, a necessary evil in these days of microscopic examination of crimes scenes down to a molecular, let alone cellular, level.

Anderson, fully suited and booted, grabbed the kitchen door handle. "It's shut, sir. Should I knock?"

"You're not a child coming to the headmaster's office for a whacking. Get in there."

"I'm afraid you can't . . ." A deep voice came from the other side of the door as Anderson turned the handle.

Robin pushed into the room. "I'm afraid we can."

"Oh, sorry, sir." A gangly constable stepped aside to let them in, carefully shutting the door behind them. "I thought you might be another unwanted interloper. We've had a few of them."

"And not all of them children, Bright." The police surgeon, Dr. Brew, straightened up from where he'd been leaning over the body. "Offers of tea or coffee or help—none of it wanted. Ghouls . . . they want to get a peek at what's going on."

"And pick up information." Or maybe even cross contaminate it. How many people had already been in here, innocently or otherwise? "It's always like gold dust around a murder scene."

Robin took in as much of the room as he could at first glance. A general impression—that's what he wanted before he got bogged down in forensic detail. Cookers, fridges, worktops, all at the right height for children. The shrubbery outside the window . . . It had grown so much in twenty years. The little table with the body slumped over it.

"Oh yes. Worth a fortune in gossiping currency." Dr. Brew sniffed.

"How did he die?" Anderson asked.

"It's strangulation, I'd say."

That seemed clear, even to a layman. No obvious signs of blood or a violent struggle. The young man looked as if he'd just laid his head down on the table to get forty winks. Only the ugly bruising just visible on his neck and the awful appearance of his face made that peaceful scene a lie.

"And," the doctor continued, "not, I think, with bare hands. Something like a knotted cord. Or a good old-fashioned stocking with a gobstopper tied up in it."

Anderson looked at his boss, mouthed *Gobstopper?* and shrugged.

"I saw that, Sergeant." Dr. Brew grinned. "You should have been at *my* school. We used to fantasise about how we were going to get rid of the maths teacher. A stocking with a gobstopper—or one of those large marbles—tied up in the middle was the method of choice."

"Ye-es. Quite." Robin had come up with a few of those ideas in his time here, but he wasn't going to admit it. "Do you think the victim was just sitting here when he was killed?"

"It appears so. There were some papers under the body, so I suppose he could have been reading them. No sign of a struggle, or at least not much of one. Some evidence that he'd tried to pull the other person's hands away—some fibres appear to be under his fingernails."

Anderson nodded. "We'll know better when the CSI has fully processed the scene. I wonder if it's Grace. She wheedles out anything that's there to be wheedled."

Robin rolled his eyes at Anderson's flight of verbal fancy. For a zealously straight bloke, he could be camper than a row of tents. "May I?" he asked the doctor, gesturing that he wanted to move the dead man's arm to get a better look at what lay underneath.

"Be my guest. The girl took plenty of snapshots and samples before I even started."

Robin knew he could have waited—those papers weren't going anywhere—but he liked to get his hands on evidence, letting it speak to him even through the obligatory protective gloves. This time the papers were mute. "This looks like it's all to do with their interviews."

The doctor grinned. "Were you hoping it might be a vital clue? I only think detectives get that lucky on the television."

Robin ignored the quip. "We saw the ambulance outside. Are the paramedics hitting the tea and biscuits?"

"I think they're in the first aid room dealing with some seven-year-old who'd been whacked on the conk with a rounders ball. Blood everywhere." Dr. Brew grinned. "Nothing else for them to do here, is there?"

"I suppose not." Robin sighed, weighing up the scene. There would be no countering the rumour mill once it started grinding. "Mr. Youngs doesn't seem that big a bloke. I guess he could have been easily overpowered by someone strong—or cunning—enough to put him at ease. Anderson, can you get behind him?"

"If I can just . . ." The sergeant manoeuvred round behind the body.

"Would you have room there to carry out murder without making your intention so bloody obvious that the victim would be able to fight back?"

Anderson made an elaborate mime of strangulation. "Plenty, sir. I can imagine someone looking over Youngs's shoulder at what he was reading, a nice innocent conversation turning into . . ." He finished off with another garrotting movement.

"Yes, we get the picture. Easier there than from this side of the table too." Robin eyed up all the likely angles. "Would an attack from behind fit with the marks on the body?"

Dr. Brew nodded. "Absolutely. Still, I wouldn't jump to any hard-and-fast conclusions. Let's see what the autopsy shows."

Robin took a close look at the body, shutting his mind—as ever—to the fact this was someone's son or lover, cut off in his prime. Pleasant-looking guy, nothing out of the ordinary, except for ears that seemed too large for his head. And yet . . . Robin sniffed, then wrinkled his nose. *Something there, some scent.* He leaned closer to Youngs's body and sniffed again. "Sergeant, can you smell something?"

Anderson leaned closer to the dead man, sniffing around like a bloodhound. "There's something there, sir, but I can't put my finger on what it is. Some sort of aftershave?"

"Maybe. It seems a bit too floral, though."

"Perhaps Mr. Youngs preferred his cologne—what's the word?—metrosexual." Dr. Brew winked, clearly thinking he'd been hilarious.

"Or possibly he's been up close and personal with one of the women here," Anderson said, easing them through a tricky moment.

"You'd better get close to them yourself then and see if you can match up the scent." Robin was quite happy to delegate that duty. "Maybe—" A sharp rapping noise interrupted him. A nod to the constable and the door got opened an inch or two.

"I'm afraid— Oh, sorry." The constable produced his usual line as an efficient-looking woman barged through the door. Grace, one of the crime scene investigation team members, was pretty, clever, always appeared to be trying her best, and was fancied by half the blokes in the division. The first three facts were unlikely to cut any ice with Robin and the last one just riled him.

"Out of the way there, Harry, I just—" The sight of the police took the wind out of Grace's sails. "Didn't realise you'd arrived, sir. We were just wondering if the doctor had finished so we can get on in here some more."

Robin nodded. "That's quite all right by me, Grace. Anything turn up so far?"

The CSI smiled, clearly arranging herself as elegantly as she could, given the disadvantages of working gear. "Not that I can see, although we've not been around the outside of the building yet. Didn't want to scare the children while they practice their sports."

"I thought sports days were a thing of the past. The perils of the little ones becoming upset at not winning and all that." Dr. Brew started to pack his stuff away.

"Oh, they still thrive around here. If you want to see cutthroat competition you should watch the average parents' race. We nearly got called out to stop a fight after the last one." Anderson rolled his eyes. "Anyway, sir, maybe it's as well they're trampling about out there rather than obliterating anything in here."

It was a valid point. A bit of thought might have ensured the children were all taken entirely off the premises, but if nobody was certain it was murder, would they have bothered to think of that?

"Constable, you did check with the teachers to find out if they'd noticed anything suspicious?" Robin kept his gaze out the window, fighting down his temper. It was probably too late now to make a fuss about sloppy procedures.

"I had a quick word, sir. They hadn't." The constable smiled nervously, like a child desperate to please the teacher. Local lad, most likely, drafted in at a moment's notice and maybe out of his depth. "I nipped round all the teaching staff. We felt it would be safer to let them take the kids out there and keep the building clear."

"You probably did the right thing." Robin sighed and turned to Grace again. "Did you by any miraculous chance find anything in the school itself? With your unimpeded snoop around?"

Grace, unmoved by his sarcasm, or unaware of it, shook her head. "Very little."

"Nothing at all show up?" Anderson, at least, was keeping civil.

"Nothing apart from a couple of smelly socks and two Top Trumps cards, no." Grace eyed the dead body eagerly. "More luck in here, I hope."

"We'll leave you to it, then." Robin wasn't convinced. What chance was there of something like a clear set of prints, with the number of sticky fingers that would have been all over everything? "Let me know as soon as anything significant turns up." He nudged Anderson, tipping his head towards the door. "Come on. We've got people to talk to."

"And sniff at, sir?" Anderson asked, almost earning himself the sort of clip around the ear that Robin had suffered more than once on these very premises.

Chapter Three

*C*an the hands on that clock turn any bloody slower?

All conversation had ceased in the classroom, leaving an uncomfortable silence, livened only by the funereal ticking of the clock in question.

"Until we know for certain what's caused the death, perhaps we shouldn't even discuss it at all," Victor had said, putting the gossipers to shame but leaving a vacuum. Adam had tried to spark a discussion about police procedures, anything rather than just go crazy with his thoughts, but that had been met with little enthusiasm. And now Adam's stomach—bereft of all its contents and horribly sore—was starting to rumble, although he wasn't ready to risk putting even a biscuit in there. He could still see Youngs's face—mottled, lifeless, horrible—every time he closed his eyes.

A dead body, in *his* school. He thought of the pupils in his class, how much this was going to upset them, how much he wanted to go out and make sure they were all right, how much he didn't want to kick his heels in here.

Oliver, inevitably, broke the silence. "How much longer are we to be kept waiting?"

"A man's dead, Oliver. We have to do what we're asked." Marjorie had fished a manicure kit out of her bag, using the enforced captivity to titivate elegant hands that had suffered under the laundry load. The coolness didn't fool Adam; at times, her hands shook.

Oliver produced something like a growl. "That's still no reason to treat us like common criminals, cooped up until called for."

Marjorie rolled her eyes. "Must you exaggerate?"

Adam would normally have enjoyed this sort of tiff, especially if he needed something to pass the time. George—his ex—had slagged him off for it plenty of times. *People watcher? Don't kid yourself, Adam. You're a nosy fucking parker.* The name-calling had started off lightheartedly, but towards the conclusion of their relationship, there'd been an edge to everything. The failure of George's sense of humour had been the first sign of the end approaching.

Well, Georgie boy, you'll be pleased to know I'm not amusing myself by people watching today. This is too serious to make a joke about.

Christine's voice cut into his thoughts. "I hope we won't be here too long, Marjorie. Who's going to look after my Rachel and Tom?"

Victor, clearly trying to sound reassuring, began, "I'm sure the police will be—" only to be interrupted by the door opening. As if on cue, the rozzers—it had to be the police, Adam thought, as no other grey-suited individuals would be lurking around the school—came through it.

"Ah, Inspector Bright," Victor said. "We were just wondering when you'd be here to tell us what's going on."

"A murder enquiry's going on." The inspector's voice preceded him into the room.

Christine clasped her hands to her mouth. "Murder? Oh . . ."

The inspector appeared, nodding sympathetically. "I'm afraid so. Which means we'll need to get a statement from each one of you before you can go."

If the policeman said anything else, Adam didn't quite catch it. He was feeling confused enough, so to have—Wright, Bright, what the hell had Victor said his name was?—walk through the door looking like *that* sent his thoughts off in ten directions. Policemen weren't supposed to be so tall, dark, and stupidly handsome. Apart from in Adam's fantasies.

Oliver's voice interrupted the unwanted germination of some inappropriate thoughts in Adam's brain. "Perhaps you could take Mrs. Probert's statement first? She has two small children at the school, and they'll need her to pick them up at the end of the lessons." His unexpected thoughtfulness earned him one of Christine's stunning smiles.

"Happy to oblige," the inspector said with kindness.

Why did Adam never seem to meet blokes who reacted to his smile the way they reacted to Christine's? Why couldn't this policeman favour him with a flash of those dark eyes?

"Perhaps you could come along now, Mrs. Probert, and my sergeant could take you through things?" The sergeant looked like that was the best news he'd heard all day. "Anyone else need to get away urgently?"

For a moment—only a moment—Adam felt like shouting, *Take me, take me now!* but this was serious business. Was it defiance or denial in the face of sudden death that made him feel like behaving like a schoolboy? Or was it simply the incongruity of somebody like the inspector walking through the door? *Instant chemistry*, that's what they called it, but he'd never come across such a sensation before. It was the romantic equivalent of being hit over the head with a sock full of wet sand.

Then he remembered why the police were here—Youngs's body, those awful teeth—and felt sick again.

"Can't you see me at the same time? I need to get my husband's tea." Marjorie got out of her chair, following in Christine's fragrant wake.

Victor slammed down the papers he'd been fiddling with for the last ten minutes. "Oh, Marjorie, can't he fend for himself for once?"

"I wish he could." Marjorie pinched the bridge of her nose, then suddenly smiled. "Actually, this might be just the thing to make him. Take your time, Inspector Bright. I'm happy to go to the end of the list. It'll be nice to have an excuse to be out later than expected."

"Put me at the end of the list too." A voice that must have been Adam's emerged from his mouth, although he wasn't sure he'd meant to speak. "I haven't got any domestic duties to rush away to . . ." *Oh God, you're blethering. Shut up before anybody notices.*

"Thank you," Bright said, maybe with a note of humour in his voice. Or was it suspicion? He hoped the policeman didn't think Adam was trying to hide anything, given how quickly the guy turned away and addressed Oliver. "Perhaps you could organise a list for me of all the people in the room, Mr. . . . ?"

"Narraway. Oliver Narraway." Oliver seemed delighted at the policeman's trust in him. "Yes, I'll do that."

"Thank you. Everyone who was involved with your recruitment *is* here, I assume?"

Victor cleared his throat. "Ah, well. I'm afraid not. Jeremy Tunstall—he's our Lead Learning Partner—isn't."

"Your what?"

"He's a sort of school inspector. Our very own." Adam's answer got him pinned by those flashing brown eyes again. Where was the verbal equivalent of Imodium when he needed it? He remembered being like this when he'd witnessed his grandfather being hit by a car: he hadn't known what to say, so he'd just gabbled. Apparently, the romantic sock full of wet sand had the same dramatic impact.

"He had to go out and make some calls to his manager," Victor explained, hurriedly. "As you can appreciate, it's going to be a difficult time for the county education department."

"For the county?" Bright's voice could have taken the paint off the window frames if they hadn't been made of plastic. "What about for Mr. Youngs's family? Please stay here while I try to locate him."

"What's so important about Tunstall that your boss has to go chasing him?" Victor asked the sergeant as soon as the door had shut. Adam wanted to know the answer too. It dawned on him, with a sudden sickening belt to his stomach, that one of *them* might have killed Youngs.

"I'd have thought it was obvious." The sergeant narrowed his eyes. "We sent the message out for everyone to stay put. There's a horde of kids all over the field and now one of you has gone walkabout? That's the sort of thing that makes Inspector Bright hot under the collar."

The inner schoolboy told Adam there were lots of things he could do to make Inspector Bright hot under the collar. But the rational part of him felt the need to go and dump whatever was left in his stomach. Again.

Robin had a volley of swear words ready, but he kept them for when he got to the playground. Old habit, developed in this very spot—never show emotion in front of people who could make use of it. He closed his eyes, took a deep breath, and tried to remember he was a detective inspector, not a schoolboy.

He opened his eyes again to find someone was out by the road, talking on his mobile. If that was Tunstall, the bloke was going to get a roasting. The conversation became gradually more audible as Robin crossed towards the gate.

"I know. It's an absolute bloody mess. Murder. I sometimes think this school is cursed." The man paused, listening. "Yes, it's all been rearranged already, although I—" He jumped as Robin tapped his shoulder. "I'll call you back later. Police, I presume?"

Robin resisted saying he was Dr. Livingstone. "Inspector Bright. Mr. Tunstall?"

"That's right." Tunstall slipped his phone into his pocket. "Well, Inspector, I was just checking in with my district manager. Awful business, never known anything like it."

Robin wasn't sure he'd ever seen such a mess, either. Except for the yummy mummy who'd got Anderson smirking and the nice-looking lad who went red every time he said anything, the denizens of St. Crispin's seemed like well-meaning middle England at its worst.

"How did you know Mr. Youngs had been murdered?"

Tunstall scowled. "Give me some credit. Victor said Youngs was dead, but I saw the expression in the vicar's eye—and how shaken that young teacher was when he came back from losing his lunch. When I saw your crime scene officer arrive, I knew it couldn't just be natural causes."

It wasn't an unreasonable answer. Everybody watched an endless parade of crime shows these days; they all knew about procedure. "We should go inside. Where I can take your statement properly."

Tunstall seemed like he was going to argue, but he shrugged and followed Robin back into the school, passing the office, turning left, and going through the big doors to the school library. Scene of many horrors of the past, when young Robin Bright—academically an ugly duckling—had been so slow to learn to read. They settled at a table, where Robin produced his notebook.

"Did you know Youngs? Before today?"

"Of course I did. We have all the aspiring headteachers on our radar. Run across them at all sorts of events." Tunstall seemed to be taking it all in his stride.

Robin would have to trust him about the radar for the moment. Shame there wasn't some convenient TV show to teach coppers about school procedures. Still, he didn't like how Tunstall had just gone wandering off. Surely ringing his office could have waited. Or been done on the school landline.

"Is there anything you can tell us about him to help our enquiries?"

Tunstall narrowed his eyes. "Do you actually mean the old cliché 'Did he have any enemies?' If that's the question, there's nothing I can tell you."

"I don't think I was being quite that blunt. Although, if there were any parents he's fallen foul of in the past, maybe one of them might hold enough of a grudge to want revenge." At least some things had changed since Robin's school days. Now the teachers were more likely to live in fear of the parents than vice versa.

"Oh, come on, Inspector. Irate letters, maybe a shouting match over the office hatchway, but murder? I don't think parents get quite that worked up." He rolled his eyes. "Not even here."

Robin had decided he didn't like Tunstall. Too much of a smarmy git, irrespective of the unhelpful wandering off. "You'd be surprised what works people up enough to make them kill someone. Especially if they're unstable to start with."

Tunstall appeared dubious. "If you say so. You'd be best to check with the schools he's worked for, past and present. I could get you a list from his application form."

He may have sounded helpful, but Tunstall looked as though doing anything to help was going to be like having teeth drawn. Did he have something to hide, or was it just a typical case of local-government-employee syndrome? What made them naturally so bloody-minded?

"As far as the county was aware," Tunstall went on, "he didn't have anything that would bring him to our notice. He's led a blameless life . . . educationally."

Robin's ears—always alert to nuance, whether it was some villain giving himself away or some bloke in a bar hinting that he was interested—pricked up. "Does that imply he hadn't outside of the classroom?"

Tunstall sniffed. "I couldn't say. We concern ourselves with a candidate's ability to do the job. Anything that is just grist to the rumour mill, we try to ignore. Unless it's about child protection—or if they find themselves on the front page of *The Sun*."

"You'd better hope this story doesn't end up there. The tabloids love this sort of stuff. Murder in rural England." Robin enjoyed watching Tunstall squirm.

"Oh God. I'll have to get through to the press office, in case my boss hasn't already. And tell those idiots here not to talk to anyone they shouldn't."

Idiots? Robin decided he liked Tunstall even less than before. "Can you tell us why the school failed to appoint last time? It's all over the Stanebridge gossip network that the candidates were sent home before they even got to interview."

"Is there really a gossip network?" Tunstall looked less than comfortable.

"It'd make our job a lot harder if there wasn't." Robin wasn't going to admit that the main source of gossip about St. Crispin's school was his mother. Shame she'd gone off to Málaga for a month of over-sixties frivolity just when he could have done with her eyes and ears. "Why didn't they hold any interviews?"

"I'm not sure I should tell you that. It's supposed to be confidential to the selection panel, and I can't believe it has any bearing on Ian Youngs being killed." Tunstall ran his finger around his collar.

Robin produced one of his favourite lines. "I think we should be the ones to decide what has a bearing and what hasn't."

"Yes, well, I'll need to consult Education Personnel and get back to you."

"If you could do that as soon as possible, I'd be obliged." Robin smiled. Not his best "I really fancy you" smile, as Tunstall wouldn't have counted as fanciable even if he'd been the last bloke in the world. This was the "I'm being civil even if I wouldn't trust you with a balloon on a stick" smile.

"Is that all, Inspector? I have a lot of things to do back at the office because of . . ." Tunstall gestured vaguely in the direction of the children's kitchen.

"You'll be free to go once we've finished this statement. It's just like the dentist: better get it over and done with before you have too long to think about it."

And before you get a chance to set any stories straight.

Chapter Four

Adam wished he'd got some marking with him. Or his laptop so he could get on with his emails, but that was in the staffroom, which was at present in the hands of the CSI. Anything that would help him to get back in touch with normality while the police were working through those present, the vicar being the latest to go in for questioning. Anything that would get his thoughts off that policeman's dark eyes.

Despite anything Victor or the police had said, the tittle-tattle had blossomed again. Adam had enjoyed it at first because it reduced the murder to something you might read in the sort of novels his mother's bookshelves were full of. But the chitchat soon lost its appeal, especially when he kept remembering the dead man was a real person and not some victim in a genteel crime drama. Ian Youngs could only be ten years older than him—they weren't allowed to put ages on applications anymore, but anyone with half a brain could work it out from when people had been at school. Only a few hours ago, they'd been chatting in the office, and now . . .

The door to the classroom swung open.

"I've escaped." Neil's booming voice made everyone jump. "Still here?"

"Isn't that obvious?" Oliver, who'd produced a book of sudoku and had been attacking them with vigour, didn't seem that bothered about having to wait with the rest. Safety in numbers, maybe? Although those numbers were diminishing as the police got on with things. "What did they ask?"

Neil looked over his shoulder. "I can't say. I'm not even supposed to be poking my nose back in here. They'll have a fit. I just wanted to encourage you to tell the truth and you'll be fine."

Adam liked the vicar—he was one of the few people in the room who didn't seem to have his head stuck up his arse. Although he seemed to have forgotten that *somebody* wouldn't be fine if he or she told what had really happened. Maybe somebody who'd been in this room.

"What was the time they were interested in?" Oliver asked lightly.

"Lunchtime," Neil said, shiftily, peering over his shoulder again. "You better remember exactly how many cigars you smoked." He ducked out of the door, clearly thinking he was making a huge joke, Dunkirk spirit style.

Lunchtime. Why was it so hard to think about one's movements from just a few hours ago? Adam had eaten his lunch, made that phone call. But would anyone be able to vouch for him while he was fannying about trying to get a signal in the famous St. Crispin's blind spot?

"They must have asked him more than that, surely? He was in there ages." Oliver was still doodling in his book, although Adam wasn't convinced he was putting any numbers into the boxes.

"You'll soon find out," Marjorie said, as Anderson appeared at the door, but it was her he called. She got up and sashayed out of the door, gathering up the needlework she'd produced from her bag in the process.

"She'll make mincemeat of him." Oliver smirked and went back to his puzzle book.

"Fancy a cup of tea? If they let us get one." Adam wanted to do something—anything—to get out of the room.

"A bloody great mug of it." Oliver sighed.

Adam leaped up, got to the door in time to catch Anderson, who was still in the corridor with Marjorie.

"Okay to fetch ourselves a cup of tea from the staffroom?"

Anderson seemed to be weighing the odds. "I saw the forensic team coming out of there, so you should be able to get in now. Don't hang about though."

The staffroom was empty, all the teachers presumably huddled up in someone's classroom or giving their statements. Adam knew the body had been taken away—Jennifer had been giving them running reports—and the parents who'd come to collect their children and stayed to gawp had been, apparently, shooed away.

"Bit of a mess, isn't it?" Neil said, coming though the door en route from the loo, given the way he was adjusting his clothes.

"Nightmare. The worst thing is that the horror won't end when we've signed our statements, will it?" The playground speculation would linger on until—and after—the culprit was caught. This place would always be tainted.

"The St. Crispin's killer."

Adam almost dropped his tea. "What?"

"I was just thinking about what people will say in ten year's time. Please God it either turns out to be natural causes or the culprit gets found soon."

Before they can strike again? Adam thought but didn't say. "Amen to that."

"It must be your turn soon. With the police. Oliver's next."

"I expect so." At least that was something to look forward to. Inspector Bright with the shining eyes to match his name.

"Do you think one has to tell the police absolutely everything?" Neil fiddled nervously with his cuffs.

Adam would have dropped his tea if he hadn't been gripping it carefully. Neil being less than honest? Unheard of. "I suppose if they ask, then yes. Or . . . is this about the confessional or something?"

"We don't have confessionals at St. Crispin's," Neil said, frowning. "Church or school."

He wants to say something. If it's a confession, I'm calling for Jennifer. "If you think the police should know something, you should tell them." Adam remembered the strange snippet of conversation earlier, about whether Neil had met Ian Youngs before.

"I suppose you're right. It's just—" The arrival of Mrs. Barnes, trying to find Victor, muttering feverishly about press releases and insisting Neil come and help, cut off any further discussion.

Chapter Five

R obin neatened up his pile of papers, which had been sprawled all over the library table, looked at his watch, and sighed. This was the part of the job he hated: the routine taking of statements, especially when they didn't seem to lead anywhere and no obvious suspects were throwing themselves at his feet. Still, it was early days.

He didn't trust Tunstall as far as he could throw him, but the man had given a consistent account of his movements. Had last seen Ian Youngs when they'd broken for lunch, just gone a quarter past twelve; the bloke had been heading out of the school front door. Tunstall had stayed with the rest of the panel until almost the end of the lunch break. Had a call to return so he'd gone out onto the school field. Usual problems with finding a decent signal. Hadn't seen anyone else apart from dozens of children. When pressed, he'd said that Simon Ford, the other candidate, had been on the field then too, looking like he was being roped into a game of British Bulldog. And Oliver Narraway had been heading off somewhere to have a cigar.

He'd asked—twice—about the time and cause of death, but Robin had been noncommittal. Better that people didn't know when or what they were supposed to have an alibi for, not that Tunstall had an alibi for anything other than his time in the staffroom.

Maybe Anderson was having better luck working through his half of the list. Robin checked the names again—just Narraway and Matthews left to do. The old buffer and the young teacher. The teacher with the cute smile and the ruffled hair and the little scar that might have been an old sporting injury above his left eye. The one who didn't look anything like the teachers used to here.

A rap on the door jolted him out of his thoughts. Narraway appeared, having hardly waited for the C of the "Come in!"

"The vicar said I was next so I came along. Save you fetching me."

Robin scowled, but there was no point in getting angry about procedures at this point. He sat Narraway down, asked about his whereabouts during lunchtime, got a story that corresponded with what Tunstall had said.

"I had to go a bloody mile just to smoke a cigar. Not allowed to do it in here and pollute the atmosphere. Bloody nanny state. They'll be stopping us smoking in our own homes soon."

Robin dived in before the hobbyhorse could be ridden any further.

"When did you go out?"

"Just before one o'clock. Maybe ten to. The children were still out on the field screeching and hollering."

"And you returned at . . .?"

"I came back at twenty past one. And I know that because I checked the time when I signed back in. It's all in the book. I don't approve of these nonsensical health and safety and whatever regulations, but this time they might help all of us."

Bugger. The old buffer had a point. "I *will* check it, Mr. Narraway. Although the book will only show what time people *said* they came in and out. Now, where exactly did you go to have your cigar?"

"Down to the end of the field and through to the lane. And before you ask, I didn't see anyone there. Not anybody I knew, anyway." The statement came a bit too readily, but Robin let it go. Mental note made, though. "There were some dog walkers about, but I didn't recognise them."

"Do you know if any members of the panel had contact with any of the candidates before today?"

"Did we know them, do you mean? That would be terribly bad form." Narraway made a comic face, evidently not wrong-footed by the change of tack. "Actually, I think the vicar said something about knowing one of the applicants."

Robin looked up from taking notes. "Really?" The vicar was on Anderson's list. Trust him to get all the leads.

"Ah, no. I think I've got that wrong. He said he *thought* he'd seen Youngs somewhere before, and Marjorie—Mrs. Bookham—tore him off a strip for not having said anything about it. The vicar said they'd probably just met briefly at some church do."

"I'll need to follow that up, thank you."

"And I believe Youngs came to have a shufti round the school before he applied. All the candidates did—seeing the place didn't put any of them off." Narraway seemed avuncular—now that he was off his soapbox—and more eager to help than Tunstall had been. Robin got the distinct impression it was all an act, though.

"Did any of the governors meet Ian Youngs when he visited?"

"Only if we happened to be in school at the time. I met Mrs. Duncan briefly. She's the candidate who was taken ill and couldn't be here." Narraway leaned forward, conspiratorially. "Can I give you some advice, Inspector?"

Whether Robin wanted advice or not, there'd be no point in refusing; Narraway was clearly going to provide it. "I'm always ready to listen to anything helpful."

"Make sure you don't just interview people here. Spread the net wider."

"I'm sorry?"

"Mrs. Duncan's no-show. Highly suspicious, if you ask me."

Robin wasn't asking. Anyway, that was already on his to-do list, and he didn't appreciate amateurs teaching him his business. He rose, indicating the interview was over.

"Is that all?" Narraway appeared disappointed.

"For the moment. You'll have to sign this statement once it's written up, but you're free to go now. So long as you don't flee the country or anything." Robin grinned, the smile vanishing as rapidly as it had appeared. Oliver Narraway wasn't amused. "Thank you, Mr. Narraway."

"My pleasure." Narraway muttered something about offering help—and having it snubbed—under his breath as he crossed the library and opened the door. As he went out, as if on cue, someone else came in.

"Excuse me, can you tell me what's to be done with me?"

"I beg your pardon?" Robin swallowed hard at the sight of the young teacher he'd spotted earlier. The one with the emerald eyes and the neatly ironed shirt. If this had been any other situation, he could have thought of at least a dozen things to do with Old Green Eyes, but at the moment, any of them would be off the agenda.

"Am I to go home or make a statement or what?" Matthews rubbed his head like a schoolboy. "I thought I'd been forgotten."

Who could have forgotten a bloke who looked like *him*?

Robin used to count just about every moment in the classrooms here as torture, but he'd have been a damned sight more enthusiastic if his teachers had a face like this bloke's. He'd have busted his backside trying to do something good and win one of those slightly lopsided, green-eyed smiles, like the one that had come round the door with him. The inspector was bombarded with voices in his head telling him how inappropriate it would have been to have those sorts of "pupil fancies the teacher" thoughts back then. It wasn't even right to have them now. Policeman fancies witness? Not allowed.

"No, you're right here on my list." Robin waved the relevant paper and tried to look professional rather than libidinous. "Come and have a seat."

Matthews crossed the library with an easy stride and swung into the chair by the table. "Thank you, Inspector Bright." The lopsided smile flashed again.

Robin concentrated on taking a drink of water to ease his throat. Why had it become so difficult to speak clearly? Or think clearly, for that matter? "We're asking everyone to tell us where they were from the end of Simon Ford's presentation to what should have been the start of Youngs's."

"I think I was in full public view during all that time, apart from when I nipped to the loo, but Victor was in there washing his hands so even that's accounted for. I suppose that makes me the chief suspect?" Matthews looked more anxious than his chipper words implied. It sounded like an act, but Bright wasn't sure which play was being performed. Nervous witness making a joke or clever double bluff?

"Give the comedy a rest." Robin didn't have time at present for jokes, even from witnesses with bloody boyish grins. "What I want is some more detail. Not about the toilet visit—the rest of it."

He jotted down the particulars as Matthews—suitably serious now—related how he'd had lunch, gone to get a signal to make a phone call, chatted to the vicar, and worked over the data analysis. So far so good; everything checked off with what other people had said, and Robin hoped the same would happen when he and Anderson compared notes. Although . . .

"Something doesn't make much sense. You said you had to go out of the school to find a signal for your phone, but Youngs's was connecting to the network all right, assuming you could hear it in the kitchen."

"He'll be—sorry, he would have been—with O2, I guess. You can get that on the premises if you sit in the right chair. Move a yard either way . . ." Matthews shrugged.

"What did you think of Ian Youngs? Did you see him when he first visited the school?"

"Only in passing to the second, and not sure to the first. He came into my class but didn't stop long. Didn't talk to the children, which is always a bit of a bad sign." Matthews reached into his pocket, produced a packet of mints, then seemed to remember his manners and offered Robin one. "My greatest sin. You can keep chocolate. Give me these any day."

Robin hesitated, but he took a mint. Suddenly it seemed very important their fingers didn't touch. "Thank you."

"When he came here it was a busy afternoon. Two of the older children showed him round. All my class really saw of him was a nose poking round the door. I met him briefly this morning, but apart from that . . ." Matthews spread his hands. "I was waiting to see his presentation before I made any sort of judgement. His data analysis was sound. He spotted which kids hadn't made progress and what interventions they might need."

Robin nodded, even though only half the education speak made any sense to him. "Do I need to understand what data analysis and interventions are?"

"Not if you want to avoid being bored." Matthews grinned, again, flashing those green eyes. "It's all to do with children's progress. Do you need any more?"

"No, that's fine." Robin lowered his eyes from out of the firing line of the teacher's piercing gaze. "Would he have made a good headmaster?"

"Headteacher, Mr. Bright. We have to be gender neutral." Matthews made a sarcastic face. He swivelled in his chair like a dog trying to get comfortable. "I honestly don't know. Good application, if a bit old-fashioned in places. He could certainly talk most of the talk, but could he walk the walk? If you'll excuse the cliché."

"You don't seem convinced."

"There were some odd off-the-cuff remarks he made. One particularly snarky one about the kids that got my back up." Matthews looked like he wasn't sure whether to add to that. Something was bothering him.

"What did he say?"

"He'd been in with the pupil panel, and he described them as being snotty-nosed oiks." Matthews spoke the words with evident distaste.

"Pupil panel?"

"We arrange for all the candidates to get the third degree from the children. It's remarkably enlightening." Matthews gave a consistent impression of liking his charges, which wasn't something Robin associated with St. Crispin's teachers. "Simon Ford's a different kettle of fish. He stepped up to the mark."

"Impressive?" A stupid, completely unnecessary pang of jealousy struck Robin at the glowing mention of another bloke. Robin tried to focus on the matter in hand.

"It impressed me that Simon Ford sacrificed his lunchtime to be with the kids," Matthews continued, probably oblivious to the effect he was having. Unless, of course, he knew just what he was doing, trying with those bright-green eyes to blind Robin to whatever was bothering him.

"You'd have expected your applicants to do what Ian Youngs did and get away?" Robin sniffed. "Maybe *he'd* have been better off if he'd gone and played British Bulldog."

"Maybe he would. Bloody ghastly, isn't it? I mean, the bloke must have set out this morning full of hopes and aspirations, and he ended up . . ." Matthews seemed to crumple before Robin's eyes. The nervous bluster had gone, and a frightened air replaced it. "Sorry. You're probably used to this, but it's been a hell of a shock for us."

"I don't think I'll ever get used to it. Professionally, yes, but there's still part of me that gets upset, rightly upset, about the taking of a life." Now, where did that come from? He'd never dumped that sort of thing on a witness before. Robin shuffled his papers together. "Right. Have you anything else to add?"

"No . . . no, I don't think so."

"Are you sure?" Robin waited. An anxious witness usually rushed to fill a conversational gap, but Matthews didn't bite, just shook his head.

"Then that's all for the moment. I'll get this typed up so you can sign it. We'll let you know if we need to see you again." Robin rose, escorting the teacher to the door. "If you come across anything we should know, call the station. Better still, call me." He fished a card from his pocket, offering it to Matthews.

"Will do." Matthews hesitated for a moment, looked as though he was going to say something, then just took the card. He set off down the corridor, being pounced on by Mrs. Shepherd as he passed the office door, which can't have made his day any better.

Robin watched him. Nice bloke. Nice backside in those chinos. In the frame for murder? Well, that was the question.

Times didn't seem to work out, but he couldn't have been under constant view when he'd been out on the field, so he could have sneaked through the shrubbery and done the deed. There were plenty of hiding places and secret paths in the St. Crispin's grounds, or there had been twenty years before.

And that caveat could apply to everyone he'd spoken to.

Motive? Nobody seemed to have one of those, either. Not yet. But Matthews was edgy about something, and he hadn't told all that he knew, Robin was certain. He'd let the bloke stew.

Note to self, one: Don't let those green eyes blind you. You've got no idea yet whether he could have killed Youngs.

Note to self, two: Even if you decide he has nothing to do with it, don't be tempted to ask Adam Matthews to be your eyes and ears at St. Crispin's. Makes him a Judas. A Judas with his life at risk if the killer's based here.

Note to self, three: Don't even think about falling for him. Too complicated.

Mrs. Shepherd had clearly done whatever was needed, and Adam—flea in ear or patted on back—set off again, neat little backside wiggling.

Note to self, four: do not ignore note three.

Chapter Six

Anderson appeared in the corridor as if by magic, a wad of papers under his arm. "Any luck, sir?"

"Depends what you call luck. No confessions. No obvious lies." Robin blew out his cheeks. "You?"

Anderson shrugged. "I've done my list. Not a lot to show for it."

Robin sighed. "I'll ask Mrs. Shepherd to get us some tea, and we can compare notes."

"I'll go in the library and organise this lot." Anderson brandished a pile of paper. "Your Mrs. Shepherd couldn't find us a slice of cake, could she? I'm famished."

"She's not *my* Mrs. Shepherd. Used to put the wind up me when I was seven. Yes, don't pretend to be surprised." Robin grinned. "You must have guessed this was my old place of imprisonment."

"Imprisonment? Sounds like Borstal."

"Get three pints inside me, and I might tell you everything. For the moment, it's tea." Robin set off to the office before the questions started. Anderson had a sympathetic ear—sometimes—but Robin didn't feel like pouring out his heart to his sergeant. Adam Matthews might be a better bet. Would he at some point fancy a pint or three and being made privy to his school's darkest secrets?

Note to self, five: Do not ignore note three. Remember?

He sighed again and went off to plead with Mrs. Shepherd.

Robin's stock at St. Crispin's must have gone up like a bull-market tracker. Mrs. Shepherd didn't just produce a huge pot of steaming hot tea in the library; she also brought along cake *and* biscuits on the side. Enough to fuel any amount of comparing police statements.

"What's Simon Ford done with himself all afternoon?" Robin flicked some crumbs off the table, feeling defiant for making the library floor messy.

"He said he'd been out with the staff, mucking in with their games session. 'All hands to the pump' or something like that." Anderson's words fought for clarity against a mouthful of custard cream.

"Glutton for punishment." Robin remembered Adam's interview and how impressed he'd been with Ford's enthusiasm. "Did Ford have any contact with the panel apart from when he was 'on parade'? Either today or previously?"

"He said, to quote, 'It would hardly have been the done thing to go around drumming up support.'" Anderson sniggered.

"And in between giving his presentation and going off to play ring-a-roses or whatever?"

"He says he grabbed—" Anderson consulted his notes "—some sandwiches and a packet of crisps, then joined the big picnic over lunchtime. After the bell went, he came in to get ready for the assembly he was leading. He says he had a PowerPoint presentation he'd wanted to load."

"PowerPoint presentation?" Robin rolled his eyes. Why couldn't they have had those when he was a boy and spared him twenty minutes of daily torture? He hated assembly when he'd been back in school, being made to sit quietly and struggling to sing hymns that were never quite in the right key. "So he gave his party piece. Until when?"

"Until nearly—" Anderson looked at his notes again "—twenty to two, then he went to put his stuff in his car. The vicar covers him for most of that. Ford said he was going to grab a cup of tea in the children's kitchen afterwards, but that plan got scuppered."

Robin's ears pricked like a racehorse's. "By finding a dead body in there already?"

"No such luck, so don't get excited. He says his phone picked up signal out in the car park, and there were a couple of messages on his mobile. Bit of a flap on at his present school. By the time he'd dealt with them and got back into St. Crispin's, there was a flap on here too. I don't know whether he ever got his cup of tea."

"I bet Mrs. Shepherd got one for him." Robin shut his eyes and tried to clear his thoughts. "Earlier on, did he get his sandwiches from the children's kitchen?"

"Just before half past twelve. Ian Youngs wasn't there . . . so Ford says."

"Makes sense. Unless Youngs put on his running boots as he got out of the front door and nipped around the back." Robin sighed. "He had nothing else to add?"

Anderson grinned. "He said he'd love to know what Oliver Narraway said about his presentation."

"Nothing to me. Plenty to anyone else who would listen, I would guess."

Robin fiddled with the last piece of fruitcake, separating raisins from nuts like truth from the lies that somebody—surely—had to be telling. "Didn't he notice anything in that kitchen?" He shut his eyes, trying to picture the little room, part of the school that hadn't existed in its present form in his time. "Was the external door open?"

Anderson consulted his notes. "Ford said he wasn't sure. Why? Youngs wasn't even dead then, so the murderer couldn't have got out that way."

Robin opened his eyes. "Don't be dense. This isn't about getting out. Getting *in*. This place is like Fort Knox—only two or three doors open from the outside, and they all have those keypads." Adam had told him that when he'd described his lunchtime hunt for a phone signal.

"Are you feeling okay, sir?"

"Yes. Why shouldn't I be?" Robin snapped.

"You're just a bit tetchy, that's all. Not your usual ray of sunshine."

Robin opened his mouth to give his sergeant a blasting, then shut it again. Anderson was right, of course. "Sorry. This place gets to me. Too much junk to dump at the gate. And no, I don't want to discuss it."

"I wasn't going to ask you to," Anderson said with a grin.

Hopefully that would serve as answer enough. He didn't want to get into the whole issue of Adam and the attraction he felt, and how that nagged at him like an itch he couldn't reach.

"Right . . ." Anderson looked at the statement again. "There was some business with a wasp hovering about near the sandwiches, so Ford opened the door and shooed it out."

"And did you think to ask whether he'd shut the door behind him properly?"

"Oh, give me some credit, sir." The sergeant looked affronted. "Didn't help, though. He said he *thought* he did but couldn't swear to it."

"Oh, great."

"Do you think this could be an inside job, sir? Everyone here's red-hot on security and not just in terms of the doors. I bet if a stranger wandered through the grounds, the kids would tie him up with their skipping ropes." The sergeant looked wistfully at the now-empty plate. "I'm glad I didn't have to interview the little buggers. They scare the pants off me."

"It may come to that." Robin groaned. "Did any of your lot admit they'd met Ian Youngs before today? Somebody said the vicar might have run across him."

Anderson shrugged. "He didn't say so. Christine Probert did, though." He smirked at the mention of her name, maybe thinking of her long legs as he fished through his papers again. "When they first put the advert up, he came to visit the school. She comes in every week to listen to some of the children who have trouble reading, and she'd seen him briefly then. He hadn't made any particular impression at the time; she'd been too busy concentrating on the children." Anderson rubbed his forehead. "And, unless she nipped in and strangled him when she said she was powdering her nose, she's pretty well accounted for all of the time in question. Shame, though—I had this daft idea about her and Youngs having had some fling in the past."

"After which he turns up here and threatens to tell her husband?"

Anderson grinned. "Something like that."

"Do you always think in clichés?" Robin groaned. "Or is it just that you always associate crimes with sex?"

"And you don't?"

It was safer to change the subject. "Has Mrs. Bookham got such a watertight alibi?"

"So-so." Anderson looked less enthusiastic now that they'd passed on from the yummy mummy. Maybe his Helen should put him in blinkers. "She went home at about ten to one. She wasn't needed for a while. They'd originally planned Mrs. Duncan's presentation for after lunch, while Ford took his assembly, and Youngs did who knows what, but they cancelled it when she got taken ill, so Marjorie and the others weren't back on duty until one fifty-five."

"Mrs. Duncan, the famous missing candidate. Mr. Narraway seems highly suspicious of her for some reason." Robin didn't like the feel of this case. Nothing he could get his mind around clearly. Where was a nice straightforward domestic crime when he needed it? "What did she do at home? And did anyone see her do it?"

"Got the washing out of the machine and put it on the line. Thrilling stuff. Nobody to verify it, though. Her husband had gone to the pub for his lunch, seeing as she wasn't there to get it for him," Anderson said, rolling his eyes. "Her words, not mine. So it was just her and the tights and the pegs and the knickers."

"You're at it again." Pot calling the kettle black, getting at the sergeant for having dirty thoughts while *he* was still feeling uncomfortable at the remembrance of Adam Matthews's smile.

"She's an attractive woman, sir. Well dressed, got the figure of a woman twenty years younger."

"Behave. She's old enough to be your mother."

"Only just, sir. Must be in her fifties . . ."

"You need a cold shower. Concentrate. What time did she get back?"

"Just gone half past one. She said she played hooky for as long as she could. Apparently it was so nice to have the house to herself for once and listen to Classic FM rather than Radio 2." Anderson wrinkled his nose. "Sounds a bit sad, really."

"Did nobody tell you that parts of Lindenshaw are still stuck in the 1950s?" Robin's school days had seemed Dickensian, but could they really have been that bad? Probably. "That makes just a couple of people who can't quite account for themselves, although God knows why they'd want to kill anyone, let alone this bloke." He stood up, grabbing all the papers in an untidy heap. "Let's leave these. I want to go look at the doors."

The school's fire-evacuation plan made for depressing reading. Fine if one found oneself at risk of being burned alive but not a lot of help if one was trying to work out how a person without the keypad code could get in and out of the school.

Robin ran a finger along the map. "Here's the main entrance. And the children's kitchen. Anywhere else have external doors?"

"Um, I think I can answer that." A deep, hesitant voice sounded behind Robin.

He turned to see Adam, who was fiddling nervously with the pile of books in his arms. "Yes?"

"Possibly too many places for your liking. Like a semipermeable membrane, this place," Adam continued.

Oh God, he's clever as well as cute. Why here, why now? Note to self, four: do not ignore note three.

"This is just the person we could do with, Sergeant." Robin tried to act nonchalant. "Mr. Matthews can tell us the ins and outs."

"It's Adam. Nobody older than eleven calls me Mr. Matthews." Adam showed off that bloody charming smile, nerves clearly settling by the moment. Maybe he'd just had the sort of jitters anybody would have had when faced with making an official statement. Maybe.

Robin turned back to the map, not trusting himself to say anything in case it came out accompanied by an inane grin. "All these classrooms have fire doors?"

"Yep. And the hall, but they're the same type—you can only open them from the inside. Like the children's kitchen. Ofsted would have our guts for garters if any old nutter could wander in from the streets."

Ofsted—love it or hate it, the school inspection system was a fact of life. Maybe if they'd been around in Robin's day, the fear of this particular government department might have made someone deal with the bullying he'd suffered.

"Doesn't this constant need for security get you down?" Anderson didn't sound impressed.

"I used to think so, until Dunblane happened." Adam turned pale. "And before you say 'It couldn't happen here,' I'll remind you that something similar already has."

"Sorry. Point taken."

Robin had never seen the wind so effectively taken out of his sergeant's sails. Clever, cute, efficient. Bound to be straight.

"In theory, the only way anyone can get in the school is if they know the key code for these doors. Like I told you." Adam tapped the map then pointed across the hall to the main entrance and then down the corridor to the far end of the school, past the staffroom and hall, where the other external entrance led to the playground.

"So how do the kids get in and out?" Robin recalled the days when he had free run of the place—even in the evenings when the field was usually the favourite venue for football and sometimes an open door could be found when the drunk of a caretaker hadn't taken proper care. Had anyone ever missed those biscuits from the staffroom?

"They line up at the classroom doors, which we open when we're ready for them. It works, surprisingly." Adam pointed to an enclosed area marked on the map with hatchings. "That's for the youngest children. They have their own playground, and the door into their classroom is always open. In case of accidents."

"Falling-over accidents or wetting their pants?" Robin remembered doing those sort of things when he was just five.

"Both," Adam replied, grinning. "But there are always a couple of adults on duty, so nobody could get in that way. Nor via the 'loo route.'"

"What?" The policemen were in perfect, if unrehearsed, music hall–style unison.

"If any of the children need the toilet during playtime, they have to come in via the hall. We have a pair of year-six kids at the door to make sure only those in genuine need are allowed in."

"The mind boggles. When I was a lad you weren't allowed in at all if you were at the big end of the school. You had to hold it in until going home time." Robin avoided Adam's gaze.

Anderson cleared his throat. "Sir, if we can stop reminiscing about the Stone Age, we've got a murder to solve."

Robin, for a moment, had been sure his sergeant was going to say, *Sir, if you two can stop flirting,* and kicked himself up the mental backside. "Having orders to keep fire doors shut doesn't mean that's what actually happens in practice. How do you stop them being used willy-nilly?"

"Us poor sods of teachers are supposed to make sure that the rules are obeyed or else we get hauled over the coals. Somebody got into the school last summer and nicked a couple of handbags, so now we're all paranoid about shutting the bloody things." Adam seemed like the nerves had returned and, with them, the need to keep talking. "Not my handbag. I keep that at home with the stilettos."

The silence couldn't have been more awkward if it had been part of a bad Australian soap opera. Anderson had begun to study a notice about fathers helping their children to read, clearly avoiding looking at his boss. What was that quip supposed to mean? That Adam somehow knew Robin was gay and was having a dig at him? Or could it be Robin's lucky day and Adam had let something slip he hadn't intended in the anxious rush to fill time with words? Robin stifled a smile. Better not dwell on that too much at the moment.

"If what you're really asking is if a murderer could have got into the school through a fire door, the answer's yes." Adam, blushing to the roots of his hair, ploughed on. "But they'd have needed someone to let them in from the inside. The children know that all visitors are to come in via the front door and sign the book like you'll have done. They're like rottweilers about it."

"And would Ian Youngs have been as vigilant?" Robin summoned up the courage to look Adam in the eye. He couldn't keep addressing his questions to the fire plan; at some point, he'd have to get his mind round what was going on.

"If he'd had any bloody sense he would. All schools are red-hot on safety. Although I suppose somebody could have come along looking like they belonged here and persuaded the bloke." Adam shrugged.

"But why would a stranger want to kill Youngs?" Robin sighed, frustrated at the lack of motive. "Let me just get this absolutely straight. Staff members don't let the key code become common knowledge."

"Yes. And it changes regularly."

"Maybe it *is* an inside job, then." Anderson almost looked happy at the thought. "At least that narrows the field."

Robin had a sudden pang of regret that his old school—no matter how much he'd hated the place at times—should be sullied with murder. An inside job? Very likely.

Bloody hell, his mother and her gossip network were going to lap this up.

Chapter Seven

Adam couldn't recall how he'd got back to his car. Nor how he'd gone from the corridor to the staffroom. He vaguely remembered asking Mrs. Barnes if there was anything he could do to help, collecting his stuff, saying good-bye to Jennifer. The next moment he'd been fiddling with his car keys, mind somewhere else entirely.

Why had he made such a stupid joke about handbags and high heels? That sergeant had hidden a smirk as soon as it broke out, and Bright, the nice-looking inspector, had looked uncomfortable.

No wonder. You're acting like you've something to hide. What's he going to think? Apart from the fact you're a pillock. And probably king of the Stanebridge cross-dressing, makeup-wearing scene, over the top and out of place even in Bosie's.

He'd never been interviewed by the police, never anticipated how edgy it would make him. Never realised how tongue-tied he'd get, either, but whether that was due to the murder or talking to Bright, he couldn't tell. There was more he could have told the inspector, about the secrecy surrounding the first time they'd tried to recruit, but he hadn't. He'd been too embarrassed to say, *Something happened, but I have no idea what.*

See? Pillock.

On the positive side, if there was one, maybe he'd got closer to finding out whether Bright himself was the sort who might hang around Bosie's. Anderson had studiously avoided looking at his boss when Adam had mentioned stilettos—he cringed again, remembering it. Surely it meant the inspector had strong feelings about cross-dressing, one way or the other? Or was Adam just clutching at straws?

Just when he could do with five minutes to get his thoughts untangled and work out what the "strong feelings" might have been, Jennifer rushed across the playground, waving her arms. He fought the temptation to start the engine and go, picking up the pieces tomorrow.

You were trying to catch me yesterday? Sorry, Jennifer, I never saw you. Concentrating on not hitting any of the other cars. You know how bad I am at reversing.

Duty won. He rolled the window down, smiling. "Jennifer. Can I help?"

"Did you tell those policemen about the paper?"

Adam racked his brain. "What paper?"

"The paper Ian Youngs slipped in his pocket when he was in my office. He'd written something on it." Jennifer fumbled for a handkerchief. "I didn't tell the sergeant about it and now I'm worried."

"Don't be. The police will search through his pockets. They'll find it." Damn it, though. Something else he should have mentioned. How suspicious was it going to look when all this came out?

"But what if it isn't there? What if it's important?" Jennifer's handkerchief was being twisted into knots.

Adam went into reassurance mode—or the nearest he could get to it, considering how crappy he felt. The contents of his stomach— nothing more than tea and biscuits, now—kept wanting to reappear. "Look, don't worry. I'll get in touch with them tomorrow and say I've remembered something. Then there'll be nothing for them to get cross with you about."

"Thank you." The secretary blew her nose. "It's just such a mess. I sometimes feel like there's a cloud over this school. We need a new headteacher to sort things out, and now it feels like we're never going to get one."

"It'll be all right. The right person's out there; we just have to get our hands on them." Adam hoped he sounded more positive than he felt; at this rate, nobody would take the school on. "It's been a bloody awful day, hasn't it? Go home and put your feet up."

"Yes. I will." Jennifer blew her nose again. "And at least we have Robin Bright on the case. He's a St. Crispin's boy, you know."

Adam didn't know, although he'd suspected as much from the inspector's familiarity with the school. And he was called Robin? Nice name. Adam couldn't quite imagine the conspicuously handsome rozzer as a spotty urchin of a child. "I did wonder."

"I wouldn't have expected it of him, doing so well. He didn't seem our most promising pupil at the time."

"The ugly duckling who turned into the swan?" Adam said, immediately regretting it, especially when Jennifer's smile seemed to be so knowing. "Safe hands, then. It'll be all right, I'm sure."

"I know." Jennifer sighed. "Sorry to be so silly. See you tomorrow." She waved before turning and wandering slowly back to the school door, anything but her efficient—and occasionally officious—best.

Such a mess. Such a fucking awful mess.

Come tomorrow morning, everyone was likely to be looking at one another with suspicion, and that would carry on until the police had run the murderer to ground. And when the bloody thing *was* solved, they'd be back to square one in finding that elusive headteacher. They could put their trust in Robin Bright—and his seductive smile—to sort out the first problem, but he'd be no help with the second.

Adam had learned a lot these last few months, throwing himself into work to help get his mind off George, and what he'd learned wasn't just about recruitment. Human nature—the good, the bad, the professional, and the stubbornly uncooperative—of every type sat around that table during governors meetings. And somehow, the process of finding a new school leader had amplified those characteristics, showing everyone's true colours. All Oliver's prejudices about modern education had surfaced, Victor had proved ineffective, Christine had become more maternally efficient, and *he'd* regressed into his shell, avoiding confrontation at all costs.

If Adam couldn't hack dealing with this sort of conflict, growing a pair and tackling things that needed tackling, then he'd never have the skills required to be a strong leader. Might as well shove any prospect of making his way up the ladder to headship in the dustbin and resign himself to standing in front of a class the rest of his working life.

He looked at the school again—the old building, the old playground, the modern additions, the little community he'd become part of and valued so much. He'd known good times and bad here, but he'd always felt safe.

Sergeant Anderson's words suddenly echoed in Adam's mind. *Looks like an inside job.*

Was somebody at St. Crispin's really capable of murder?

Chapter Eight

"This one's okay." Anderson finished tugging at the door. "I suppose we should check them *all*?"

"Yes." Robin grinned, knowing his sergeant wouldn't really leave anything to chance; he was already heading for the last of the external classroom doors.

"You can't get any of these open without using a jemmy. Like I said, inside job." The sergeant looked horribly smug.

"Unless Simon Ford did leave the kitchen door open." It wouldn't do to let junior officers get too full of themselves. "And call me cynical, but I bet that wasn't the only one that could've been open. Think how warm it's been today—it wouldn't surprise me if a few of those classroom doors were wedged open to let some air in."

"Open or not, sir, I'm not convinced the stranger theory runs." Anderson had his belligerent expression on, which was all to the good. When he looked like he wanted a fight, then he was *really* thinking. "Nobody's reported seeing a *stranger* today. But they wouldn't necessarily have mentioned seeing someone they recognised in a place where that person could legitimately be."

"And Ian Youngs could have opened the kitchen door for a familiar face, someone like a member of the panel." *And please God, don't let him have opened it to Old Green Eyes.* "Do you see that row of bushes outside the kitchen?"

"Think they're thick enough for someone to hide in? Maybe." Anderson didn't look convinced.

"And to obscure the view from the field. As I said, call me cynical. Simon Ford might just have left that door open deliberately, for someone else to get in—something about his story makes me think *wasp, my arse*. Don't write off a mysterious stranger just yet." Although who and why was as big a conundrum as ever. "Any luck with that unusual smell?"

"Not a sniff. Yes, bad pun, sorry."

"You should be. Not Mrs. Shepherd's, nor any of the teachers I had on my list." Robin didn't feel the need to report that it hadn't matched Adam's cologne, either.

"And I didn't get a whiff of it from either Mrs. Bookham or Mrs. Probert. It must have been something Youngs was wearing, then." Anderson wrinkled his brow. "Do you think he might have been gay?"

"Oh, bloody hell, sergeant. Just because somebody wears a bit of Issey Miyake or whatever doesn't make him a screaming queen."

If he says, You should know, sir, *I'll deck him.*

"Maybe—" Anderson was cut off from whatever unsubtle thing he was about to say as Victor Reed came running around the side of the school waving a piece of paper.

"Oh, great. Neville Chamberlain."

"What?"

"Never mind."

"Here's the candidate timetable I promised you, Inspector." Reed looked like a little boy trying to suck up to teacher with a bar of chocolate. "One copy for each of you."

Anderson turned his from side to side, as though the murderer's name might fall out of it. "It's going to be interesting comparing this to the statements."

"This looks like the sort of school timetable I had as a lad." Would Robin ever be able to separate the memories of his own school days from this case?

"Did they have them on paper in those days, sir? I thought it was slate." Anderson grinned.

"Very funny. Can you explain this to us, please, Mr. Reed?"

"Of course. It's to keep both ourselves and the candidates clear about what's going on at any given point of the day." Reed's index finger performed an intricate dance on the paper. "Everyone gets to do each of the activities at a different time."

"Some of the sections are blank." If only *his* timetable had contained blanks, a bit of space for him to go and think, and get away from the constant jibes.

"That was my idea. To allow candidates the opportunity to look around the school, talk to staff, or just put their feet up. What they choose to do with that opportunity can influence our opinion of them."

"Never off the catwalk?" Robin sniffed. "Did you keep to time?"

"We did." Reed seemed to visibly swell with pride.

"Good." Robin looked at the paper again. "You tried to recruit someone three months ago, didn't you? Without success."

Now that they'd strayed off the safe ground of charts, Reed appeared uncomfortable. "We had to cut our losses and start again. Owe it to the children to make sure they have the right captain at the helm."

Anderson jabbed his finger at the timetable. "But this wasn't what actually happened today, though, was it? Your third candidate didn't turn up."

"We still kept to the plan, though. It would have been too late to revise it this morning when Mr. Duncan rang up."

"*Mr.* Duncan? Mrs. Shepherd told us you had two men and one woman on the short list."

Reed looked at Anderson as though he were in a special needs group. "Mr. Duncan is the husband. You're not likely to be in any fit state to ring when you've got a suspected ruptured appendix, like she had. Still, I'd have preferred her to be here. Better to have three horses to run against each other than just two."

"I hear you let the pupils loose on them. The two horses in your race," Robin added, puzzled. It was like having candidates for chief constable be interviewed by the inmates of Wormwood Scrubs.

"But of course. Most schools do now, Inspector." An almost evangelical light appeared in Reed's eyes. "We need to put our candidates under pressure or else how can we know whether they'd cope with the real thing?"

"It sounds like a day in the trenches," Anderson muttered.

Reed, clearly impervious, carried on. "I think if you were faced by a horde of parents irate about something that has or hasn't happened to their little Sophie or Archie you'd wish you *were* in the trenches, for a bit of peace and quiet. It's a very different world from when you and I were at school."

Don't I know it? With all this talk of their school days, Robin was afraid he'd break out in a sweat. Long-buried memories—teachers calling him stupid because he was a bit slow learning to read, some hooligan calling him a sissy—had begun to disinter themselves, feeling all too real when everywhere evoked memories.

"My parents only went up to see the headmaster if I was in trouble," Anderson said, as though he was proud of the fact.

"What time did Mr. Duncan ring?" Robin had to bring things back to the present day.

"At about nine thirty, although he'd left a message on the answerphone much earlier. He was rather cut up about his wife missing the interviews. Kept asking whether we couldn't defer recruitment until another time so she could take part."

Oliver Narraway's insistence that they follow up with the missing candidate rang in Robin's ears. "And what did you tell him?"

"That it was out of the question." Reed frowned, his precious protocol and procedures clearly under threat. "As I said already, we couldn't afford to delay the decision any longer. It's ironic, of course. We'll have to do exactly that, now."

"Will you advertise again?" Anderson asked.

Reed shrugged. "I hope not. Jeremy—Jeremy Tunstall—says he hopes we can just go ahead with Simon Ford and Lizzie Duncan. We're rearranging for a fortnight's time."

"Only a fortnight? Will she be up and about by then?" Robin remembered how his mother's appendicitis had laid her out for a month.

"Oh, yes. Turns out it wasn't really appendicitis, just some form of food poisoning." Reed's turn to roll his eyes. "She'll be fine for the new dates."

"How can you be so sure?"

Reed had the grace to look embarrassed. "You might think I'm precipitate but we had Mrs. Shepherd ring up Mr. Duncan to pass on the good news."

"Good news?" Robin looked at Anderson. What *was* it with these people?

"I mean, it was good news for her. Bad news for us, clearly. And for Ian Youngs," Reed added, almost as a flustered afterthought. "Excuse me. I have to help get an email out to the parents explaining exactly what's gone on."

They didn't stop him.

"This bloody school. It's always thought it was a law unto itself. More concerned with its bloody reputation than the fact some poor sod's been murdered." Robin stopped, aware that his sergeant was giving him a strange look. "Don't you think it's odd?"

"I do. But I'm not sure I'm as up in arms about it as you are." Anderson's heavy brow furrowed, giving him an apelike appearance. Not his best look. "I was just thinking that killing one of the other candidates is a good way to get an interview panel deferred until a more convenient time."

"And I thought I was the cynic. You can't really believe that?"

"I've learned to believe anything, sir." He was right; they'd have to explore every avenue, no matter how pointless some of them seemed to be. "What now?"

"I'd like another look around here but not until tomorrow. So back to the station to start the usual balls rolling."

Robin thought about the other, strictly nonconstabulary, ball he'd like to set in motion.

Note to self, four: do not ignore note three.

Chapter Nine

W*hy does the phone always ring just when I'm in the middle of dinner?* At least Adam wasn't in the loo with his trousers around his ankles, which was another customary time for the curse of the phone call or the doorbell to strike.

"Hello?"

"Is this Adam Matthews?" The voice down the line was vaguely familiar, although not enough to immediately put a name to.

"Ye-es," Adam replied, ready to change the answer if this turned out to be an irate parent who'd somehow got hold of his number.

"Inspector Bright here. I'm not interrupting your dinner or anything?"

Adam looked at the plate he'd brought from the kitchen to the hall with him, a plate half full of rapidly cooling spaghetti bolognaise. "No, I'm done." He hadn't had much of an appetite for it, anyway. "How can I help?"

"I wanted to pick your brain."

"Go ahead, if it'll help." Adam tried to sound intelligent and sensible, neither of which he felt. It had been a long day.

"I had no idea recruiting a new headteacher was such a complicated business, and I don't know anybody else to ask about some of the detail. And before you suggest Tunstall, I'd rather not; he's a hard nut to crack."

Adam could hear the frustration seeping down the line. "I can understand that." He didn't particularly like Tunstall, either. "Would it be easier to come round here and talk? I hate talking on the bloody telephone."

There was a momentary hesitation and an intake of breath at the other end of the line. *Is he weighing up whether I'm too much of a suspect to fraternise with?* "I'll be around as soon as I can get the satnav to tell me how to get there."

"Okay. But if you're coming from Stanebridge, just ignore the name it gives you for the road. Hanger Avenue is off Old Mill Road, not Church Road."

"Sound like you lose a lot of visitors." Robin chuckled. "Be there in about half an hour."

"I'll have the coffee on." Adam laid down the phone and looked at his plate. Murder putting him off his food or a dose of the collywobbles because he'd be seeing Robin again? Better channel his nerves—and excitement—into tidying the place up and rooting out some decent biscuits.

When the doorbell rang—almost exactly on the half hour from the phone going down—Adam leaped from his chair, where he'd been flicking aimlessly through the TV channels. It had been about the only thing he'd settled to, once he'd got the coffeemaker on and run a Hoover over the carpet. He had to make a good impression.

Inspector Bright, looking just as attractive as he'd had earlier—maybe more so, given that his collar had clearly been loosened a bit—stood on the step, smiling. "Thanks for seeing me. I know it's a bit late, but the more we can get sorted early on, the better."

"Not got your sergeant with you?" Adam, trying not to sound too pleased about that fact, ushered his guest into the hallway.

"He's got the job of contacting Ian Youngs's family. I got the long straw for once."

Adam wasn't sure how to answer that, apart from showing the way to the kitchen and hiding his grin. "Bloody awful job that must be. How can you bear to do it?"

"I was going to say you get hardened to it, but I suspect if you did, you'd be no use at it." Robin slipped onto one of the stools at the breakfast bar, then took out a notebook and pen. "Black coffee, please," he said, in response to Adam's gesture towards the coffeemaker. "This house is really nice. I thought teachers were poorly paid."

"We are." Adam poured the drinks. "This was my grandparents' cottage. As their only grandchild, they left it to me. I'd rather still have them here and be a lodger or something." *Oh God. Already pouring my heart out.* "Sugar?"

"No. Just as it comes, thanks." Robin took the mug. "Have you always lived around here?"

"God no. Born and brought up in Hampshire." Adam fetched his drink and a plate of biscuits—maybe he'd get his appetite back?—over to the breakfast bar. "One of life's coincidences, the job at Lindenshaw St. Crispin's coming up just about the same time I got this place. And a bit of a promotion—inclusion coordinator as well as class teacher." Nerves were getting the better of his tongue. *Shut up with the life story.*

"I bet you think that's a two-edged sword, now. Being at St. Crispin's."

"You mean because of this murder?"

"Not just that." Robin took one of the biscuits, tapping the crumbs off but not eating it. "It's not exactly a high-flying place."

Adam shrugged. "I knew it wasn't all the local reputation cracked it up to be. It was going downhill even before I got there, in case you think I'm the one who scuppered it."

Robin laughed, wearily. "It's always had a high opinion of itself."

"I don't know, it's . . ." A scratching noise at the back door made them both turn round. "Excuse me. That's Campbell." Adam hopped off his chair.

"Campbell?"

"The dog. I inherited him with the house too. Come in, boy." He opened the door for a large Newfoundland to make a regal entrance. "Does he bother you? I'll lock him in the bedroom if he does."

"No. I like dogs." Robin tapped his leg, encouraging Campbell to come over for a pat. "I don't have the regular hours to let me keep one."

Adam slipped back onto his chair. Funny how the arrival of the dog had eased the atmosphere immediately, creating a common point of contact that had nothing to do with dead bodies or schools. "Unlike us teachers with our allegedly short days and long holidays."

"I didn't say that." Robin smiled, caressing Campbell affectionately behind the ear.

"You've made a friend. Just don't give him any biscuits. He's spoiled enough."

"Noted." Robin flashed another one of his devastating, dark-eyed smiles. "You were saying?"

"I was going to say that there are plenty of people who'd leap at the chance to run the school." Adam watched the interaction of dog and rozzer. George had never really established more than a wary truce with Campbell, even when he'd been living here for weeks on end. Didn't they say that animals *knew*? "If someone comes in and turns us around, it'll be a real feather in his or her cap. Campbell!"

The dog, suitably chastened, took his nose out of Robin's pocket where it might have hoped to find a stray custard cream.

"Where's your chewy toy? Go find it. Go on, boy."

Campbell, reluctantly, went to his bed, rooting around under it.

"He's a daft beggar. I'm sure it's not there. Still, it'll keep him out of mischief." Adam sighed. "For whoever gets the headteacher job, there's every chance it'll turn out to be this year St. Crispin's, and two years down the line some failing inner-city primary school with a mega salary to boot. People should be falling over themselves to get it."

"Really?" Robin made a sour face, swiftly hidden. "If the job's such a plum, then why did nobody decent apply the first time?"

Campbell, proving his owner wrong, waddled over with a teddy bear firmly clenched in his jaws, depositing the vile object in Robin's lap.

"I said you'd made a friend. You'll have to pretend to be pleased, even if it's revolting." Adam found the sight of dog and man together strangely comforting. "And the answer to your question's simple. On the surface, anyway. We didn't offer enough money the first time we advertised. Oliver Narraway insisted we draw in the purse strings."

"Why doesn't that surprise me?"

"And of course, it's cost us more in the end. Not just the wasted time but double the recruitment fees." Adam took a swig of coffee. "He used to be a headteacher himself, you know. God help his school and all who sailed in it."

"Did he really?" That was evidently news to the police. "I can't decide if that helps or hinders you."

"I can tell you: hinders," Adam replied, wondering how much of what he said was relevant to the case and how much was just about getting things off his chest and into a sympathetic ear.

"You said the money thing was the superficial answer. What's the deeper one?"

"No bloody idea. Staff governors aren't privy to the discussions." There'd been something going on that round of recruitment, and he'd never got to the bottom of it. "Sorry, shouldn't dump this on you. Anyway, you can't blame us for being picky. Have you any idea how hard it is to get rid of a headteacher if he or she isn't up to the job?"

"No, but you can enlighten me." Robin managed to take a bite of his second biscuit without Campbell trying to get a look in.

"You pretty well have to pray they'll go in the classroom and wallop one of the kids, or dip their hands in the school budget. Plain incompetency isn't grounds enough. Except, we—" Adam stopped, aware he'd let his tongue run on again.

"Yes?" Robin clearly wasn't the sort to miss even the merest whiff of a clue, like Campbell when he was on the trail of a lost sweet. And just as endearing.

"Look, we were told our last headteacher, Mrs. Stephenson, retired for medical reasons, but I have the impression the governing body got rid of her because she wasn't doing a good enough job. Not quite sure how they managed it, because there's always a risk of being sued for wrongful dismissal." Adam felt uncomfortable discussing this. "You'll keep that quiet, won't you?"

"What do you think?" Robin shook his head, evidently not offended. "It's a common enough story in schools, isn't it? Right, I should get down to what I came for."

They spent the next twenty minutes discussing the riveting business of exactly how schools went about recruiting a new leader—who met whom and when, what information (official or otherwise) people had on prospective candidates—all against a background of Campbell trying to ingratiate himself with the policeman.

"Do you ever look them up on Facebook or anything?"

Adam threw his hands up in mock horror. "That would be a cardinal sin. Doesn't stop people doing it, of course, but if somebody discovered they'd lost out on a job because they'd been stalked round the net, we'd all end up in front of the beak."

Robin leaned over the breakfast bar, his dark eyes twinkling. "If you just happen to run across any gossip about Ian Youngs, let me know, will you?"

"As a good, law-abiding citizen, it would be my pleasure. Nothing to tell you at present, though."

"No dirt to dish on the rest of your governor cronies? What about Mrs. Probert?"

Adam remembered Robin's response to Christine's hundred-watt smile. Why did they have to put a damper on things, just when they were getting on so well?

He drank some of his coffee, mentally counting off the reasons Robin would turn out not be gay, despite the little flickers of something or other that had been going on when Adam had made his earlier remark about stilettos. Adam's luck couldn't be that good. Anyway, why was he even thinking such things? He was a witness, if not a suspect. Policemen—decent policemen—didn't mess on their own doorsteps, so even if Bright happened to be gay, Adam had no chance.

"Christine? Oh yes, all the blokes have the hots for her," he said, putting down his mug.

"*All* the blokes?" Robin asked, biscuit halfway to his mouth and half a smile on his face.

"Except the older ones, who have the hots for Marjorie." Adam tentatively returned the smile.

"She doesn't strike me as pinup material."

"I've seen pictures of her twenty years ago. Very classy." He was rambling again, nerves getting the better of him. "Still said to get the blokes with a Mrs. Thatcher fetish going."

"Husband a bit old-fashioned, I hear?" Robin, giving up on the biscuit and rubbing Campbell under the ear, had found a soft spot, eliciting a deep canine rumble of pleasure from him.

"Hang-and-shoot-'em type. Military family, although he was an accountant. Maybe that was his act of teenage rebellion—numbers rather than guns." Adam smiled.

"Right. Noted." Robin looked at his watch. "You've been a great help, but I think I should be going." Despite the slightly theatrical call to action, he stayed rooted in his seat, having just started another mutual-admiration session with Campbell.

"You've made a conquest," Adam said, immediately regretting it. He didn't have any coffee left, so the strategy of hiding his burning cheeks with the pretence of draining his mug wasn't an option.

"Have I?" Robin gave him a piercing glance that lingered just a bit too long.

Under any other set of circumstances, Adam would have taken that glance—the sort of glance that could make both a man's heart and the contents of his trousers leap—as an amber light. *Get ready. Your shout.* Surely Robin wasn't giving him the come-on?

The inspector turned his attention back to the dog, and Adam could breathe again. "Maybe I should invite *you* out for dinner, Campbell. I'm sure I can find somewhere with two Michelin stars for dog biscuits."

"You'll have to do better than that," Adam said, relieved at an awkward corner negotiated. "He turns his nose up at them."

"He's got taste, then." Robin gave the dog a final pat, then slid off his stool.

"Oh, just one more thing . . ." Adam stifled a grin. Images of his mother's favourite detective show, *Columbo*, flashed in his mind. The most important question always came at the end of the interview, although in most cases it was the detective asking, not the witness offering evidence. "I'd forgotten about this, and I doubt it's important, but when I was in the office this morning, mending the buzzer, Youngs jotted something down on a piece of paper and stuck it in his pocket."

Robin's expression changed to sharpened interest. "Any idea what it was?"

"Seeing as I'd left my x-ray glasses at home today, no."

"Well, it wasn't in his pocket when he got himself killed. Thanks for telling me."

"I'd say it was my pleasure but given the circumstances . . . Oy!" Adam tugged at Campbell's collar as the beast tried to block the kitchen doorway. "The nice policeman has to go. You're worse than the kids when we have a class visitor."

"Do you prefer Campbell to the kids in your class?"

"Absolutely. Just don't tell them that." Adam reluctantly showed his guest to the front door. "And you can't blame me. Dogs are much more biddable than children."

Halfway out, one foot on the step and one still in the hall, Robin stopped. "Where do boyfriends come on that scale?"

Adam, temporarily stunned, felt his mouth working but not a lot coming out. He finally managed, "That would be telling."

Robin raised his eyebrows, turned, and walked down the path to his car.

Adam made a mental note not to go leaping in with both feet and ending up flat on his face, having put two and two together to get five. He'd known at least one friend who fell foul of a copper whom he'd mistaken as gay and just turned out to be *bent* in the wrong way. Bright wasn't necessarily giving clues about himself; he might just have been telling Adam that he knew *he* was gay.

Why did life have to be so bloody complicated?

Campbell, who didn't want to be left out of the good-byes, had come to the door, suffering his owner—who'd clearly come second in the current popularity contest—to rub his ear.

"Always said you had good taste, boy. We need to work out how to get him round here again. Legitimately. Think you can go and root up a clue to this case? Or should I do what they do in films and volunteer to be his mole?"

Campbell turned up his nose and went back to his bed in the kitchen.

Chapter Ten

The next morning, Robin took his time getting out of the car and into the school car park. St. Crispin's looked calmer now, bereft of most of its usual occupants; at least the police would be able to get another decent look at the school and ask another round of questions without little ears wigging. But he still had to fight a wall of reluctance—the memories the place had stirred up, combined with the coffee he'd drunk at Adam's, had meant a sleepless night.

Perhaps some of the thoughts he'd had about Adam had contributed to the sleeplessness. This was the first time work life and private had overlapped, that he'd fancied a witness—suspect?—to the point that it was clouding his thinking. He wasn't sure he liked the experience.

Anderson's opinions, freely given all the way here, had kept Robin awake at the wheel when the yawns threatened to engulf him. The sergeant had been working hard—helped by Davis, one of the keenest detective constables in the department—to build up a picture of the victim. Youngs didn't have any criminal record, he'd been universally liked at his existing school—or so the headteacher had said—and his only close family was his mother down in Cardiff.

"The local family liaison officer rang me back to say she's devastated."

And now Davis had the unenviable task of trying to sniff out any scandal about the bloke, a whiff of which, as yet, there was not a sausage. Maybe after she'd been out talking to the man's neighbours and drilling down into his bank accounts, something would turn up. Maybe.

"I know you said it looks like an inside job, but I can't believe it was one of the governors who killed Youngs. Seems like they're desperate to get someone to run this place." And yet something nagged at Robin about that, something to do with the mysterious first attempt to recruit. He stopped the engine, staring out at an empty playground.

"Are you coming, sir?" Anderson was already out of the car.

"Give me a chance. Need to lock it. In my day, the kids here would have had the stereo out as soon as look at it."

Anderson grinned. "You won me a fiver, yesterday, sir. I've had a bet with Davis for ages that you'd been to a village school. Either St. Crispin's or Tythebarn. She was convinced you were inner-city primary material."

"Cheeky cow. I'll have to have that out with her. And *you* can buy me a drink out of your winnings." Robin went into the school playground through the gate, making sure he closed it securely behind them.

"None of the present crew here in your day, I guess?" They made their way over to the main door.

"Only Mrs. Shepherd. She's been around since Noah sent his kids here." Robin waited until he'd finished speaking before he buzzed the intercom. The continual ringing tone suggested Cerberus had temporarily abandoned her post.

Anderson, as dogged in pursuit of something as Campbell had been the evening before, carried on. "You don't suppose one of the people here did it to open up the field? Maybe they thought killing off one of the weaker candidates would make it easier?"

Robin wondered if he could thump his sergeant without ending up the subject of an internal investigation. There'd be no witnesses if he did it now.

"Only a joke, sir." Anderson grinned.

"Splitting my sides, Sergeant."

The sarcasm flew over Anderson's head. "I'd love to know exactly why they couldn't recruit before."

"So would I. They're being very cagey about it, and I don't like people being cagey around a murder." If only Adam had been able to shed light on it. "I think I'll try to butter up Mrs. Shepherd on the subject while you talk to Mr. Narraway."

"Narraway?" Anderson didn't look like he exactly relished the prospect.

Robin grinned. "He's just coming around the corner. See you later." He buzzed the intercom again, but still no reply came.

"Inspector Bright!" Narraway's voice rang out, cutting off any chance of escape.

"Mr. Narraway!" Robin tried to look enthusiastic. "Just the man we need. Do you know the code to get in?"

"I'm afraid mere governors aren't privy to that. Jennifer not about?"

"Doesn't seem like it."

"Just as well. I was hoping to have a word."

"We didn't expect to see any of the nonstaff governors here today." Last bloody thing they needed was that lot poking their noses in.

"Someone had to come in and make sure things were being done properly. Newspapers have been on the phone and all the rest of it." Narraway snorted. "Maybe it's as well I volunteered. Some of my fellow governors wouldn't be up to the job."

"I'd have thought that would be Victor Reed's role. Dealing with the media."

"Victor's in with the staff, doing the touchy-feely stuff." Narraway rolled his eyes. "Governance isn't what it was. Legions of do-gooders and soft-centred liberals. England's schools are going to pot and taking the country with it."

Robin wondered if Narraway would ever get down off his soapbox. Why, at this of all times, had Mrs. Shepherd not sprung to open the door? He cast a swift, surreptitious glance at Anderson, who just shrugged.

"The worst thing that ever happened was taking away the cane. We need a prime minister brave enough to stand up and insist we be allowed to use it again."

Oh God, what if he's a serious nutcase? What if he starts singing 'Land of Hope and Glory'? Time to stop this right now.

"I didn't realise, when we spoke yesterday, that you used to be a headteacher."

"I was a *headmaster*." Narraway scowled. "In my day, there were headmasters and headmistresses, not this headteacher lark. Children learned facts—good, solid, sensible facts. The only time parents came to the school was because their child was in trouble. I can remember—"

"I'm sure you can." Robin knocked the soapbox from under the man's feet. "Are you sure you never came across Youngs before, when you were still in education?"

"*Still in?*" Narraway looked as though he were going to explode.
"I never left it. This is what I'm doing now, making sure St. Crispin's
benefits from the wisdom I've accrued over the years."

Anderson had edged behind Narraway, rolling his eyes and
mouthing, *Nutter.*

"You haven't answered my question." The more Narraway ranted,
the calmer Robin made his own voice. It seemed to work.

"He never taught for me, and if I've seen him at some educational
event, then I don't remember it." Narraway leaned forwards, jabbing
his finger at the intercom button. "Is that all? I have jobs to do."

He'd changed his tune, but Robin let it ride for the moment.
Narraway had seemed to want a word with the police, but unless it was
the plea to return to the 1950s, he'd not had it. Well, let the guy stew
in his own juice for a while; if they pressed him now, he'd probably put
the barriers up.

"Hello?" Jennifer Shepherd's voice finally sounded, brightly, in
response to the buzzer. Narraway's finger had evidently succeeded
where Robin's had failed. Maybe the fabric of the building remembered
him and wanted to get its own back for any havoc he'd wreaked on it.

"It's the police. Can we come in, please?" Robin got in before
Narraway could. A loud *click* indicated the lock had been released.
"Thank you."

Robin let Narraway go in first, theatrically offering to hold the
door for him. While Anderson signed them in, Robin watched the
educational dinosaur stride off down the corridor.

"Back again, Inspector?" Mrs. Shepherd's voice came through the
hatchway, shortly followed by her head. She must have had a poor
night's sleep: those bags under her eyes hadn't been there the day
before.

"We're making the most of having free run of the place. Everyone
keeping to the hall and staffroom as agreed?" Maybe they'd run into
Adam en route—although whether that would be a good thing all
round was a moot point. Last evening he'd got a bit too familiar—
if only with Campbell—and at least once he'd let his gaze linger on
Adam a bit too long. And that throwaway remark about boyfriends.
He cringed at the memory.

"I hope so." Mrs. Shepherd cut into his thoughts. "Most awkward
for the staff."

Anderson snorted. "Murder usually is, not least for the victim."

The school secretary either didn't hear or didn't want to hear the remark. "I've had reporters on the phone. We even had the local television outside this morning before Oliver sent them off with a flea in their ears."

"They'll be back. As we drove up, they were in a lay-by down the road, looking like they were regrouping." Anderson grinned, although Robin felt a pang of sympathy for Mrs. Shepherd. Murder was bad enough without the intrusions of the media.

"Worse still, I've had parents on the phone all morning wondering what's going on. Despite the bloody email we sent."

It must be bad. Robin had always assumed Mrs. Shepherd didn't know any swear words, let alone use them. "It'll pass. This week's hot news is next week's chip paper. Would it help if we held a meeting to reassure parents that their children are safe?" Not that they could guarantee that yet, not until they knew what the hell had happened.

"I'll ask Mrs. Barnes," Mrs. Shepherd said. "Although she'll probably want to handle it in-house. You know, at least one set of parents said they might withdraw their child. We used to have a waiting list a mile long, back in your day." She lowered her voice, looking around as though to check if anyone might be eavesdropping. "Some people used to cheat to get further up it."

"I assume you mean bribery?" Robin would have cheated to get out of the place. If he found out his mother had done anything underhand to wangle him into this house of horror, he'd have to disinherit the old girl.

Mrs. Shepherd managed a smile. "Not by that name, no. 'Donations to the school library' or 'items purchased for the benefit of the children' was how it would appear in the accounts. The last headteacher put a stop to all that." The rueful note in her voice made it plain she didn't believe that was an entirely good thing.

"That would have been Mrs. Stephenson, I believe?" Robin tried to sound insouciant.

"Mary Stephenson, that's right. She retired last October." Mrs. Shepherd fussed with the array of things on the shelf next to the signing-in book, avoiding eye contact.

"October? Isn't that a bit unusual, retiring halfway into a new term? And just after a new school year started?"

Mrs. Shepherd looked over Robin's shoulder nervously, clearly worried about being overheard. "I don't normally indulge in gossip, although I suppose in a case of murder, it's acceptable. Mrs. Stephenson wasn't due to retire until next August, but she was unwell for a lot of last year. The official line said she was suffering post-viral fatigue syndrome, only I'd heard it was stress."

"And the 'stress' made her take early retirement?" The way Anderson used the word made his implication clear: she wasn't up to the job.

Mrs. Shepherd lowered her voice again, still keeping watch. "Either that or pressure from the county. As I said, this school was top of the heap once, and it went to being bottom of the pile."

That seemed to solve one mystery. *Something just on the legal side of constructive dismissal?*

"Just one more thing for the moment, Mrs. Shepherd," Robin asked. "What exactly is Mr. Narraway doing here, apart from shooing away the TV cameras?"

"He came in to make sure I was all right." She smiled at the thought of her knight in shining tweed suit. "And he brought in a tin of biscuits for all the staff. He's not as bad as everyone makes out."

"Really?" Not sure Adam would agree with that, but—to be fair—Adam's viewpoint was the only one Robin had obtained in detail. He'd have to stop assuming everything the guy said was true. "Is he always so thoughtful?"

"Well . . . not always. We do get a card at Christmas." Maybe the weight of evidence wasn't in Narraway's favour, then.

"Thank you. We'll try not to disturb people too much." Robin nodded his head in the direction of the children's kitchen, indicating for Anderson to follow him. "Sounds like this sudden outbreak of generosity was just an excuse to be on-site. We saw him coming round the side of the building. Surely he wasn't delivering biscuits or chasing cameramen at the back of the school."

"Do you think he might have been poking around where the kitchen comes out?" The sergeant shrugged. "He's one of the people without an alibi."

"I think we need to get out on that field, see what the lines of sight are like. Maybe—"

Adam Matthews, emerging from the staffroom with an armful of files, stopped Robin in full flow.

"Oh. Hi." Adam smiled, hesitantly.

"Hello." Robin felt Anderson's eyes boring into the back of his head. He wasn't going to give him the satisfaction of turning round and showing his face, not until he'd controlled the awkward look that must be smeared all over his gob. And his voice, which was at risk of sounding like a desperate teenager. He took a deep breath. "Busy?"

"Supposed to be. People's minds aren't really on 'differentiated planning.' Feels like we've been under a steamroller." Adam jiggled the files, smiled again shyly, then lowered his eyes. "Got to get these to the hall."

"Want us to hold the door?" Why the hell couldn't Robin come up with some brilliant case-related question that would keep Adam here for just a few minutes more and get those eyes to look up from the floor?

"No, that'll be okay. Thanks. You soon learn how to manoeuvre through with just your backside." Adam exchanged a brief glance with Robin, clearly horrified at his choice of words, then was off. Something like a snort came from Anderson's direction.

Robin spun on his heel. "Yes, Sergeant?" Maybe he should try to find a sidekick who was less cheeky—only Anderson was a good copper, or a lucky one, or something. And however much they grated on each other at times, they got results.

"We need to get out onto the field," Anderson answered. The sergeant sounded suitably sheepish.

"Lead the way." Robin, with a pang of regret that he couldn't find a reason for having to search the hall top to bottom, followed.

Robin stood on the school field, outside the children's kitchen, and took a deep breath. This was the very spot where a large, spotty oik and his equally repulsive pals had regularly made Robin's life a misery by calling him a pansy or a poof or something cruder. Had the oik known then what *he'd* taken another five years to conclude, or had it been just a random set of insults, the way that kids today called everything *gay*?

"Righty-ho, sir." Anderson's voice, faraway and slightly muffled by the shrubbery, brought Robin back to the present day and something nastier than name-calling.

"How much can you see?"

"Not a lot from back here. The ground sort of dips and obscures the view even more."

The trees and bushes had grown a lot since his day—maybe the kids didn't even go in there to make dens anymore. Or, as he had done, to hide away from Ryan Atherley. "Come closer."

"Right." The sergeant's voice grew gradually louder. "No, I still can't see anything, not until I get—" his face was just visible through a small gap in the branches "—right up here, sir."

"So that confirms it." If the children and staff were mostly in the middle and far end of the field, there was no chance of them seeing anything. Not unless they were up a ladder.

"You can't see the other side of the school, either," Anderson added. "I mean, where the lane is."

The lane where the vicar said he'd been walking and where Adam had been looking for a phone signal? Maybe that would be a good enough reason to go back and question the bloke a third time. Not now, though, as the bloke was up to his eyeballs in differentials or something...

Anderson, who seemed to have a penchant for breaking into blossoming daydreams, was trying to get into the kitchen. "I wonder whether Youngs let himself in this door if Simon Ford didn't close it properly. No one seems very clear about how our *victim* got back into the school, let alone the murderer. No one saw him after he was on the playground, supposedly going off to take a walk."

"Or if they did see him, they won't admit it." Robin eyed the door. "You'll never get that open. Perhaps Youngs arranged to meet somebody back here. Any sign of what Narraway might have been up to today?"

"Not that I can see. The police tape across the kitchen door has not been touched by the look of it. Maybe he had something hidden away out here, in those bushes?"

"Grace was all over them like a rash once the kids had gone. Turned up nothing more suspicious than some stray fag ends."

"If this had been the centre of Stanebridge, it would have been needles and used condoms." Anderson turned up his nose. "Why can't villains leave us clues anymore?"

Robin looked into the kitchen. "How can somebody be murdered in the middle of the day with people milling around everywhere and nobody sees anything?"

"I still need to get the dinner ladies' statements, sir. They'd all gone home by the time the body was found."

"That's the rest of your morning sorted, then, once we've finished here. Got your list of names and addresses?" There had been a gaggle of dinner ladies trying to keep order in the playground over lunchtime back in Robin's day, not that they'd ever really succeeded.

"List, map, and shoe leather, sir. Saving the planet and using Shanks's pony, seeing as they all live in Lindenshaw."

"And are you using the bus to return to the station or expecting me to come back here to get you?"

"Only if it's on the way from wherever you happen to be going, sir." Anderson was the sort who'd have been happy to jog all the way to town and regard it as nothing more than a bit of light exercise. "Where are you off to while I'm chasing dinner ladies?"

"Me? I'm in search of a mysterious appendix."

Chapter Eleven

If Adam's house had given the lie to the "poor, underpaid teachers" viewpoint, then the Duncans' house in Kinebridge—large, detached, and with an unusually spacious front garden for such a modern property—carried on the theme. Mrs. Duncan was a headteacher already, apparently, so maybe she earned more than he thought, or maybe Mr. Duncan had earned himself a mint before he'd been made redundant. That was stop-press news: DC Davis, hard at work looking for dirt, had somehow turned up that little gem and texted it to him en route.

No sign of someone to care for her coming to answer the door, and while Robin tried the bell three times, it went unanswered except for the barking of a dog somewhere on the other side of the property.

"Hello?" A woman's voice, faint and indistinct, came from the back garden.

Robin managed to find the side gate. "Inspector Bright, Mrs. Duncan," he shouted, causing another outburst of barking.

"Shut up! Not you, Inspector. Reach over and unlock it."

After a bit of a struggle, and wishing his arm were two inches longer, Robin got through the gate. Lizzie Duncan was sitting in a comfortable-looking garden chair, a bag at her side and a big black Labrador at her feet. "Mrs. Duncan?"

"Inspector Bright? Have a seat." Mrs. Duncan indicated the chair opposite hers.

"Thank you." There had to be a lot worse places to conduct an interview than in an English garden in the sunshine. "I appreciate you seeing me so soon. You must still be feeling the effects of yesterday."

"Only a bit. I've been signed off work until the middle of next week, but I'm feeling much better already, thank you." Although drawn, she certainly didn't look that ill. "I'm almost at the 'sitting here and fretting about the weeds I can see but I'm not allowed to pull out' stage."

Robin wondered how much of this was just an act, being unwell and hiding it or quite the opposite. "That's always a sign you're recovering—frustration at what you're not allowed to do. Did you spend long in hospital?"

"They discharged me yesterday afternoon, once they'd prodded and poked me to their hearts' content. I must apologise for not being able to make you a pot of tea, but—"

Robin cut the niceties off midflow. "No problem. I've been awash with tea and coffee this last week." He'd never enjoyed playing at tea parties with witnesses, although last evening had been an exception. But Lizzie Duncan wasn't Adam, and by the way it was eyeing him up malevolently, the Labrador wasn't a patch on Campbell. Why was he acting—and thinking—so out of character where Adam was concerned?

"Well, let's not beat about the bush. Straight to the questions," Mrs. Duncan said, with unconvincing brightness.

"I've clearly come here to ask about yesterday, when you were supposed to be at St. Crispin's." Robin waited for a reaction but only got a nod. "Did you know that one of the candidates was killed?"

"I heard it on the local news. Such a terrible thing for the poor children. A murder in their school."

More lack of concern for the victim. Why? Nobody gave the impression that Ian Youngs was unpopular, so maybe he just left people . . . underwhelmed?

"Luckily, none of them would have seen the body. I don't think the younger ones would have realised what had gone on unless their parents told them."

Mrs. Duncan snorted. "I bet the parents knew almost as quickly as you did. Sometimes I think they know about things before *I* hear of them. Perhaps they open my post."

"That wouldn't surprise me." Bit of an eye-opener, this case. Adam had dropped a hint or two about the truth behind the "nice little schools" image. Was everything in this case going to be calibrated against what Adam had said or done? *Note to self, four: do not ignore note three.*

Robin met Mrs. Duncan's eyes, guiltily cleared his throat, and continued. "Are you happy at your present school?"

"Very much so. I wouldn't want to move if it wasn't for the commuting. Only having to travel to Lindenshaw would knock the best part of forty minutes off my journey, both ways."

"Would the pay be better too?" Robin asked, relieved to see that the vile-looking dog had at last settled at its mistress's feet.

"You've done your homework, haven't you?" An edge had appeared in her voice. "It certainly would. There are more children at St. Crispin's than at my present school. More children on roll generally means a higher salary for the head."

"I believe your husband was made redundant last year." Robin liked questions that silenced his interviewees. They cut through the preprepared answers and might get him somewhere.

"He was," Mrs. Duncan said, eventually, weighing her words. "This recession's affected an awful lot of people in our circle of friends. Somehow you don't think accountants in a thriving firm will go under the axe."

"So a better salary for you would come in very useful?"

"I think every one of us could say that. Who'd turn their nose up at the chance of more money? And the challenge, of course," she added, hurriedly. "The challenge of turning that school around and making it what it should be."

Seems like you've just remembered what you're supposed to say. "Restoring its glorious name again?"

"Glorious name? Do you know the school, Inspector?" Mrs. Duncan laughed, holding her side as though it hurt to do so.

"Too well, I'm afraid. I was being ironic. Or sarcastic." Or something.

"I'm not interested in its glorious name or trying to knock the spots off the local independent school. I'm concerned about the children. Apart from one or two classes, they're getting a raw deal there at the moment."

Robin ignored the urge to clarify that Adam's class was one of those where the kids did well. Oh fuck, why did everything still have to be calibrated on the Matthews Scale? This was worse than having a teenage crush, and Robin had forgotten how distracting that could be. He had to get a grip. "Raw deal? Is it that bad?"

Mrs. Duncan narrowed her eyes. "I could bore you to death with stuff about progress data, but I won't. Let's just say that most of the kids would probably be better off at the nearest inner-city primary and most of the teachers could do with the sack. I'm sorry. I'm preaching at you. You're investigating a murder; this is no time to be putting the world to rights."

No, it wasn't, although it gave another interesting slant on things. Could it have been possible that one of those teachers had been scared that Ian Youngs's new broom might sweep so clean it took him or her with it? And could that teacher have resorted to killing him? Surely that was too far-fetched.

"Is your husband around, by any chance? I'd like to clarify a few things with him." Mrs. Duncan may have been flat on her back the day before, but the same didn't apply to her other half.

"Brian? I'm not sure how he could help you." Mrs. Duncan looked worried. "He's not here at the moment. Every Friday he handles the finances over in Stanebridge at the charity secondhand bookshop just off the high street. Keeping his eye in for when he finds another job."

"I thought he'd have been at home looking after you."

Mrs. Duncan laughed, unsettling the annoying Labrador, who eyed up Robin malevolently once more. "He'd love to be here, but he didn't want to let them down. Anyway, I couldn't bear him under my feet all the time. I'm feeling much better today, and he can fuss over me all he wants this weekend."

"He clearly looked after you very well yesterday." Robin wondered if his hostess would notice if he gave the dog a sly kick.

"Well, of course he would. I'm afraid he can be a little overprotective at times. I was pleased he had to go and run some errands, instead of fussing over my bedside all the time."

Robin liked the sound of this. "Errands? When was that?"

"Late morning, I think. It's all a bit of a blur. He fetched me a bag of things like toiletries when it seemed like I was going to be kept in hospital for several days. Although first of all he had to ring the school to explain why I hadn't got there. Then there was walking Branston. The poor thing had been cooped up in the house since the previous evening."

"He must have been fretting by then." Robin mustered up a forced smile for the nasty-looking beast. "Where's his favourite walk?"

Mrs. Duncan leaned down, gingerly, to pat the dog. "Down the road here to the village green and then out into the little copse. He thinks he's a hunting dog and goes after rabbits at times, the big ha'porth. If he's too frisky, we stick him in the car and take him over to Lindenshaw or Tythebarn. Anywhere he can get his nose in a bit of dirt and run off some energy."

"Right. Thank you for your help, Mrs. Duncan. I won't tire you any more." Robin eased from his chair, hoping to escape before Branston, who'd started to growl, could decide to take a lump out of him. "No, don't get up. I'll let myself out by the side gate."

"If you're sure . . ." she replied, although making no effort to leave her seat.

Robin took one last glance over the gate, checking that Branston hadn't sneaked after him. The dog was looking smug, but his owner was rummaging in her handbag, sending stray items flying in the hunt for her mobile phone, which she jabbed at with her finger. Lizzie Duncan had clearly felt the need to ring somebody, and quickly.

Robin had driven to Stanebridge like the wind, but now he felt welded to his car seat, sitting staring at *his* mobile. Why the hell did he feel the overwhelming, illogical need to ring Adam Matthews and arrange to see him later?

Investigation-related answer? No reason at all. There were questions to ask but he could pop into St. Crispin's at the end of the day to do that. He could tell himself that the less time *he* spent in the school the better, given the rate at which childhood memories were starting to resurrect themselves and that interviewing Adam at his home was more conducive to clear thinking. But that would be lying.

Lust-related answer? Because he fancied him. Fancied him like he'd never fancied a witness. Fancied him to the point that he was tempted to put aside all his rules—the force's rules—about relationships with people related to a case.

Possibly the most honest answer? Because Adam taught at St. Crispin's and might just be the one person Robin had ever met who would truly be able to understand what he'd gone through there as a boy.

He looked at the phone like it was a grenade, pin released. He dialled the number. Sadly—or was that luckily?—he got some stroppy automated bint telling him that it was unavailable. The infamous Lindenshaw signal blackout spot playing up again at Adam's end, probably, and Robin left a message for the man to ring him. Mr. Duncan was next in the firing line and the longer Robin left seeing him, the longer he'd have to get his story straight. Proper work had to come before something that was more like play.

He'd never had cause to visit Stanebridge's "premier charity bookshop" before—which was what the place advertised itself as in the window. He couldn't see how it was any different from every other charity bookshop, except that there seemed to be a collection of particularly obscure tomes on display to the left of the door. Somehow, Robin couldn't imagine them outselling works by Stieg Larsson or Kathy Reichs. Much more interesting was the window to the right, which was full of murder mysteries.

Once inside, he had to give the place some credit. It was neat, the books appeared to be in good nick, and it didn't have that stale, dreary smell that routinely infested the world of the secondhand. The two customers browsing the shelves seemed like they were genuine, not the usual crop of pensioners getting out of the rain while they waited for the quarter-past bus. Maybe the lack of rain was weeding out the idlers.

"Can I help you?" A sharp, well-spoken, but not particularly friendly voice came from behind the counter.

Robin produced both his warrant card and a semicivil grin. He'd taken an instant, irrational, and probably unprofessional dislike to the man addressing him. "Inspector Bright. I'm looking for Brian Duncan."

"You've found him." Duncan seemed to suddenly find his misplaced manners, smiling obsequiously and pushing aside a pile of forms and receipts he must have been working through. Clearly the communications from Casa Duncan hadn't included a pen portrait of what the police would be like when they appeared.

"I've just been talking to your wife about St. Crispin's school. We're investigating the murder there yesterday."

Duncan appeared suitably aghast. "That young man? Absolutely tragic. I'm just so grateful my Lizzie was taken ill or else it might have been her." He sounded genuine—or maybe he was just a good actor.

"Really?" Robin became aware that the customers' browsing activities in the background seemed to have ground to a halt. "So you think this was just a random killing and Youngs was in the wrong place at the wrong time?"

Duncan, clearly aware they were being listened in on, dropped his voice. "Wasn't it? I'd assumed some lunatic was running mad in the place, like you hear of in America. Am I wrong?"

Wrong? Robin hoped so. He'd no evidence of anyone else being at risk, but then he'd no idea what motive lay behind Youngs's killing. "It's too early to say. Although wouldn't you think it unlikely someone would go to all the trouble of sneaking into a school, killing a stranger totally at random, and then just going away again? Your American high school killers seem to want to go out in a blaze of what they think is glory."

Duncan rubbed his chin, casting a quick glance at the customers, who weren't even pretending to browse anymore. "I suppose so. Anyway, what can I tell you?"

"I'm trying to get my timelines clear. Can you confirm when you first rang the school?"

"At about seven o'clock. I left an answerphone message so they'd know about Lizzie as soon as possible. Then I rang back at half past nine to explain in a bit more detail. It's usually quieter in a school office by then."

Robin nodded. "I hear you were on dog-walking patrol too. The poor lad must have been bursting, being left home alone for so long."

"He was. I've never seen a dog go flying out the back door so quickly. I'd been expecting to come home to a puddle in the kitchen, but he'd crossed his legs and thought of England."

"Bless him," Robin said through gritted teeth. "Did you take him far?"

"I bundled him into the car at lunchtime, and we headed down to—" he hesitated, just long enough for Robin's nose for a lie to twitch "—down towards Tythebarn. There's a patch of grotty old ground that used to be the battery chicken place. He loves rooting around there. It must be the smells."

"Right." Robin didn't believe a word. "Your wife must have been very disappointed not to be able to take part in the interviews."

"Yes. It would have meant a lot to us if she'd gotten the job." Duncan ran his hand across his brow.

"Would the change in salary make such a difference to you?" The browsers were listening in again, but Robin wasn't concerned. Something was bothering Duncan, and he wanted to get a handle on it.

"Of course it would when you've been used to two lots of wages coming in and you're making do with one. Have you any idea how hard it is to find a job in this area?"

Actually, Robin did—his sister was in the same boat—but he wasn't going to let on. "So you'll be pleased they've just rearranged the recruitment days without readvertising? Still a two-horse race."

"Are you insinuating something, Mr. Bright?" Duncan leaned across the counter, irrespective of the fact that the "browsers" were now openly gawping.

"Not that I'm aware of," Robin replied, trying to sound convincing rather than delighted that he'd rattled his witness. "Just stating the facts as I understand them and making sure I'm correct. The odds are shorter now."

"If you think that Lizzie faked her illness in order to somehow affect the headship interviews, you're quite mista—" He stopped, banged his fist on the counter, and gave Robin the sort of look he used to get in the headmaster's office at school. "No, that's not what you mean at all. You're saying that we might have had something to do with the murder. That we set out to reduce the field somehow. Fucking cheek."

The customers may have been happy to listen to scandal, but the unexpected oath sent them scuttling through the door. Duncan scowled after them.

"I never said anything like that, Mr. Duncan. Please calm down. This isn't making my job any easier. And if your wife gets the post, she doesn't want to inherit a school with an unsolved case hanging over it."

"Good God, no! Think of the adverse press. Parents would be taking their children away in droves." As usual in this case, the victim was last in line for any sympathy.

Robin put his hands on the counter, leaning forwards conspiratorially. "You know how these local government departments work, there's always tittle-tattle going about but they close ranks when we try to stick our noses in. Anything you should happen to hear about St. Crispin's, or about Ian Youngs, would be helpful. Strictly in confidence, of course. I'll give you a number to contact me at."

Robin drew a card from his pocket, which Duncan took, looked at dubiously, then placed by the till. Without speaking, he picked up a briefcase from behind him, opening it en route to the counter. "I'll put this somewhere safe."

He slipped the card into the case, then snapped it shut, but not before Robin got a glimpse of a pair of surgical gloves in amongst some paper and files. What would an accountant, marking time in a bookshop, need with surgical gloves? Duncan had large hands—did he need extra talc to ease them on and had that been the source of the fragrance on Youngs's body? Or was Robin getting desperate to find any lead?

He thanked Duncan, then made his way back to the car, disgruntled. Where was a jealous ex-girlfriend or a drug dealer who'd been crossed when he needed them? Not even a strictly-against-the-rules snog with Adam Matthews behind the bicycle sheds would make up for the lack of a credible motive in this case.

Chapter Twelve

"So, how are you getting on with the dinner ladies?" Robin had waited until he was in the car before using his phone; he couldn't bear the shouting in the street that mobile phones encouraged.

"They're not called *dinner ladies* anymore, for a start." Anderson's broad grin was almost audible.

"I beg your pardon?"

"They're lunchtime supervisory assistants, or so the first stroppy lady told me. Anyway, I'm four down and about one thousand thirty-seven to go."

"Anything to report?"

"Nothing new. All the movements of people on-site are accounted for. No gossip, no scandal. Except . . ."

Robin always liked the sound of *except.* "Yes?"

"Nothing about Youngs, but Oliver Narraway's name got mentioned a couple of times today and not just for going through the school field to have his cigar. Apparently he gives some of the staff the creeps."

Robin couldn't blame them. Narraway struck him as unsavoury too. "Did they say why?"

"Yeah." Anderson chuckled. "They think he's a dirty old man. Gets too close when he talks to them. A bit too free and easy with the hugs and the hands."

"And here's me thinking he didn't approve of touchy-feely." Robin grinned.

"Your jokes get worse, sir."

"Right. Ring me when you've finished with the din— whatever you call them, and I'll come and get you."

"Are you going back to the station?"

"No." Robin smiled. "I'm going to go scratch an investigative itch or two."

"I don't follow."

"You're not supposed to, seeing as I'm not sure what it is that's bugging me except that Tunstall's holding back something. I'm not far from the county offices so I think I'll get onto Tunstall and see if I can squeeze some more stuff out of him." He wouldn't elaborate on the other itch, the nagging presence of Adam's lopsided smile in his mind's eye.

"Maybe you should find out the name of Tunstall's boss and ring him or her instead. That might carry a bit more weight."

"As if I believed I carried that much weight with you. And stop rolling your eyes. I can hear it from here."

The county education department looked as if the local government cuts had passed it by. The building was modern, clean, and smothered in the typical sorts of notices—unions, health and safety, whistle-blowing, all the hot topics. Robin was carefully following the directions given him by the nice-looking lad at reception, counting off the office doors, when he spotted Tunstall heading for him.

"I thought I'd come and meet you. It's a bit of a rabbit warren. We can talk in here." He opened a door into a small meeting room. Modern table and chairs, a couple of potted plants—now Robin knew where his council tax went. He waited until Tunstall took a seat before he settled himself.

"I spoke to my boss after you rang me."

Robin waited, but the pregnant pause wasn't giving birth to any words. "And?"

"And he says I'm clear to discuss the previous unsuccessful recruitment attempt at St. Crispin's, so long as it remains confidential. The candidates' names are all here."

The sheet of paper, with handwritten notes on, didn't yield a lot. "If something's not relevant to our investigation, it'll stay as confidential as you want. If it becomes important, I can't guarantee it wouldn't come up in court."

Tunstall snorted. "I can't see how it *could* be relevant. We had three candidates, and I'm not aware any of them have any current links to Ian Youngs. Nor can I see how they could be linked to his death."

Robin couldn't see it yet either, but he wasn't going to explain about his hunch. "Isn't it our job to check that?"

"You can double and triple check it." Silence descended again.

"Back to last time then. None of the three got even as far as the second day?"

Tunstall nodded. "I'd have sent one of them home at ten o'clock the first morning if I'd had my way. Good on paper but rubbed everyone up the wrong way from the minute he walked through the door. Despite what his references said."

"Maybe his school wanted shot of him if he was that bad?" It must happen in schools as anywhere else, easing the problems onto someone else's turf.

"Nothing would surprise me." Tunstall sighed, as though he'd lost the will to fight.

"That accounts for one of them. What about the others?"

"One failed on his data analysis. Hopeless. And the third, Claire Waites, got into an argument with one of the governors."

Now they were getting to it, the thing everyone had clammed up about. "I don't suppose it was Oliver Narraway?"

Tunstall grinned. "You don't miss much, do you, Inspector? Actually, not this time. He was his usual pugnacious self, but it was started by something Marjorie Bookham asked. No, not Marjorie, she got involved later. The vicar asked a question; the candidate had taken enough and couldn't resist getting into a squabble."

Adam had mentioned something awkward happening that he hadn't been told about. Was this it?

"Isn't that the sort of strong leadership you want? The ability to deal with the Oliver Narraways and Marjorie Bookhams of this world?"

"Ah, but there are ways to deal with them and ways to *deal* with them, if you get me. This candidate couldn't manage it, poor girl. Ended up in a blazing histrionic row. If she couldn't cope with that, she'd never cope at St. Crispin's."

"Governing body meetings get lively there?"

"Not in the right way. But there are plenty of parents at the school who are itching for the chance of a stand-up fight. If you can't manage them without resorting to a slanging match . . ." Tunstall shrugged.

"That place sounds more like Borstal every minute." Felt like it too, twenty-odd years ago. "So you sent her home along with the rest?"

Tunstall looked uncomfortable. "I didn't have to. She withdrew. Came and saw me privately to say she couldn't continue with the process as she had a personal connection to one of the panel, and it made for a conflict of interest."

"Which panel member?"

"Oliver Narraway. He used to be headteacher over at Tythebarn."

"The one they shut down?" And how all this linked to Youngs, he had no bloody idea. But when murder was concerned, if people seemed so determined to hide things, then you had to probe.

"Yes. Donkey's years ago, lots of children were there, but the area became a place where people retired to, and the number of pupils dwindled. It was amalgamated with another school the best part of a dozen years ago."

"Did Claire Waites teach at Tythebarn?"

"No. It was a personal association. She used to live in the village, and as a teenager she was involved with helping out at the Brownie pack. Many of those children attended the school."

"And that was enough for her to withdraw?"

Tunstall looked as though his chair was sprouting tin tacks. "That was what I told the panel, but there was more to it. She told me, in strictest confidence, that she'd heard stories about Oliver Narraway—enough to make her feel uncomfortable about working with him."

"You have any idea what it was about?"

"She wouldn't tell me, and I didn't feel I should press. There's such a thing as the law of slander." Tunstall had got his fight back. "Is that all?"

"Unless you've got some equally enlightening dirt to dish on Youngs, yes."

Tunstall spread his hands. "Not a spot."

Robin sighed; it was going to be that sort of a case.

Chapter Thirteen

"Is that wire behaving itself now?" Adam popped his head round the office door.

"Yes, thank you. Clever boy." Jennifer sounded like she was talking to her pet dog; maybe that's how she regarded all the teachers.

"Magic." Adam tried to sound appropriately pleased, although that wasn't the point of the visit. "It's bad enough for you at the moment, without any extra niggles."

Jennifer sighed. "I only wish everyone was as sympathetic."

"Police giving you a hard time?" Adam asked, edging the conversation nearer where he wanted it.

"No, they've been poppets." Prejudice in favour of St. Crispin's boys? Or boy. "It's the press and the parents and all the rest of the troublemakers."

"You give me some names, and I'll have them done over." Adam waited for her to realise he was making a joke before he cracked on. "That poor inspector must feel a bit awkward. His old school and everything."

"I know. It must break his heart to think of a murder taking place here."

Adam didn't believe a word of that. Robin hadn't seemed that concerned for his alma mater when they'd spoken the evening before. In fact, he'd seemed oddly cagey on the subject.

"I remember him like it was yesterday," Jennifer continued, getting up and heading straight for her beloved books of pictures. "Let's see . . ." She considered for a moment, then selected one, flicking through the pages and hitting the jackpot almost instantly. "Here he is."

"Where?" Adam tried not to be too eager.

"This weaselly-looking thing in the front row." Jennifer pointed at an unpromising specimen, less weasel than ugly duckling.

"He doesn't look happy." Something troubled lurking behind the eyes. Adam had seen that expression a couple of times before, and followed it up to discover some child was being bullied, at school or at home.

"He never did." The secretary cocked her head to one side, evidently trying to remember more about it. "Always a quiet little boy."

"Top of the class?" Adam could imagine a keen mind being picked on for "swottiness."

"Not especially. *He* was the high-flyer." Jennifer pointed to a gawky lad, but Adam had no interest in whoever that was.

"Did . . . did anything happen to Robin Bright while he was here?"

"What do you mean?"

"Bullying, I guess. He has that troubled expression."

"There was no bullying at our school back then." Jennifer closed the book and, with it, the conversation.

No bullying? Adam didn't believe it. Every school had bullies; it was how the school dealt with them that counted. Maybe the attitude here had been to sweep it under the carpet or deny it.

That anxious expression on young Robin's face was going to haunt Adam all day.

The St. Crispin's blackout spot never seemed to extend quite as far as where Adam left his car. The insistent bleeping in his pocket, just as he got his keys out, had become part of the routine. These days, it was usually either a message from his mum or an advert from his phone provider, but this time it was an answerphone message. From Bright.

Adam's heart briefly sank—what did the rozzers want with him now?—then resurfaced again at the thought of Robin's smile.

He rang back, getting the inspector's answerphone in return. Yes, it was convenient to talk to him this evening. Did he want to come round again or had Campbell put him off? Seven o'clock would work best as the week's marking would be done by then. And a bottle of wine probably opened, although he didn't add that. Would the call of duty allow a glass or two? Was drinking—or flirting—allowed on the job?

Surely there was a code of conduct surrounding the ethics of policemen getting up close and personal with witnesses, but he couldn't figure it out clearly with a brain distinctly fried by the end of a particularly gruelling week. He tried to persuade himself that, seeing as he was innocent of anything to do with Youngs's death, he could simply help Bright solve the case, in the capacity of expert witness.

There couldn't be anything wrong about that, could there?

When the grandfather clock—another heirloom—struck the seventh chime, the doorbell sounded and the race for the door began, Campbell winning by a paw's breadth.

"Let me open the door, you stupid thing," Adam said, pushing the hound's bulk aside.

"I hope you're not calling me a stupid thing. I could have you up for insulting a police officer." Robin, standing smiling on the doorstep, seemed relaxed, although the suit and tie spoke of business as usual. Had he practiced that smile, to try to put witnesses at ease? If so, did he realise the unnerving effect he was bound to have on some of them? Or—wishful thinking—was that smile for Adam alone?

"If you're going to arrest me for that, then let me lob in some proper insults en route to the station." Adam ushered his guest into the lounge. The kitchen was cosy, but the pile of washing-up wouldn't create any sort of good impression. "Have you eaten?"

"I'm fine. I grabbed some chips on the way back to my desk."

"So I can't tempt you with a bowl of chilli? Homemade. As a special treat, you can eat it in here on a tray. If you're allowed to. Duty and all that." Adam bit his lip. *Shut up.*

"No, like I said, I'm fine. I could murder a cup of tea, though."

"Your wish is my command." Adam decided to study his shoes, wishing he didn't keep sticking them in his own gob. "Your part of the deal is keeping Campbell out from under my feet."

"Best bargain I've had in ages," Robin said, visibly relaxing. The dog seemed happy with the arrangement too, resting his head on their visitor's knee.

When Adam returned with coffee for himself and Robin's steaming mug of tea, Campbell had settled at Robin's feet, eyes closed, and it looked like the policeman wasn't far behind. His tie was still knotted—just—but the top shirt button had been undone. "You look all in."

"I feel all in. Thanks." Robin took the tray. "Always the same with murder enquiries, unless you get the big break early on. Lots of legwork and very little to show for it." He blew on the tea, then took a swig. "This is great."

"Glad to hear it." Police business appeared to have been put on the back burner for the moment. Conversation turned on Campbell's occasional disgusting habits, the provenance of the Welsh dresser in the kitchen, and the watercolours on the wall. Anything and everything except murder. It was like a first date, finding things to talk about while you sussed out whether there was going to be a second one. The disappearance of the last bit of tea put an end to that, though.

"I need some inside gen, and I'm not sure I trust anyone else to give me it. Like getting the gen from a stableboy in the run-up to the Grand National."

"Ask away," Adam replied, trying not to show how delighted he was at Robin's remark.

"I'm trying to work out the likelihood of something." Robin put his mug on a table, taking evident care not to wake the dog who'd long succumbed to slumber, and got out his notebook. "Would any of the runners for the Great Lindenshaw St. Crispin's Headteacher Handicap go so far as nobbling their rivals? Just so the recruitment race got rerun?"

"Have you been putting the Duncans in the frame? No"—Adam put up his hands—"I'm not psychic. Our mutual friend Oliver Narraway was in school this morning and told us all how he'd tipped you the wink about them. In short, I don't think so, although that's no guarantee." It didn't seem much of an answer, but it was his best shot at an honest one. How the hell did he know what made people kill? That was Robin's job.

"Okay, so here's my other long shot. If someone at your school was worried about losing his or her job under a new headteacher who'd be rooting out all the rubbish, might he or she have turned violent about it?"

"Violent enough to kill someone? I doubt it." Adam was going to leave it there, but the disappointed look in Robin's eyes changed his mind. "Look, between you and me, there are three teachers in the school who need to pull their socks up. Mrs. Barnes is working with them, but it's like flogging a dead horse. But all three of them were out on the field over lunchtime, and then they'd have gone into class."

"So you've thought about it?" The keen, amused expression on Robin's face made Adam's day. There was something to be said for being an expert witness.

"Of course I have. I'm not just a pretty face." *Oh hell. Rambling again.* Adam finished off his coffee, hoping the mug would hide his embarrassed expression.

"Thanks for the heads-up." Robin studied his notebook. If Adam had been a betting man, he'd have said the inspector was deliberately avoiding replying to the last remark. "We've got to look at every avenue, although it feels like clutching at straws, if you'll excuse my mixed metaphors. Are you sure you haven't suddenly remembered a big burly stranger cornering Youngs in the playground?"

"No such luck." Adam got up, reached over, and took the tray. "Glass of wine make it any better? I've got a bottle in the fridge."

"I shouldn't while I'm on duty." Robin's face belied his words. The man was torn, no doubt about it. He fidgeted with his pen, dropped it, picked it up, then sat upright, as though that would get him back into the proper investigational zone. "Leave the tray. Sit down, and let me ask the rest of my questions first."

First? Then you'll take off your tie, and I can crack open a bottle?

Where did that *first* rate on the Flirtometer? On the positive side, even just a level-one flirt must mean the police reckoned Adam was in the clear, unless this was some sort of bizarre entrapment game. Or did entrapment only happen in the sort of movies with plot holes you could drive a truck through?

"Okay, but please let me get rid of this before Campbell wakes up and decides to lick out your mug." Adam cleared away the dirty crockery, returning from the kitchen with the biscuit tin. "You can have one of these on duty, surely?"

"Nothing in the rules about—" Robin looked into the tin "—custard creams. Did you know they're my favourites?"

"I guessed you had good taste." Adam dithered about where to sit, wondering if parking his backside next to the inspector was allowed. Eventually he decided on plonking down in the same comfy chair he'd been on previously. "Right. More questions."

Robin balanced pen, notebook, and a small pile of biscuits. "Yesterday I asked you about the previous occasion when the governors had tried to recruit. Why didn't you tell me about the row they had with Claire Waites?"

"It didn't seem relevant. Especially as I didn't have any of the details." That sounded pathetic, but it genuinely hadn't seemed significant.

"So you didn't know she pulled out because of something she knew about Oliver Narraway?"

"Blimey."

Robin grinned again. That smile took years off his age. "I was told in confidence, so don't snitch. I just wanted to see if it was common knowledge."

"I'm not a telltale tit." Adam's innocent little remark had an unexpected effect: Robin's smile coming to an abrupt end. A sudden flicker of pain registered in the policeman's eyes, like a child in the playground, hurt by name-calling. That same look Adam had seen on the school photo.

Say something or carry straight on as if he hadn't noticed? Discretion—or cowardice—won. "And it wasn't common knowledge in this house. I had heard some rumours about Oliver, though. That he'd done something wrong back at his old school."

"You didn't think it might have been useful to tell me about those?"

"Not being Sherlock Holmes or Hercule Poirot, no. And I've no bloody idea what form this misdemeanour took. Did your confidential informant not tell you?"

"What do you think?" Robin waved a biscuit, scattering crumbs for Campbell to find when he woke up. "He didn't even deign to say what Marjorie Bookham and Claire Waites had their spat about. Was it a discussion on using the cane?"

"That's the bee in Oliver's bonnet, not Marjorie's. She's far too meek and mild for that." Adam paused, a bee of a thought buzzing in *his* bonnet. "When I was in the office yesterday, mending the buzzer wires, Youngs said something odd, just as he left. The sort of little off-the-cuff aside that makes the person saying it smug and is only meant to be half heard."

"You're going to tell me what it was, presumably? Not make me come back a third time?"

"I couldn't be that cruel." Even if the prospect was enticing. He'd tape the inspector to the chair, if he could. Why did fate have to be so callous as to bring this guy into his life under this set of circumstances, putting him straight into "look but don't touch" territory?

"Jennifer was talking about us being strict on something— procedures or timekeeping or whatever," he continued. "I'm sure I heard some snide remark along the lines of us enjoying being strict about all sorts of things."

"No idea what he meant by it?"

"Bugger me if I know." Adam flushed. Not the best choice of words. "I mean, I wondered if he was having a pop at me for being gay. People do."

"Tell me about it. It's—" Robin stopped, sat up straighter. He'd let his guard slip.

Adam, trying not to show his delight at Robin's near miss on the "I'm gay too" front, carried on as if nothing had been said. "As for Marjorie and her candidate baiting, rumour has it that it was about the stupidest of things. Whether people who hold positions of importance within a school should behave in their personal lives to the same standard you'd expect in their professional. Caesar's wife and all that."

"Bloody hell. Given those rumours about Narraway, no wonder that set the fists flying." Robin leaned forward. "Look, I have to ask this. That stuff about teachers' private lives. Could it have been a sideways dig at you?"

"God no," Adam said, too quick and too loud. Campbell opened an eye, murmuring in protest at being disturbed. "If Oliver or Marjorie wanted to have a dig, it would be straight at me. And I've had both—or all four—barrels by now. I always assumed what Marjorie said was just a jibe at Oliver. He's always telling us what an upright citizen he is, but he's got feet of clay."

Robin nodded, took a deep breath, then put his notepad to one side. "Are you out of the closet? At the school?"

"Sort of." Adam sighed. "To my mother and my mates, I'm out. I'm trying to keep things quiet at Lindenshaw St. Crispin's, though. Last headteacher was a bit of a bitch about it."

"I understand that. I don't shout it round the station, either."

So the admission had been made, at last.

"I'd have thought in these days of political correctness that would guarantee the fast track to the top." Adam held up his hand. "Sorry. Stupid joke."

Robin didn't seem to find anything funny in it. His voice lost some of its relaxed quality. "Nobody suspects?"

"If they do, they don't say anything. Even the kids don't seem to have twigged, and they're sharp-eyed little buggers."

"Nothing changes at that bloody place, does it?" The serious edge to Robin's voice intensified. "There was a teacher in my time—he'd been in a POW camp and it had left him a bit odd—and they always called him an old poof behind his back. And to his face, when they got the chance. I made the mistake of standing up for him once. Never did it again."

"Took a bit of a fallout?"

"Enough to teach me to keep my trap shut. The kids in your class never ask you personal questions, then?" The subject had been signally changed. Whatever lay behind that haunted look in the little boy's photo was going to take a lot of time and trust to surface.

"They do. They've even invented a girlfriend. Saw me talking to my cousin in town one day, and they're convinced she's my partner. I shouldn't be so good at encouraging their imaginations when they're writing stories."

"So what do you tell them? About the girlfriend?" Robin had turned slightly, tucked one leg underneath him. The interrogator pose had—at last—gone.

"My standard answer to the boys is that she'd be out of their league, even if they were twenty years older."

"And what's your standard answer for the girls?"

"She's an air stewardess. Long-haul flights. I'll have to give her the virtual dump soon, though." Adam sighed. "Then I can pretend to be heartbroken for a year or so. Not ready to commit again." He looked up. Robin had him fixed with a particularly searching look. Should he say something about his pathetic love life? Would the policeman want the long sorry tale of the long sorry breakup with George and how Adam was over the heartbreak and more than ready to get back into dating again?

"Not easy living a lie, is it?" Robin sighed, picked up his notebook again, and looked resigned. "You said Oliver Narraway had feet of clay. I understand he was a bit free and easy with his hands with some of the female staff. I know it's the hot topic at the moment, but I have to consider it. He couldn't have been abusing children at his old school, could he?"

"Bloody hell, I hope not." Adam thought of the children in his class, how Oliver sometimes came in to hear them read. How friendly he seemed with them, despite all his bluster in governors' meetings and yearnings to return to the days of the cane. "That's all the school needs. The parents would haul their kids out."

"Would it be as bad as that?"

"What do you think? You know what villages are like for running the rumour mill. The playground's like *The Sun*'s newsroom, if not worse." Adam had managed to avoid being at the butt end of it, thank God, but he'd long dreaded it. "Supposition becomes fact by the time it's gone through three sets of parental mouths and ears."

"And if it turned out to be true? Would they have let him be a governor if he had a record like that?" Campbell had decided that sleep was impossible with all the hoo-ha going on; his head was on Robin's lap now, being stroked absently by his nonwriting hand. Adam felt a sudden pang of jealousy. How nice it would be to have Robin's long fingers going through *his* hair. Best to keep his mind on the conversation, even if it left a sour taste in his mouth.

"No way, if he's on one of the lists. Mind you, people didn't used to be so forward about reporting those sorts of incidents, or even taking the allegations seriously. Maybe nobody said anything, or if they did, he or she was just ushered out quietly. That's how things used to be done." Adam drummed on the table, fingers beating a vehement tattoo. "I hate to think of all the children who suffered in silence because nobody would have been prepared to believe it could have been 'that nice man' and 'in our school.'"

Robin put down his notepad again. He kept one hand for Campbell, resting his chin on the other. He had a five-o'clock shadow now, although it only added to his allure. "I've never seen you so passionate about something."

"It makes me wild. Dirty old men getting their kicks at the expense of the innocent." The drumming became more incessant. "If I found anyone was mucking about with one of my little mob, I'd kill him."

The drumming stopped, silence coming down like a sword. Robin showed no sign of breaking it.

"Oh God, that's just a figure of speech, you know that." Panic now, the desperate wish to do the impossible and get those words back. Especially if Robin's unhappiness at school had been caused by abuse.

"Is it? It's not one I like to hear. Maybe if you'd seen as many victims as I have, you'd think twice about saying it." Robin's face had hardened. He'd even stopped caressing Campbell. There was no way the tie—or anything else—was going to be coming off now, unless by some miracle the situation could be rescued.

"I'm sorry. I'm an idiot." Apologising had never been Adam's strong suit, but what choice did he have in the circumstances? "But it's not like I found out that Youngs was a kiddie fiddler and exacted revenge."

"And was *he* a paedophile?" Robin used the word with deliberation, as though to distance himself even more. "Or is that just another flight of fancy?"

"Oh, fuck it." Adam suddenly didn't feel inclined to pour any more oil on troubled waters. It seemed pretty pointless, anyway. He'd shot his bolt. "I'll answer your questions when you're being more reasonable."

"I wasn't aware I was being unreasonable." Even Campbell had noticed the change in the atmosphere—ears down, easing away from Robin, and looking at his master, worried. "You've got a bit of a habit of not telling us everything you could have. What else are you keeping hidden?"

Us. Back entirely to policeman mode, then? "I've never deliberately kept anything from you. I may be an idiot, but I'm not a liar."

"I'll reserve judgement on that. For when you've told me whether you're holding back something about Narraway."

"Of course I'm not." Adam's voice was sharp enough to make Campbell jump. "Is this your normal tactic, trying to bully answers out of witnesses? Well, I've seen bullies that would have you for breakfast."

"Oh, go to hell." Robin leaped from his seat, sending Campbell running for cover behind Adam's chair. "I'll see myself out. I'll get Anderson to come round here and see if he can get a sensible answer. Maybe he can work his charms on you. I bet you're a sucker for a pretty face."

"What the fuck do you mean by that?" Adam shouted, although Robin was halfway through the door. "Are you going to answer me?"

He wasn't, as the slamming of the front door bore witness to.

Oh God, how could things have turned so sour so quickly?

Campbell appeared from the lounge, cowering a bit at the unexpected turn of events, sticking his muzzle into Adam's hand. He stroked his head. "Sorry, boy. I'm not sure what happened there. Except I've been a complete and utter idiot. Again."

Chapter Fourteen

Lindenshaw, again. The village, not the school, and thank God for that. Robin shut his eyes and tried to clear his brain. How could he have let last night go so tits up?

Okay, he hadn't planned on ending the evening making a pass at Adam on the sofa—he wasn't stupid enough to go risking his career like that—but it had been important they part on friendly terms. Friendly terms that could develop into something else when all this mess was cleared up and Adam was free of any suspicion. Robin kept telling himself that Adam wasn't in the frame, couldn't be in the frame unless all the statements were wrong or the bloke had perfected the means of moving faster than light. But until Robin had the person under arrest who did do the deed, he had to keep Adam at arm's length. Not least because of his value as a witness, even if at present he was a hostile one.

Why the fuck had Robin gone and lost his temper so spectacularly? And over something that didn't really matter? Everything had been going along so well—the tea, the biscuits, the dog, having Adam to talk to. That little line about being a telltale tit had niggled, of course, putting him on edge. He'd been called that at school, after he'd stood up for Mr. Doyle, the guy who'd endured a hell of a lot during the war. And who, Robin had realised with the eyes of maturity, had likely been gay.

Funny how hearing the insult from Adam's lips could unearth such emotions. Add to that the "I'd kill him" line. Why the hell had he let himself react in such a spiky way? Almost like he'd been looking to pick a fight.

Well, you found one, didn't you?

He gripped the steering wheel, Adam's gentle voice, suddenly harsh, echoing in his brain: *Bullies that would have you for breakfast.*

I'll have you for breakfast, Robin ragged-arse. Teacher's pet.

Hearing that phrase again had hurt—the insults he'd suffered in the course of his job had never cut so deep. Robin looked down at his hands, knuckles white with tension, holding on to the steering wheel as if it were someone's throat. Was he always going to let the past screw up his life?

He focussed his attention on where it should have been all along—Oliver Narraway's house. The cottage looked almost as old as Adam's and was even more chocolate-box pretty. More time spent on the garden, probably, and fewer predations at the paws of a large hound. Whether the interior would also reflect the man's businesslike, dapper appearance remained to be seen.

Narraway hadn't seemed put out at the request for a Saturday-morning interview, making some attempt at a joke about policemen not getting the weekend off. For once, Robin was glad of that usually annoying fact. Anything to take his mind off last night's debacle. He got out of the car and shook himself—literally—to the surprise of an elderly woman walking past.

Right, Mr. Narraway. You wanted to talk to me. Well, I want to talk to you.

If the cottage and garden had seemed attractive from the car, they looked stunning as Robin reached the front gate. Masses of spring colour in the garden, much of it from plants he couldn't even try to name, and Narraway himself hard at work trimming some shrubs. He looked up, seemed pleased to see his visitor, then motioned for the policeman to enter, secateurs waving about dangerously.

"Inspector! Come to grill me?" The joking tone showed a sharp contrast to the man's bombastic manner the day before.

Robin opened the well-kept gate—neither a chip on the paint nor a squeak from the hinges—and walked along the noticeably weed-free path. "I've certainly got plenty of questions for you."

Narraway indicated a pair of garden chairs, then seemed to think better of it. "I suspect it's still a touch too early in the season to sit out here, especially in the morning."

"I suspect you're right." Robin didn't mind; the setting wasn't conducive to razor-sharp questioning, anyway. He followed Narraway into the cottage.

"Tea or coffee? The kettle won't take long to boil."

"No, thank you." The thought of something to drink paled, after being spoiled with Adam's excellent brew the other night. He hurried on, aware of both the flush rising from under his collar and the uncomfortable feeling hot on its heels.

Time to use the subtle approach. "I wanted to ask if you remember the last time Lindenshaw St. Crispin's tried to fill the headship vacancy."

"Remember? I'm never likely to forget." Narraway ushered him into a living room whose furnishings and decor were surprisingly modern given the owner's dinosaurian tendencies. It was homely, immaculately clean—maybe the house proudness was some sort of deliberate memorial to his late wife, whose picture had pride of place on the mantelpiece? "Shocking time. We had to send all of the candidates packing."

"Not all of them, I believe. One withdrew of her own accord." Robin, despite being in the process of taking his seat, kept his eyes fixed on his interviewee, but the anticipated shocked reaction wasn't forthcoming. If anything, Narraway looked amused.

"Was that the one who got into a fight with Mrs. Bookham? I've never seen our meek and mild Marjorie get so agitated." Narraway sat down, slapping his knees, clearly enjoying the woman's discomfort. "Mind you, Inspector, take what you've been told with a pinch of salt. That candidate may have said she withdrew, but I assure you—"

"No, I can assure *you* that Claire Waites jumped before she was pushed for arguing. Have you any idea why?"

Robin hadn't believed Narraway could look quite so shaken. And furtive.

"Should I? Tunstall from county dealt with all that."

"I know. He told me." *Time to dig the barb home.* "We understand that you knew Miss Waites from when you were headteacher"—he deliberately avoided the title *headmaster*—"at Tythebarn. She lived in the village."

"She may have done, but I didn't know *all* of the local residents, Inspector." Narraway was getting some of his spirit back. "As far as I'm concerned, I'd never met her before she turned up at St. Crispin's."

Robin weighed up whether to probe that, but let it ride; Narraway cornered was liable to come out fighting harder than ever. And if the speculation was in the offing that there'd been something untoward concerning children, then they'd run it to ground in Tythebarn soon enough.

"You said yesterday that you had something to tell me?"

"I do. I think it's important." Narraway leaned forwards, hands on knees, face softening as though he were trying his best at a jovial pose. "Thursday lunchtime, when I went for a cigar, I walked out to the back of the school grounds and down the lane to the place where it bends. There's a lovely vista away over the fields."

"Very bucolic." Robin bristled. *Why the sudden travelogue?* "I assume there's a point to this story, apart from recommending the local viewpoint?"

"Of course there is. You needn't be so rude."

No, he needn't. Last night was still niggling. "I'm sorry, but you must realise that at this point in a murder investigation, we need focus. Time's of the essence." So why spend two evenings with a not-particularly key witness? Robin was glad he wasn't in court, in the box, having to account for the time he'd spent with Adam.

"Very well, I won't hold you up any longer." Narraway sniffed. "I saw someone, a stranger, walking a big black Labrador. He was hanging about at the bottom of the school field for quite a while."

Black Labrador? He'd met one—rather unpleasant—black Labrador, and it supposedly had been at Tythebarn, along with its owner, on Thursday. "Why didn't you tell me this when I interviewed you?"

"Because I'd forgotten. We're not all as young as you, Inspector, and anyone can be a bit absentminded."

Despite Narraway's apologetic smile, Robin wasn't sure he believed the man. Too shrewd by far to be allowed to play the senior-moment card. "Hm. Where did this man with the dog go?"

"I thought he went up the footpath, the one that goes along the other side of the school field and comes out beside the playground. I wouldn't swear to that bit, though." The sudden vague note in Oliver's voice didn't ring true. Robin waited, to see if silence would elicit anything further, like it often did with a witness who had to fill the vacuum with something, anything. But this time, the only effect was Oliver fidgeting in his seat. Something was agitating him.

"This man. Would you recognise him again?" *Oh, for a photo of Duncan to whip out right now.*

"Possibly. I have a good memory for faces, if I can't always remember names. Do you have someone in mind?"

"Possibly. I'll get back to you." Robin scribbled some words then shut his notebook. Narraway heaved a sigh of relief that the interview was coming to a close. "And I'll want another chat with you when I've spoken to Claire Waites and found out what she has to say."

"Oh. Oh, yes." Oliver dithered, as though there was more to add, but this too came to nothing. "I'll see you then."

"You will." Not for the first time, Robin wished he could read minds, because Oliver was still holding back, and he wasn't sure which strategy would open the floodgates.

Adam, having fought Campbell back into the house, set off on his late-morning run. Normally he'd take the dog with him, but juggling the lead and a large envelope full of budget reports wasn't going to work. Still, he'd promised Jennifer he'd take Oliver's governor post round, as it was quicker and easier than posting it from the school. He'd usually just bung them through the door and run away before Oliver even realised Adam was there, but this package seemed particularly bulky, so that option might not be available.

He eased open the gate to Oliver's cottage garden, still debating whether to force the package through the letter box or ring the doorbell when the sound of Oliver's voice—raised and heated—brought him to a halt.

"Sorry," Adam started before realising it wasn't him being addressed but somebody in the cottage. The noise floated through the open lounge window. Eavesdropping wasn't something Adam approved of, but if Oliver was saying something important, then maybe *he* could report it back to Robin Bright, as a sort of investigational olive branch. He slipped out of sight of the window, if not out of earshot.

The one-sidedness of the conversation soon made it plain that Oliver was talking over the phone, although, frustratingly, he didn't use a name for whomever he was addressing.

"I don't think it *can* wait until tomorrow," Oliver said, voice getting louder by the moment. "I've just had the police here, and they know what happened."

Adam swallowed hard. Maybe Robin himself had walked out of the door not long ago. Thank God he'd had that fight with Campbell or they might have run into each other, and Adam wasn't ready for that.

There was a pause, then Oliver said, "Yes, *then*. I think we need to talk, soon."

That definitely sounded significant. Adam looked over his shoulder, guiltily, in case anyone was watching him from the road. He must seem as if he were casing the joint—or lurking like a loony—but he was in a terrible snake-and-mongoose moment, rooted to the spot.

Oliver was talking again, this time about not being able to keep something covered up. Adam hadn't heard him say what that *something* actually was. He'd have to keep playing the lines out in his mind until he got home and could make some proper notes. The exact details might be crucial.

The conversation sounded like it was coming to an end, so he dumped the envelope on the doorstep and set off as quickly as his legs could carry him. At least the running gear made him look innocent enough, even if he was sprinting. Now, was he going to ring Robin or go into Stanebridge to visit the station? And how was he going to swallow his pride as part of the process?

Driving into Stanebridge, Robin debated whether he should just ring Adam, and make a huge apology for being an oversensitive idiot. Watching the shoppers crossing the road, he wondered whether Adam was out with them, buying a nice tight shirt to wear at Bosie's, getting ready to pick up someone who was less of a dickhead than *he'd* been. Back at the station, he'd finally screwed his courage up enough to get out his mobile, only to have all plans scuppered. The office door opened, and a pile of paperwork, followed by Anderson, came into the room.

"Hello, sir. I thought I saw your car out there. Useful morning?"

"Possibly. If you call finding out that Lizzie Duncan's husband might just have been walking their dog behind the school Thursday lunchtime *profitable*. And that's just for starters."

Anderson whistled. "What is it with you that everyone wants to tell you their secrets?"

Robin grinned. *You don't know the half of it, mate. You should see it when the old queens get going on their life stories.* Maybe he had *too polite to tell you to fuck off* tattooed on his forehead.

"I hope Claire Waites does the same, then." Robin related the story of the first disastrous round of recruitment. "So, could you get Davis to add having a dig around in Narraway's past to her list of jobs?"

"She'll enjoy that." Anderson dumped his papers, then got himself comfy in the chair at his desk, arms behind his head. It smacked of indolence, but Robin knew by now that it meant his sergeant was thinking. "Right. Could Narraway have a motive?"

Robin got up, went to the window, and took a breath of fresh air to clear his mind. "Let's imagine he screwed up big-time in the past, thinks it's all been washed away with time, but Ian Youngs somehow finds out about it. Then he says something on Thursday—maybe even suggests Narraway should make sure *he* gets the job or else he'll tell everyone what he knows."

"That could work. We've known murders done for less."

And it would be enough of a link to that first recruitment round to explain Robin's "itch."

"In which case, what happens to the story about the man with the dog?" Anderson asked.

"It's a deliberate lie to put us off the scent, or there was really a bloke, but he's just being used as a red herring, or it *was* Duncan and it's just coincidence." Or a million other things. This horse could run. "Right. Did your dinner ladies say if they'd seen Narraway lurking around the kitchen at any time?"

Anderson mimed shooting himself in the head. "Lunchtime supervisory assistants, sir. You'll get lynched if you don't use their proper job title. They didn't say they'd seen anyone near the kitchen door, though we know that doesn't mean a lot, given the visibility."

"Shame."

"Actually, sir, I've been through all the statements again"—he tapped the pile of papers—"and while nobody seems to have seen Youngs after he appeared on the field, or at least won't admit to it, a couple of people said they got the impression that when he did appear, he was looking for somebody."

"Narraway, maybe?" Robin tipped his head from side to side, easing his neck muscles and the nagging, stressful ache spreading over his head. "Okay, but I'll tell you something else interesting. Brian Duncan carries around latex gloves in his briefcase, just the handy sort of thing you need lying about if you want to hide your fingerprints."

Anderson whistled again. "Right, so we *do* need to find out where he walked his dog on Thursday. Do you think he was lying to you?"

"Through his teeth." Robin laughed. "I could have sworn he changed what he was going to say right at the last minute. He didn't go to Tythebarn. I'd put a fiver on it."

"Do you want me to get over there and talk to him?"

"Yes. He's had time to stew overnight. And I need to get hold of Claire Waites."

"No luck yet?"

"I just spoke to her boyfriend. She's gone on a girls' shopping trip to Bristol and won't be back until the wee small hours." Inconsiderate, going off on a hen night or whatever it was, without your phone on, just when the police needed you. "I suppose your lunchtime supervisors have all got cast-iron alibis and not a motive between them?"

"That's about the size of it, sir." Anderson fished a sheet of paper out from his pile of documents. "Here." He set it on Robin's desk. "What I was doing last night while you were out ale-ing it up."

"I was on the case too," Robin said, just a touch too quickly and both of them knew it. How soon would it be before Anderson started to apply his brains to where his boss had been and why Adam's evidence was suddenly so important?

The sergeant raised an eyebrow but didn't say anything. "I ended up with this diagram—who was where and when and with whom. Looks like the bloody Tube map."

Robin leaned over the plan. "That confuses me as much as your diagram does. What does it mean?"

"It means all the assistants are accounted for, both during lunch and after, as are the rest of the St. Crispin's teaching staff. And Simon Ford."

"What about our redoubtable Mrs. Shepherd?" Not that she seemed to have any motive, but she loved the school with an almost unnatural passion. He'd known women like that to kill to protect their children. "Dangerous."

"Sir?"

"Sorry, I was thinking of she-lions and their cubs." Robin grinned.

"Well, if this particular she-lion was nippy enough, she could have slipped along the corridor and performed the deed. But—" Anderson consulted his chart "—I'm not sure she'd have had a lot of time, what with keeping the panel supplied with lunch and making a long phone call to county about the computers. Which checks out."

"Just covering all the bases." Or grabbing for a life belt like a drowning man? "Davis hasn't turned anything up, I assume?"

"I'd have told you if she had, sir." Anderson shrugged. "Not a sniff of scandal or anything about Youngs, so far. Been at three schools and they all liked him well enough. Mind you—" he rummaged through the papers, coming to one marked with a yellow sticky note "—I did turn up something odd."

Robin had a sudden, completely irrational fear that whatever it was would involve Adam. Him and Youngs having an argument outside Bosie's or something.

"You all right, sir? Want that window shut?"

"No, just someone walking over my grave." Awful place, Bosie's. To be avoided like the plague and not just when it was screaming queens' night. One of the boys who'd made Robin's school years misery was—surprise, surprise—a regular there.

Anderson sniggered to himself, as though he'd taken to reading minds. "One of the lunchtime staff said she's got a good memory for faces. Apparently she'd seen Youngs at a brass band concert in the Stanebridge Abbey last Christmas."

"Blimey. Good memory? It must be an astonishing one if she can remember that."

"I'm only feeding back what she told me. Actually, I think she was a bit embarrassed by the whole thing. Remember Youngs's ears?"

"A bit on the large side, weren't they?" He'd had a boyfriend like that once. Big ears, small everything else.

"Nicely put, sir." The sergeant sniggered again. "Apparently he was two rows in front of her at the concert, and she couldn't keep her eyes off them—the ears. When they broke for an interval, she got a good look at his face."

"I bet she did. Wanted to see if he had a big nose to match them?"

"Well, you know what they say about noses, sir. Maybe it's the same with other things. Big ears, big—"

"Thank you, Sergeant." Robin wasn't going to enter his personal testimony into evidence. "I assume there's more to this?"

"Oh yes. Youngs wasn't the only person our witness saw at the concert. Neil Musgrave was sitting two seats away from Youngs, and they were chatting on and off."

"Were they? Were they indeed? Right, get your prayer book ready." Robin picked up the sergeant's car keys, swinging them like a censer. "You can drive me to church."

Chapter Fifteen

They were on the road back to Lindenshaw village for what seemed the umpteenth time, Anderson driving because Robin had insisted, even though he was never the happiest passenger. He kept his eyes fixed straight ahead, especially when his sergeant took a shortcut up the lane where Adam's neat little cottage stood.

"Wasn't that the teacher from St. Crispin's?" Anderson asked, head turning like an owl's to follow a passing pedestrian.

"Didn't see. And keep your eyes on the road. I don't want to end up in a hedge." *Don't want to talk about him, either. Still trying to remember note to self, three.* "Drop me off at the vicarage."

Anderson pulled in without answering. If he'd noticed anything in his boss's tone, then he was still keeping his own counsel.

"Get yourself home after you've seen Duncan, unless something new comes up." Robin leaned on the car door. "I've a feeling we're in for the long haul with this one, and we need to conserve energy."

"Are you sure you don't want a lift back, sir?"

"There's bound to be a bus to Stanebridge, even in a godforsaken place like this." Robin slammed the door, ending any debate, and headed up the path to the vicarage. He didn't want to have to explain what else he needed to do here and why he wanted to be alone with his thoughts.

If Adam's and Narraway's cottages had presented an image of England that had seemed too good to be true, then Lindenshaw church carried on the theme. It must have had Norman roots; local historians, like his mother, said this had been an important settlement at some point in the past until, like the school, it had started to slip and fade. But the graves were well tended, with patches of longer grass in between which had been left for the butterflies and other wildlife to flourish in, as the notices posted around the vicarage informed anyone who felt like complaining. The insects were flourishing now, darting about as Robin crossed the churchyard in search of the vicar, who seemed to be trying to tip gravestones over.

He looked up as Robin reached the sort of crunchy gravel that prevented a stealthy approach. "Ah, Inspector. Don't mind me. I'm just checking that these old things are still safe."

"Mrs. Musgrave said I'd find you here. On health and safety patrol, she said."

Neil Musgrave grinned. "It's the bane of all our lives. We'd had a complaint that some of the stones were working loose. Risk of them falling over and crushing someone's bunions, so I've the unenviable task of giving each one a jolly good heave."

"All of them?" There seemed to be acres of the things, generation after generation of Lindenshaw's good, bad, and mediocre.

"All the ones on the south and west sides. My church warden is doing the honours for the other two sectors." The vicar gave a time-worn, ivy-clad headstone a particularly hearty shove, worrying it in its socket like a child with a milk tooth.

"And what happens if they wobble as much as that?"

"Over they must go. We have to lay them flat so they can't topple unexpectedly. Could you lend a hand?" They carefully manoeuvred the stone to the ground, resting it in the grass where it couldn't wreak havoc on anyone's toes. The vicar produced a pen and paper, noting down the miscreant's location. "I have to keep a record and try to contact any living relatives of whoever's in this plot. The world's going mad. Still, you have questions to ask me. Do you mind if I carry on while we talk?"

"That's fine, so long as you don't topple one on me." They walked along to the next memorial. "When we spoke on Thursday, you said you couldn't remember where you'd seen Ian Youngs before."

"I think I actually told your sergeant that I had the feeling we'd met before, which is not quite the same thing." Musgrave gave a marble cross a violent shove, then moved on to his next victim.

"And Marjorie Bookham apparently told everyone you'd had a run-in with him."

The vicar stopped, hands on a sad-looking angel. "I think that remark was meant to be just a joke, Inspector, but it seems to be taking on a life of its own. Come on, out with it. You've something to say, and I'd rather you said it right now than pussyfoot about."

Robin narrowed his eyes, uncomfortable when on the back foot. "We've been told you were with Ian Youngs at a concert in Stanebridge Abbey, December the fifth of last year. Brass bands. Christmas music."

Musgrave looked genuinely puzzled. "I was certainly at the concert. I remember it very well. But I didn't go with Mr. Youngs. Whoever told you that got it horribly wrong."

"They seemed entirely certain. They saw you speaking to him."

"I wasn't— Oh!" The vicar slapped the angel's arm. "You're quite right. *That's* where I'd seen him before. I was attending the concert with my sister, Gwen. I'm afraid my wife can't stand brass bands—she much prefers folk music—and Youngs was, I think, in the seat next to Gwen's. He was extremely knowledgeable about the intricacies of adapting film music for brass ensembles to play."

Robin wasn't sure he believed a word of it; too much detail was almost as bad as too little. "Your sister would remember him too?"

"She would, I'm sure. She was very taken with him." Musgrave smiled, indulgently. "I'd give you her phone number, only it's back at the vicarage. Perhaps you could ask my wife to rouse it out?"

"I will do when I've finished here."

"There's more?" The vicar stopped, halfway to attacking the next gravestone.

"There is, and it's a bit of a delicate question." Robin lowered his voice, even though there didn't seem to be anyone about to listen in. "Are you aware of anything in Oliver Narraway's past which may have an impact on this case?"

Musgrave's amiable face turned wooden, his voice tense. "I am aware of certain stories that have been in circulation about Oliver, but I'm not sure they have any bearing on Mr. Youngs's death, nor do I believe they're true."

At least he hadn't pleaded the secrecy of the confessional. "I promise I'll treat anything you tell me in absolute confidence if it turns out to be irrelevant to our investigations." How many times had Robin turned out that line, and how rarely had it produced any dividends?

The vicar leaned on the gravestone, deliberately avoiding Robin's eye. "He was headmaster at Tythebarn. One of my parishioners used to live there, and she told me it was as well the school closed when it did. For Oliver. Otherwise he might have been given the boot."

"Did she say why?" And seeing as the vicar surely dealt in miracles, did his parishioner have a way of making a link between that and Youngs?

"She didn't know for certain, although she speculated it might have been because of inappropriate behaviour towards the children and staff. I told her that she should make an official complaint—if there *were* children involved, she has a duty to blow the whistle, no matter that it was years ago." Musgrave lunged viciously at the stone. "And I also told her that if she was making up stories without any evidence to back them up, she should keep her mouth shut. I put it more politely than that," he added, finding a smile again, although a forced one.

"Which of those options did she choose?"

The vicar attacked the next headstone. "To shut up, for which I'm very grateful. The expression 'There's no smoke without fire' is a wicked one, especially when the fire is no more than a malicious streak in someone's nature." He gave the stone an almighty heave, tipping it onto thick grass that softened its fall.

"I just hope, for his sake, that's all we've got here."

Child protection—it was the most emotive topic and no policeman worth his salt would ignore any hint of it in a case. If Youngs had found out that Narraway had something to hide along those lines, and had let him know the fact, it could have led to a disastrous chain of events. Not that Robin had anything other than that bloody pillar of gossip smoke to guide him.

"So do I. Mr. Bright, believe me, if I had any evidence that he'd abused children over at Tythebarn, I'd have blown the whistle myself." He looked Robin in the eye, steadily. "Even if parts of the church have got a history of covering things up, I wouldn't. And if anything happened to the children at St. Crispin's, I'd forget about turning the other cheek or forgiving anyone their trespasses."

Robin swallowed hard. Why the hell did this case have to keep hitting so close to home? He left the vicar to his gravestones, then took the back exit from the graveyard, nipping down the little lane and finding the spot he used to go as a child, when things got too much and he needed to think. A large flat stone, set into an old hedge—his mother had said it had some sort of historical significance, lost in the mists of time, but for him it was the place he could sit, look over the woods, and try to work out his next move.

The trees had grown, and he didn't remember the little development of houses next to them, but otherwise it felt like stepping back into another world. He slumped onto the stone, shut his eyes, and tried to clear his mind, but the past wouldn't let him go so easily.

Name-calling, that's how it had started. Robin had told the teacher, and he'd told Robin to grow up. *Sticks and stones can break my bones but names will never hurt me?* Whoever had come up with that wasn't a frightened little boy.

Then there'd been a bit of rougher stuff, outbreaks of fisticuffs in that shrubbery behind the kitchen. Robin had told his mother, and she'd created merry hell with the headmaster, although he hadn't really done much. Bullying at *his* school? Just a bit of innocent horseplay. His mother would have pulled him out of the school, but Robin had wanted to stay, with his friends. And things *had* got better, for a while.

He pulled up his sleeve, stared at the little white line along his skin, still vivid after twenty years. A going-away present from one of his tormentors, Ryan Atherley, just before they'd left school. Robin had told his mother he'd fallen on some wire. That last fortnight in year six had been fourteen days of hell.

Let it go.

He took another deep breath, opened his eyes, and looked out over the woods. He'd be happy to let it go, but who would take it from him?

Luckily, the Lindenshaw signal blackout spots, which took in the church, didn't extend to the high street, although there must have been an equivalent one wherever Anderson had got himself to. Robin overcame his dislike of answerphones, left a message, and got on with ringing Musgrave's sister.

Yes, she remembered the concert. Yes, she remembered the man with the large ears. No, he wasn't a friend. They'd just happened to be sitting next to one another, and she resented any implications otherwise. They'd just chatted to each other, as people did who had an ounce of Christian spirit in their bodies. No, her brother hadn't known Youngs, and didn't the police have something better to do than annoy decent law-abiding citizens?

Robin gave profuse apologies and cut the call off as soon as was polite. He had other fish to fry, if he could refer to Marjorie Bookham that way.

Despite the glimpses he'd had of newer properties hidden away in little side streets, as though they weren't allowed to show themselves on the main road, Robin had begun to believe that just about every house in Lindenshaw had been old enough for Cromwell to knock it about a bit. He'd expected the Bookhams' house to be of a similar vintage, but it was clearly a 1950s build, immaculately looked after given the external paintwork, but a bit stuck in the past. Like the school. No wonder Marjorie Bookham felt at home there.

Still, one thing all the houses in the area seemed to have in common was the ability to leak sound. Robin waited after ringing the doorbell and could hear a gruff, masculine voice bellowing, possibly from upstairs. A curt "Door, Marjorie" suggested Mr. Bookham was as much of a dinosaur as Oliver Narraway. Like the old fogeys who had infested Lindenshaw during his childhood, spoiling all the fun.

"Yes, I'm going." Mrs. Bookham opened the door, her look of surprise swiftly turning into a smile and the crossness in her voice being toned down. "Oh!"

Robin smiled, something usually guaranteed to melt the stony hearts of women of any age. *If you've got it, why not use it?* "I'm sorry to call unannounced, but that's what my job's like at times. I've got a couple of things you might be able to clarify. About St. Crispin's school."

"Oh, of course." She didn't look enthusiastic. "Come in."

"Thank you."

Mrs. Bookham called up the stairs. "It's only the police, Derek."

"About these bloody shed burglaries? About time too. Shoot the lot of them, that's what I say."

"No, dear," Mrs. Bookham said through gritted teeth. "It's about Thursday."

"You won't need me, then." The disembodied reply clearly gave Mrs. Bookham the message she wanted to hear.

"Shall we go through?" she sounded more relaxed and pointed to a half-open door. "It's comfier in the lounge."

Like the house—and maybe Mr. Bookham himself—the decor in the room seemed trapped in the fifties, another bulwark against the steady tide of progress and change. Everything was spotless, if a touch in need of restoration. Perhaps that reflected on the man of the house too. Robin took the seat he was offered—a slightly sagging comfy chair—while his hostess perched primly on the edge of the sofa.

"Please ignore Derek. He gets a bee in his bonnet about things, but he's basically harmless."

"Been a lot of burglaries round here?" Robin's local gossip network had let him down; he'd not heard about this Lindenshaw crime spree.

Mrs. Bookham rolled her eyes. "Only a couple of plant pots and some tools taken as far as I know, at least around here. He saw something on the local news about Stanebridge—which he thinks is a den of iniquity—and has convinced himself that gangs of armed robbers are about to park their white vans by the village green and go on the rampage."

"If that happens, I'll send Anderson straight round to let down their tyres." Robin's deliberately charming smile seemed to put his hostess at ease.

"About Thursday, then. I'm not sure there's anything I can tell you that I haven't already put into my statement."

"I didn't say it was about Thursday, Mrs. Bookham." Robin tried the winning smile again. "I want to pick your brain about last term, the first time you tried to recruit."

Mrs. Bookham shuddered, slightly overdramatically, and closed her eyes. "That awful, awful time." Her eyes flashed open, revealing a piercing blue gaze. She certainly must have been stunning in her younger days, the equivalent of Christine Probert in the playground of twenty or thirty years prior. "I'm not sure I have much to tell you about that, either."

"Really?" Robin found the woman's shrewd gaze slightly unnerving. He concentrated on returning it steadily. "What about your argument with Claire Waites?"

Whatever Mrs. Bookham had been expecting to be questioned about, it wasn't this. Her usually confident tone became tentative, and the shrewd gaze fizzled into uncertainty. "I thought all that sort of discussion was supposed to be strictly confidential? Who told you?"

"When we're dealing with murder, nothing's confidential anymore," Robin got in quickly before his interviewee found her fighting spirit again. "I know you quarrelled about the difference between private and public behaviour for school staff. Could you give me a bit more detail?"

"It was outrageous." The fight was well and truly back. "That Waites woman said what people did in their own time, off school property, was up to them, so long as it wasn't illegal. I was up in arms— Imagine having teachers at St. Crispin's going out and getting drunk or living in sin."

Or being gay. Robin shuddered to think what sort of mutterings there'd be behind Adam's back if the Lindenshaw mafia got wind of that fact.

"She was living with a man, of course, which is why she was so adamant about it," Mrs. Bookham rattled on. "She seemed almost proud of the fact they weren't married."

"You have it written into their contracts that they have to live like monks?"

"There's no need to be flippant, Inspector. Caesar's wife should be above suspicion and all that," Mrs. Bookham bridled. "And I think it's appropriate to set expectations of our teachers. How else can we make sure the children get shown a good example? Standards are falling rapidly enough in St. Crispin's."

Robin was getting tired of the onslaught of self-righteousness, especially as it seemed to have some sort of undefined agenda to it. If that agenda was about gay teachers—or policemen—then he was going to get his retaliation in beforehand. "I'm not sure you should be telling me if you've given any of your candidates the heave-ho because of his or her marital status. Or anything else that would be discriminatory. I'd have to report my concerns."

The threat stopped her in her tracks. "Oh. Yes, of course. I mean, that's not why we didn't carry her forward for interview. Wrong attitude. Now, is there anything else? I need to get on with starting Derek's dinner. He'll want it put out before the football comes on. If there's a match on Sky, morning, noon, or night, he wants to see it."

Lucky sod. No way Robin was going to get to see the teatime kickoff—or spend two hours in front of the box—anytime soon. "Nothing else at the moment. Thank you."

Plenty to think about, though. Not least the fact that the accounts of what went on with Claire Waites weren't consistent. What would be her take on it?

Robin stood at the end of the Bookhams' road, wondering which way to turn. The nearest bus stop was outside Narraway's cottage, but he didn't fancy hanging about there, especially as the next bus to Stanebridge wasn't for another hour. Stump up for a taxi or try to get one of the local patrols to come get him? Or wander down to the main bus stop? And why the hell had he dismissed Anderson for the day and let himself be cast adrift here?

Because he'd wanted time to think. That and that alone, he told himself, not believing a word of it.

He *did* like finding room to let his mind work—room away from the station and the constant buzzing of phones and clamour of voices, places like the old stone at St. Crispin's but with a more positive connotation. Especially for a case like this one, where it didn't look like the solution was going to be obvious. But why did he feel the need to find that space here? Or, perhaps more pertinently, why couldn't he admit to himself the real—blindingly obvious—reason?

It would be so easy to just walk up to Adam's door, knock, and say he was sorry. Maybe he'd get invited in for a mug of tea, maybe he could explain what school had been like for him, how even the mention of St. Crispin's set every nerve on edge. If Adam couldn't understand, then nobody would. Just as nobody had really understood during all those years he'd suffered.

The moral high ground was that he should go back to the station and get on with the case. He could go along and see if the Olive Tree Café just off the high street still existed, grab a pot of tea and a cake, then catch the bus from outside the Bear and Ragged Staff without letting himself run into temptation. Apologies could lead to reconciliations. And reconciliations could be dangerous, especially when he was feeling so vulnerable. Robin had a case to solve, not a romance to run.

He turned right along the main road. It had to be the Olive Tree.

The café was there, the pot of tea arrived quickly, and the cakes were just as good as he remembered them. By the time he was ready to nip up to the bus stop, the world seemed a better place, although not even a fruit scone could bring the solution to Youngs's murder into his mind. His mellow mood came to an abrupt end, though, as he left the café, and saw Adam Matthews—and all the enticement he represented—coming along the street, wheeling a bike in a direct line between him and the bus stop.

Echoes of being in the same street twenty years ago, trying to work out how he could avoid crossing Ryan Atherley's path, hit him like a punch in the stomach. Robin knew the back way, the old footpath behind the shops and houses that emerged on the other side of the pub, but it risked losing a lot of time—especially if it had been developed away at some point—and so he could miss the bus. Sod's Law said today would be one of the few occasions the bloody thing would actually be on time.

He'd have to face it out, try to be polite, plead that he had a bus to catch. Just looking down at his feet and pretending not to notice Adam's presence was only going to make things worse.

Eye contact came when they were twenty yards apart, and Adam held it until they were face-to-face, although at the last minute, he looked away.

"Hello again." Robin hadn't meant to say anything, but the bloody words were out of his mouth before he knew it.

Adam stopped, just past him, turning half-round and addressing a point to the left of Robin's ear. "Hi."

"I didn't realise you had a bike." Bloody facile thing to say, but Robin's mouth seemed to have a mind of its own at present.

"It's all teachers can afford." It was a pretty standard sort of jokey response, although Robin wasn't sure he meant it like that.

"Right." Why couldn't the bloody bus come and put an end to the torture?

"I was going to ring you," Adam said, still not looking Robin in the eye.

"Really?" That sounded hopeful. Maybe *he* was going to hold out the olive branch and save Robin's face.

"No, I just said that for the hell of it." Adam pushed his bike to and fro, like he was about to get going again. "Although maybe you can solve this case all on your own without any input from us mere mortals."

"Oh yeah. I thought I'd use my crystal ball."

At last Adam looked at Robin, as though he wasn't sure if he was joking. "I have something to tell you. Are you interested or not?"

"Only if you bloody get around to telling it." Robin took a deep breath. This could be important. Whatever else was—or wasn't—going on between them, Adam could be a key witness. "Sorry. That was uncalled for."

"Too bloody right it was," Adam replied, looking like he was forcing back a grin. "Don't make that puppy-dog face. It's not fair trying to make me laugh."

"I wasn't aware I was doing anything." Robin couldn't help smiling too. "Come on, what's this about?" If it was important, the bus could wait—which it wouldn't, of course, so he'd have to hang around for the next one.

"I popped down to see Oliver Narraway this morning. Not for the sake of pleasure—I always take his governor post round as I'm local." Adam grimaced. "I usually just push them through the letter box and make a quick getaway. But today I heard him shouting. The window was open a bit; I wasn't earwigging, if you're wondering."

"I wasn't. Who was he shouting at?"

"No idea. He must have been on the phone. He just said he didn't think it could wait until tomorrow. Something like that. I don't know what *it* was." Adam shrugged. "Then he said he'd had the police here and that they knew what happened."

"Is that exactly what he said?"

"I haven't embellished it to make a good impression on you. I'm not that desperate," Adam added, flushing to the roots of his hair.

"Okay, sorry." Robin put his hands up in a classic gesture of surrender. Were they always going to be this spiky with each other? And had he blown any chances of finding out after this business was done? "Anything else?"

"Whoever it was must have asked something, and he said 'Yes, then' and something about needing to talk to them soon." The flush was subsiding. "Normally I wouldn't have listened, but given the circumstances . . ."

"That's okay. It could be important. Thank you."

A rumble behind them indicated the arrival of the bus. Robin looked over his shoulder, torn.

"You look like you need to catch that." Adam was still smiling, which was starting to tip the balance.

"I did, but I can wait, if you've more to tell me."

"I have, if you've got time. Where's your car, then?"

"Back at the station. Long story, don't ask." Robin suddenly felt like even more of an idiot marooned here. *Change the subject.* "What's the problem with the bike?"

"Bleeding great puncture. I was going to cycle into Stanebridge to the police station when I went over a nail. I'm taking it down to an old bloke who used to have a bike shop here so he can mend it."

"I remember him. Scared the crap out of me." It felt like everything had scared the crap out of him twenty years ago. And Adam was looking at him as though he knew all about it.

It was a key moment, and Robin knew it. He could still get the bus if he ran, then he could treat Adam like any other witness. Or he could grow a pair, see if Adam had any other inside information he could draw on, and then maybe even allow himself the luxury of pouring his own heart out. Didn't he deserve a friendly ear after all these years of holding things in?

The bus pulled away from the stop, and the decision was made by default. "Did you hear Narraway say anything else?"

"Yes. I made some notes." Adam fished a slip of paper from his pocket and studied it. "He said he didn't think he could keep it covered up much longer. Don't be smutty," he added, with a comic grimace.

"I won't be." Was Adam flirting? "You didn't by chance hear anything about this meeting he was trying to set up?"

"No such luck. Oliver was talking about either this afternoon or tomorrow, then he was saying good-bye, and I had to leg it." Adam produced a sheepish smile. "I felt like I'd been knocking on doors and running away. Something about Oliver Narraway always makes me believe I'm just a schoolboy again."

Robin couldn't resist the green eyes or the boyish grin any longer. "I'm sorry. About last night. I made a complete dick of myself."

"No. It wasn't you. I kept opening my gob and sticking my size elevens in."

Robin looked down; Adam did have unusually large feet for such a slim, wiry bloke.

"I saw that." Something about Adam's voice had changed. There was no way he used that lascivious tone with the kids. "Yeah, big feet, big..."

"Shoes?" They both looked up, caught each other's eyes, and laughed. Peace had well and truly broken out now.

"So, are you here chasing witnesses or something?"

"You've got me bang to rights." Robin put up his hands in surrender again. "And, like the bloody idiot I keep being, I've let myself be stranded here and need to get back to the station for a team briefing at eight o'clock. I can't even hijack your bike if it's got a puncture."

"I'll give you a lift back." Adam nodded towards the top of the high street. "Let's get rid of this first." He got the bicycle moving again. "You can wait outside if Mr. Rogers still scares you."

"Not on your life." Robin fell into step alongside Adam. It was time to start putting his childhood fears behind him. "I'll whip out my warrant card if he starts anything."

Robin had never appreciated quite how nice a late Saturday afternoon in Lindenshaw could be. Perhaps it was the balmy weather. Perhaps it was just the company for a pleasant stroll back to Adam's house. Perhaps it was even the anticipation of seeing Campbell and apologising to him too. There'd been a tentative offer of a meal, which Robin had refused, adamant that he'd imposed on the teacher's hospitality two evenings running. He had a case to solve too, but he couldn't do that on an empty stomach.

"I'd suggest going out for a bite, but we'd have to steer clear of any of the local places," he said.

"Good point." Adam didn't seem to need further explanation. He must have known they were straying into dangerous waters. "I could drive us over to Tythebarn. There's a good Indian takeaway where the chip shop used to be."

Much as the thought of chicken Madras, with saag dal on the side, appealed—especially if Adam was going to be across the table—the sheer thought of going out anywhere suddenly felt exhausting.

"Or we could get takeaway. Then you wouldn't have to worry about me slaving over a hot stove."

"I think you just read my mind."

When they returned to the cottage, Campbell couldn't decided whether he most needed to dash into the garden and relieve himself or lick Robin—who'd obviously being forgiven without the need to apologise—to death. The garden won, but he was soon back, sticking his nose into Robin's hand as he tried to find a seat on the settee, Adam fussing round and clearing away piles of marking and preparation.

Robin eventually settled himself against the cushions, which Campbell somehow interpreted as a sign to join him on the settee. "Is he allowed?"

"Not really, which he knows. Get down, Campbell." The Newfoundland, suitably chastened, slipped down onto the floor again. "I'm claiming that for *my* place, anyway." Adam parked his backside on the settee, close but not *too* close. "Any news about that bit of paper?"

"Paper? Oh, the one Youngs put in his pocket? No." Like everything else in this case, it remained nebulous and unhelpful.

"Maybe it was just a note he made to help him with one of the recruitment things." Adam wrinkled his nose. "Look, tell me to bugger off if you want to, but I'd like the opportunity to scoot the elephant out of the room."

Robin sighed. "If it's the same elephant I'm thinking of, I'd be surprised."

"There's more than one, then?" Adam leaned closer.

"I can think of two." It would be so easy now to let his scruples go, to ease nearer to Adam and take whatever comfort was on offer. "Which one did you have in mind?"

"That something happened when you were a pupil at St. Crispin's."

"That's one of them." Robin, disappointed that Adam didn't choose the other elephant—their clear mutual attraction—first, took a deep breath. Yes, better for both of them to clear the air, but the clearing process wasn't going to be pleasant.

"And my guess is that you were bullied." Adam said, voice still low and reassuring. "Or something worse."

"Good God, no." Robin remembered the conversation of the evening before. Was it only less than twenty-four hours ago? Because it seemed half a lifetime. "It wasn't sexual abuse or anything like that. Physical. A little—well, not so little—scrote called Ryan Atherley had it in for me. Beat the crap out of me in that shrubbery. Did this with a compass point." Robin rolled up his sleeve, showing the mark.

"Bloody hell." Adam reached over, briefly touched the scar, then drew his hand back hastily. "Did anybody do anything about it?"

"What do you think? My mother made a fuss, but it was smoothed over. I didn't tell her the worst of it."

"The good old days, eh? I'm pleased it wasn't sexual, though," Adam said, hand hovering as if it wanted to touch the scar again.

"Yeah, well, it still felt bad enough to me."

Adam drew his hand back again and ran it over his forehead. "I'm cocking things up again, aren't I? It's not this hard when they ask me to have a heart-to-heart with one of the junior kids."

"I wish you'd been at St. Crispin's back then. Somebody who'd have listened rather than just pretended it was character forming, telling me to stop being a coward." Robin shut his eyes. Wasn't it supposed to help, talking through your problems? Why did it feel so difficult?

"Want to talk about it now?" Adam's hand had edged along the back of the settee, almost touching Robin's shoulder.

"Yeah. No. Don't know." Robin shifted slightly, easing into Adam's touch.

"Okay. Well, that covers all the options." He gently rubbed Robin's shoulder.

"I was hoping that finding somebody who understood would be enough to lift some of the weight from my shoulders."

"It will, eventually. There's no magic key to turn that'll make everything better at once." Adam's fingers drifted along Robin's neck. "You can pour your heart out to me anytime you like."

"I'll take you up on that, sometime. In the meantime, what I'd like is . . ." Robin lifted a hand to Adam's face, running his fingers along a jaw that was showing the first signs of a dark- blond five-o'clock shadow.

The kiss was sweet, knowing without being needy. A secure point on a bewildering day. A step across the line into territory he—they—really shouldn't be in.

The sudden buzzing of Robin's mobile saved his bacon, sending Campbell crazy and forcing the pair to spring apart.

"Sorry." He might have ignored it, later told whoever was trying to call that he'd been in the bath and left the thing in the bedroom, but when a big case was underway, he was expected to have his phone almost welded to him. And it gave him thinking time. "Hello? Oh, right. Wait a minute."

He mouthed, *Work, sorry,* to Adam, got up, and resumed the conversation when he was in the hall. "Okay. Free to talk now."

"Having fun without me?" Anderson laughed.

"Just a drink with a friend." Near enough to the truth. He hurried on, in case Anderson started interrogating him about whether he'd managed to catch a bus back to the station. "Any news from Duncan?"

"He keeps insisting he was at Tythebarn with the dog, but there's more. Enough for you to buy *me* a drink on the strength of it."

"I'll be the judge of that. Give me a briefing, and if it's good enough, I'll stand you a pub lunch tomorrow."

Robin could almost hear Anderson's grin through the phone. "I picked up the Duncans' draft statements from the station and took them over, to go through and sign." Always a useful, easy start to a second interview. "I had to park outside the neighbour's house and she nabbed me. Asked if I was with the police."

"It's your flat feet. Makes it very obvious." Interesting, though, that somebody would be perhaps on the lookout.

"This woman, Mrs. Burton, knew you'd been by. The Cordelia Close gossip network must be as—"

Robin lost the last bit in a crackling burst of static. "What? Can you say that again?"

"The gossip grapevine must be as effective as the one in the Lindenshaw St. Crispin's playground."

"Or the hedges are particularly easy to hear over." That whole interview in the garden between Robin and Lizzie Duncan hadn't been conducted at a volume low enough for a determined snooper not to listen in.

"However it happened, Mrs. Burton said she wasn't sure if it was important, but she'd overheard an—" Another burst of static cut in.

"Yes? I keep losing you."

"Sorry, sir, I was walking through the car park. I see you've not picked your car up yet."

Robin ignored the remark. "Stand still for a minute. Mrs. Burton overheard . . .?"

"An odd conversation from the Duncans' house."

Earwigging seemed to be the activity of the moment, given the favourable conditions. Warm weather, open windows, sitting out in the garden to make the most of the sunshine, people forgetting to keep their voices down.

"It seems they were out in the garden. She reckoned Mrs. Duncan was irked because Mr. Duncan had been fussing over her too much. Started as a bit of a squabble—apparently they've been having a few of those recently—and it escalated. Mrs. Duncan said they had to decide what to do."

"The neighbour didn't happen to hear what they had to decide about?"

"She said she'd either missed that bit or it had already been said. Before she could get her ear close enough to the hedge, maybe." The sergeant paused as a police car screamed past, siren wailing. "That's one of the things that makes me think it's genuine. If she was embroidering the story, she'd have filled in the holes."

It was a valid point; Robin believed that less was often more, and he distrusted too much detail laid on.

"Anyway, the rest almost makes up for it. Reckon I'll earn my ploughman's."

"You haven't yet."

"When Duncan said his wife was to leave it to him, she bit his head off. 'Like we left it to you before? Look at the mess things have got into.' She said something like that. Shame Mrs. Burton didn't get the chance to write it down verbatim." Anderson chuckled. "I can imagine her wondering whether to go get a pencil and paper or stay and listen to the rest."

Robin leaned against the front door, trying to make out what the Duncans could have been discussing.

"And, there's more," Anderson continued. "Mr. Duncan said something about the police not knowing anything, and she went mental again. 'Don't they? I suppose you think it's just pure coincidence that inspector came straight round here?'" It wasn't a very accurate impression of Mrs. Duncan's voice but it got the point across. "He wanted to talk about it in the morning, and she said they'd got past the point of just talking."

"Did you think about confronting them with it?"

"I *thought* about it. But I decided I didn't have enough to make it worthwhile. They'd have just put up the barriers."

"And the rest of it?"

"Can keep, probably. I'm not sure I got any more out of Duncan than you did. Insists that neither of them were near St. Crispin's on Thursday, and Davis says that the hospital bears that out. At least for the wife." Anderson sighed. "That girl's been working her socks off. I suspect she deserves a drink, not me."

"Then take her out and buy her one after we're done tonight. Get Helen to come along and act as chaperone." Robin sighed. Who else had to go into work again at eight on a Saturday night except rozzers to discuss updates on a case? Forensics, legwork—whether door-to-door for Youngs's neighbours or trawling through his bank accounts and computer records—sometimes the key fact arose from sharing the mundane rather than a brilliant deduction.

"Nice to have your blessing for something enjoyable. I hope your evening turns out as much fun." Anderson cut off the call before Robin could make a rude response.

By the time he'd got his brain back in gear and his body back into the lounge, Adam was poring over a takeaway menu, the sheer sight of which made Robin's stomach rumble.

Adam looked up, grinning. "Hungry?"

"Was it that obvious?" Robin clamped his hand over the offending midriff. "I didn't really get lunch." And breakfast seemed a lifetime in the past. "When does it open?"

"Half an hour. Will you last that long? I can make you a sandwich . . ."

The dog, who seemed to ignore his master's voice much of the time, lifted his head, expectantly.

"No, thanks. Don't want to spoil my appetite. And do Campbell's ears always prick up like that when someone says 'sandwich'?"

"They go like that anytime food gets mentioned." Adam smoothed Campbell's ears down, much to the dog's annoyance. "We can go and wait on the doorstep of the takeaway, and they might show pity on us. Like when it's piddling with rain and we let the kids in early."

"You really love teaching, don't you?"

"To borrow your phrase, am I that obvious?" Adam addressed Campbell. "People see right through us both, don't they, boy?" He turned his gorgeous green eyes back at Robin. "I've never regretted a minute. Not even when Youngs was killed. Especially when it meant you turned up."

It should have been the right time for a second kiss, but the moment was gone—phone call and rumbling tummy, let alone Robin's nagging conscience, had put paid to it. He held out his hand for the menu. "Let me give the place a call. We helped them a few years ago when some thugs were causing trouble. Maybe I can persuade them to open early."

He could, and did. By six o'clock, there were two pretty well empty plates, two half-consumed glasses of wine, and Campbell was tucking into a bowlful of things he probably shouldn't have.

"If heaven doesn't have chicken tikka masala, I don't want to go." Robin mopped up the last bit of sauce with a corner of chapati.

"Just so long as heaven doesn't have interminable school governors' meetings, we'll be all right." Adam picked up the wine bottle, offering to replenish their glasses.

"I'd love to say yes, but I'm not going to the briefing stinking of wine. And won't we look a pair of dicks if the traffic police pull us over for weaving across the ring road?"

"I guess we should leave now." Adam put down his glass. "Shame. How long do these things go on?"

"How long's a piece of string?" Robin, reluctantly, put his plate and glass on the table. "Depends if anybody's turned up anything that's worth going out for again. Otherwise I'm recommending we all get an early night. Back in again tomorrow."

"We could have the rest of the wine later. I'll stick it in the fridge." Adam kept his eyes on the bottle. "I bet I could find some pudding while you're getting updated on Youngs. If you fancy a bit of company for an hour or two when you've sent the team home?" He looked up.

Robin took a deep breath. Go home and catch up on much-needed sleep? Or come back here and see what "afters" consisted of? No debate, if Adam hadn't been involved in this case. *Note to self three, remember?* But surely he could have another—small—drink and something to eat. It was helping to clear his mind, having somebody to talk to.

He tossed a mental coin.

"You're on."

Chapter Sixteen

Robin's meeting turned out to be little more than going through the motions. Nothing new had turned up. No gossip about any of the principal players, no hint of a motive. Robin sent the team home and asked them to reconvene the next day; perhaps something different would appear in the light of a new day. Perhaps.

He wasn't sure going back to Adam's house was such a great idea—by the time he hit the outskirts of Lindenshaw, he found himself barely able to keep his eyes open—but he could always just have a coffee, then drive the remaining five miles home. To his own empty, cold bed.

He swung the car onto Adam's driveway, stopped the engine, put out the lights, and sat, thinking. *He's a witness. You're a copper on a case he's up to his neck in. You shouldn't be here.* He thought about the empty bed at home again, took the keys from the ignition, and got out of the car.

Adam had been true to his word: the wine was chilled, he'd dished up some tinned mango and vanilla ice cream on the breakfast bar, and the house was pleasantly warm against a night that had turned unseasonably chilly and wet. Maybe he'd also sussed out that Robin wasn't entirely at ease. Conversation over the food was kept light, parochial, nonflirtatious.

"My parents wanted me to go into engineering or something," Adam said in response to Robin's question about a group photo, clearly taken at his graduation. "They didn't want me going into the family business. They're both lecturers."

"What did they think when you made your act of rebellion?"

"Let's take these through to the lounge, and I'll tell you." Adam grabbed the glasses and, with a deft sidestep and a quick hand on the kitchen door handle, managed to avoid Campbell joining them. "My parents reacted how they always do. Came over disappointed but stoic and assumed I'd be teaching at A level, so going into the primary sector was a double blow for them."

"Being a governor's got to be a good career move, surely?" Robin perched on the settee, memories of their earlier kiss niggling at him. *Repeat performance?* In any other circumstances he'd have been in like a rat up a drainpipe. *Note to self four. Yeah, well.*

"Maybe." Adam hovered by the fireplace, clearly unsure where to sit. "Some of our meetings resemble the Somme."

"That bad?"

"Cattier than a drag night at Bosie's."

"That I wouldn't know." Robin took another sip of wine. "I've only been there the once. Never went back."

Adam feigned horror. "Aren't you a disgrace to the Stanebridge gay community? Isn't going to the gay club mandatory?"

Robin rolled his eyes. "If it is, I've failed. Can't stand the place."

"Not your scene? Even on a normal night?"

"Maybe if I had the right company." Robin smiled, then turned his attention to his drink. This was leaning too much toward flirting. He should go.

"You should have been there the night the touring cricket team came in by mistake. They'd been playing over at Applehurst and had wanted to hit the nightlife. They'd heard the name and thought the place was going to be some sort of cricket-themed bar."

Robin had to look at Adam, hearing that. "Had the locals been winding them up, telling them a load of crap?"

"Most likely. By the time the poor buggers realised it wasn't an homage to the googly, they'd already bought their drinks and had to finish them."

Robin wrinkled his nose. "Can anyone really be that dim?"

"I suspect they were at least three sheets to the wind to start with. And it was a bears' night, so the clientele must have reminded them of Dennis Lillee." Adam grinned. "At least one of them stayed—maybe he'd always had a secret yearning for moustaches."

Robin drained his drink and cradled the empty glass. "Does the name Ryan Atherley mean anything to you?"

"Didn't you mention him earlier?"

"Probably. The guy who blighted my days at school. The only time I went to Bosie's, he was there. Looked like he was a regular."

"And does that surprise you?" Adam caught Robin's eye, a spark of understanding and recognition flying between them.

"Nah. Bullying others for the thing you most hate in yourself—textbook."

"Top that up?" Adam came over for Robin's glass.

"I should be getting home."

"Got your mobile on, still?" Adam hovered, a faint hint of his cologne hanging in the air between them.

"Yes . . ."

"Then they can get hold of you if they need to. Have another, then doss down here. I've a spare bed, and I'll make sure you get a good breakfast inside you in the morning. You can borrow a clean shirt and boxers, if you want. We must be a similar size."

It all sounded so logical and so . . . right. He could tell himself he was here as a friend, that was all. They'd *be* friends, surely, if fate had thrown them together in any other setting. Only it hadn't, and they weren't. And was Robin going to put his career in jeopardy for the sake of dossing down on a spare bed?

"I'll have the drink, but then I need to go home," he said. "Sorry."

"No worries. I understand."

While Adam was in the kitchen to refill their glasses, Robin took off his tie, slipping it into his pocket. Off duty at least in terms of his clothes, if not in terms of that bloody mobile. The second glass of wine was welcome, as was Adam, who'd decided to sit next to him now, turned sideways with an arm along the back of the couch.

"I liked that kiss," he said, "up until your phone going off. It feels wicked, kissing a rozzer."

"Not as naughty as kissing the teacher." Robin leaned over the arm of the sofa, put his wineglass on the side table, turned back, smiling. "Only this *is* sinful. Or at least unethical. I'm right at the boundary of what's acceptable by just being here, anyway."

Adam inched away. "Sorry. I didn't mean to get you into trouble. It's just . . ." He shrugged. "It can't be easy for you, having to run a killer to ground, but it isn't easy for those of us who found him, either. I keep remembering those eyes. Horrible." Adam's hands trembled around the stem of his wineglass. "I feel safe when you're here, you know. I guess that's why I asked you to come back tonight, so I wouldn't have to be alone with my thoughts. I should have realised it wouldn't be the done thing."

"I get that. Things seem less intolerable when I'm with you too." Why the hell did fate have to be so cruel, putting them in a room together when the sparks of attraction couldn't help but fly? "It's been too long since I met a decent bloke."

Adam smiled. "You too? I thought I was the only person in the county not getting any."

There was an easy way to rectify that, for both of them. Too easy, though.

"I've not wanted to kiss anyone as much as I want to kiss you. Not in a long time." Robin picked up his glass again, to give his hands something safe to do. "But I might as well want the moon. Ain't going to happen."

"Why not?" Adam leaned across and made it happen. A prolonged, almost-desperate kiss, mellowing into affection. "See? You got the moon."

"Aren't you listening to me?" Robin wasn't sure his own conscience was listening to him anymore. "We can't get involved. Not till this case is done and dusted, and maybe not then."

Adam pulled back again. "Because you think I did it?"

"Don't be an idiot." Robin didn't mention the one percent of doubt that remained in his mind; that would stay there until the real killer was identified. "I meant that, if and when it gets to court, I don't want your evidence tainted by association with me. Or else some clever defence lawyer will discredit our case." That sounded better than *I don't want to jeopardise my career.*

Adam thought for a moment, then nodded. "I can't see how I could possibly be a key witness to anything, but I'll try not to lead you astray."

"Thanks." The way Robin felt, he'd be easily led. Not just because of how much he fancied Adam. Being in his bed would take Robin's mind off a murder he had no bloody idea how to solve. Not fair to either of them.

"Want to call it a night? Not that I want you to go just yet . . ."

"I don't particularly want to go." Robin took a deep breath. "I just don't want us to have any regrets tomorrow. Professional or personal."

"Tell me about it." Adam took Robin's hand. "Look, I'm tired and I'm upset and I'm fed up with sleeping alone. I can't see beyond my own needs. Just like one of my pupils," he added, with a weary smile. "I don't fancy waking to an empty house."

It would be so easy for Robin simply to give in to servicing Adam's desires, to relax and let himself be led rather than always chasing and searching. From the settee to the door, into the hall, up the stairs, into the bedroom. How simple it would be. How simple and how devastating.

"My car's outside. People notice these things." Robin felt the fight ebbing from him. How long had it been since *he'd* woken to somebody else being in the house?

"You hardly get anyone down this road, not outside of the rush hour. But if you're worried, you could put it in my garage."

"You're not making it easy for me to leave, are you?"

"I'd like to make it impossible," Adam said, but he let Robin's hand go. "If you want to sleep over in the spare bed, do it. No catches. If not, I won't mention it again."

Robin's legs felt like lead. It would be so much easier just to put his head down here, but the easiest option wasn't always the right one. He fished out his car keys. "I should go."

Robin took Adam's arm as they got to the front door. "When it's done and dusted, I promise we can try and make a go of it. If you'd still be interested."

"I'll be interested." Adam rubbed Robin's shoulder. "Don't you worry." He opened the door and grimaced. "I didn't realise it was chucking it down this hard. Need a brolly?"

"No. I'll make a dash for it." Robin ran to the car, got in, started it—before he could change his mind about the evening—and put it into reverse. The grating, crunching noise, allied to the strange feeling through the steering wheel, made him slam on the brakes. Just what he needed.

"What the hell's the matter?" Adam, still by the door, said, as Robin swung back onto the drive and opened his door.

"Flat tyre. Must have picked up a nail or something. I'll have to put the spare on."

"Come in. You can ring the RAC or whoever you use and get them to do it. You'll catch your death trying to change it out there now."

Adam was right. The night was filthy and even sitting in the car waiting for the breakdown people would be unpleasant. By the time he got back through the door, he was dripping and ready for the hot drink Adam offered. And when the breakdown company man said it could be three hours before they got to him, because there'd been a multicar pileup on the A road and another accident in the queue of rubberneckers, he told them not to bother. By then he'd be asleep, even if it was on Adam's settee. They could sort the tyre out between them in the morning.

"Staying?" Adam asked as Robin put his phone away.

"Looks like it." And with the weather and the accident and the evidence of the phone call, he had a perfect audit trail for explaining why.

Chapter Seventeen

The spare bedroom was the larger of the two in Adam's house, but as it had been his grandparents', it was laden with too many memories for him to have taken it over. Adam's own room had been his favourite part of the cottage ever since he'd stayed there as a child. It exuded warmth and welcome, as though echoes of its days as a guest bedroom lingered on. Not that Robin was going to experience them. At least, not tonight.

Robin took the room in as Adam shut the curtains. "It's lovely."

"You should see the view—especially in the morning," Adam rushed on, in case what seemed like an innocent remark provoked something. Bullying, jokes about murder, guilt at being here, even as a friend—why did everything have to make Robin twitchy? The bloke clearly carried around a ton of baggage. "I used to come in and have morning tea with Gran and Grandfather when I was little."

Robin's eyes lit up. "Does it face Hanger Hill?"

"Yes. At a sort of an angle, but yes." Adam took Robin's arm, pulling him over to the window and opening the curtains again. "If this bloody rain ever stopped, you might get an idea of the outline of it."

"That's the way my bedroom faced when I was a boy. If I'm staying over at Mum's, I still look out at the place. Always used to play there as a kid. Happy days."

Adam smiled, pleased to learn that the inspector's childhood hadn't been entirely bleak.

Robin rubbed the pane, as though that might give him a better view. "We must have been looking at the same sight, at the same age. Weird, isn't it?"

"Weird and wonderful." There was a song with those words, buzzing about in the back of Adam's mind, but he wasn't going to rack his brain over it now. Not with Robin's lips within twelve inches' leaning distance and having to resist leaning.

"That bed does look comfy," Robin said at last, turning from the window. "It seems a shame we can't use it."

"Get that right out of your plans, even if they're way ahead. That was my grandparents' bedstead, even if the mattress is different." Rogering anybody stupid in there would have felt like a betrayal; in his own room, it felt safe and right, although there wasn't much chance of that happening at the moment. "Nothing happens in here," he added, gently punching Robin's shoulder.

"Just as well, then." Robin seemed reluctant to say good-night, even though some pyjamas were already laid on the bed and he'd been shown where he could find a spare toothbrush.

"So . . . I'll see you in the morning?" Adam dithered. Should he just take the initiative and go?

"Yeah. Thanks." Robin cuffed Adam's arm, then withdrew his hand as if it had been stung.

Time to call it a night.

Adam sat bolt upright in bed, suddenly waking from an unpleasant dream in which the person who'd killed Youngs had come to kill him. He'd heard a noise, he was sure of it, and now he listened for it again. Funny, Campbell hadn't barked, so if there was an intruder, he must have pacified the dog. Or killed him, like in the dream.

Idiot.

He remembered then that Robin was in the house. The bloke had probably just gone down to get a drink of water or was on his phone. Whatever it was, he should go keep him company.

"You okay?" he asked from the top of the stairs as Robin came up them with a glass of water in his hand.

"Yeah. Just a bit dehydrated. Thank goodness you put a light on, or I'd have had a heart attack seeing you standing there."

Adam smiled. "You almost gave *me* a heart attack. I could hear someone downstairs but had forgotten you were here."

"Am I that unmemorable?" Robin had stopped, one stair short of the top. He looked tired, tousled, and vulnerable.

"Stop fishing for compliments and go back to bed. You need your sleep. You look awful."

"If that's what I get for fishing, I won't try again." Robin stifled a yawn. "Sorry I scared you."

"Nah, it's not you. I'd been having a bit of a nightmare, and it made me jumpy."

"Want to talk about it?"

Adam wondered how awful *he* must look for Robin to make the offer. "I'd rather not think about it, to be honest. It was about Youngs. I got up for breakfast and found him dead on my kitchen table."

"You don't have a kitchen table," Robin said, coming to the top of the stairs at last.

"You tell my dream that. I was shit-scared."

"It'll pass." Robin laid his hand on Adam's arm. "It doesn't feel like it now, but it will. Time's the best healer."

Like it's healed you about what happened at school? Adam thought, although he kept it as just that. "I'll believe you. I should get back to bed. Hopefully I won't dream this time."

Robin opened his mouth, as if to speak, then shut it again. Adam stayed where he was, afraid to break the moment—whatever "the moment" signified. If only he could take Robin back to bed with him, just for company in case the dream returned, but that would be a step too far.

"Want me to sit with you for a while?" Words were coming from Robin's mouth now, and Adam wasn't imagining them. "Just till you get settled?"

"Would you read me a bedtime story?" Adam, smiling, took his guest by the arm.

"No. And I won't sing a lullaby, either."

Some awkward smiles were shared, fear of saying too much too soon or too little too late.

"I'll settle for just being tucked in."

The bed was comfortably hard, the wooden frame only creaking slightly in protest at two occupants instead of the one it had been accustomed to for so long. The night had turned cold, too cold for being uncovered.

"You'll catch your death, sitting on top of the bed. Snuggle under the duvet. I'll stay on my side of the mattress."

"It *is* parky." Robin manoeuvred under the duvet, keeping half-upright, back resting against the pillows, tense.

Adam felt good—if guilty—having someone else alongside him again, filling the empty acres left when George had buggered off. Every atom of romance in his body screamed that Robin would be a damn sight more interesting and accomplished in that bed than inhibited, unimaginative George had ever been. Not that they would find out tonight.

Adam tried to relax, but it seemed impossible. Not because he was afraid of what dreams might come—Robin's presence felt reassuring enough to keep any worries at bay—but because that very presence spelled temptation. It would be easy, oh so easy, to break his promise about keeping his distance, to put an arm round that tense waist, to say, *Stay. It'll be fine. Nothing will happen.*

"Are you all right?" Robin whispered.

"Yeah. Just having trouble settling. Sorry." Adam moved slightly farther away.

"That's okay. I can't get off, either."

"The case buzzing round in your mind?"

"Yeah. I need to clear my thoughts. See if my subconscious can work on it because I'm not getting anywhere." Robin sighed, shifting uneasily against the pillows.

"Sleep here if you want." Adam turned over. "Bed's big enough for you not to bother me."

"What about you bothering me?" Still Robin didn't leave, adjusting himself against the pillows.

Adam lay for what seemed an age, afraid to move now that Robin was next to him, the both of them drifting around the fringes of slumber. He heard his guest's breathing slow, soften, and descend into what seemed like sleep, then let himself settle, going out like a light.

He woke, with the earliest rays of the sun filtering through a crack in the curtains, to find Robin curled next to him, arm thrown protectively over Adam's shoulder. It would be so simple now to wake him with a kiss, to slip a hand down the bed to where he was hard—they were both hard—and give them both some release. It wouldn't be the great sexual encounter that a romantic novelist might insist on, the realisation for them both that they'd found Mr. Right or any other cliché, but it might make them feel better.

Or would, if it didn't come laden with a heap of guilt.

Robin moved restlessly, as though his sleeping mind had read Adam's thoughts. Reluctantly breaking the comfortable embrace, Adam rolled to the edge of the bed.

"Morning," a mumbling voice sounded behind him. "Sorry. Did I take all the bed?"

"No. I think I was cramping you." Adam tried to sound cool, but it wasn't easy with Robin's body so close. "I'll go put the kettle on. I'm probably heading for the gym, so you can have all the time you want in the shower."

"Shame I can't ask you to share it with me."

Adam reached over, took Robin's hand, and pressed it to his face.

"When it's all over, we'll make that a date. I promise," Robin said, leaning into the touch.

The next hour passed in a strange mixture of affection, awkwardness, and the shared knowledge that they'd barely escaped overstepping the mark. Adam produced some clean underwear, a shirt—just as well they were much the same size—which eased the domestic side of things, even if the social side remained a touch prickly. Breakfast—with Campbell trying to get his nose into everything—felt more comfortable, perhaps because of all the meals they'd already shared. By the time the second cup of tea had gone down, they were ready to tackle the tyre.

It didn't take long, the day being clear, dry, and bright, and Robin didn't quite clean all the muck off his hands afterwards. Making sure he preserved the circumstantial evidence?

"I should be on the road," he said, coming out of the toilet and looking at his watch. "I owe you. For looking after me in my hour of need."

"My pleasure. And I won't say anything. I promise. You had a flat tyre, that was all."

"Yeah. Sorry."

"Stop saying that. Any other circumstances . . ." Adam shrugged. "I'm not sorry I met you."

"Same here. But we can't do this again. Not even just sharing a bed. Not until—"

"You've got the killer bang to rights. I know. I'm not thick. And I can wait." Adam put his hand out to be shaken. "Drive safely."

"You too, whatever you're up to. Precious cargo." The serious look on Robin's face made Adam's heart leap. "I'll ring, I promise. Don't worry if it's not for a few days."

"I'll look forward to it." *Look on the bright side.* At least they'd avoid all those early-relationship thoughts that made you want to live in the other person's pocket. They'd have to. "If I can help any more, let me know."

"Like be my mole?" Robin stopped at the door, car keys in hand. "That would be useful, but not if it put you at risk."

Memories of Adam's nightmare flooded his brain. "Do you honestly think there's a danger of anyone else being killed?"

"I have to consider all the angles. If this conversation you heard is important, and somebody realises you overheard it . . ." Robin fiddled with his keys. "It could change things. Look, I don't want to make you paranoid, but just take care. Okay?"

"I know," Adam replied. "I'll set Campbell on them, right?"

"And have them licked to death?" Robin swung on his heels and headed for the car.

Adam closed the door, locked it, and for the first time he could remember, bolted it as well. Please God that this murder would come single spies.

Time to sit down with Anderson and a coffee and take another look at all they'd found out so far. But the meeting proved only semiproductive, sealing off some alleys and getting into a debate about whether absence of evidence was evidence of absence. Postmortem results were conclusive—Youngs had been strangled with some sort of man-made material, probably knotted around something small and hard to help with the job. No evidence of underlying disease, and the lab was still struggling to identify that bloody floral fragrance. "Unlikely to be cologne" was all they'd got so far.

Robin's feeling of getting nowhere fast wasn't helped by his guilt, nor by their losing time—a bus had aquaplaned on standing water and gone into a lorry right at the business end of the road from Stanebridge to Lindenshaw. Anderson had arrived half an hour after he should, muttering about how the traffic had been a fucking nightmare. Running late and running round in circles with a case that didn't seem to be going anywhere, and now he and Anderson had to work out how they could quiz the Duncans on what the neighbour had overheard and ask Narraway about what Adam had earwigged. Hearsay evidence—always dodgy ground, as people could easily protest that they'd been misheard or find an innocent interpretation.

Of course I said the police know what happened, Inspector. I was explaining how we'd made sure to tell you all about what that poor chap Youngs had been doing at St. Crispin's.

There'd also been the delicate matter of explaining to Anderson about the night before. Anderson had an eye like a hawk and must have spotted how his boss looked more crumpled than usual. Would he have been able to spot any signs of lingering post–not-coital-but-a-damn-close-run-thing bliss? The sergeant had accepted the matter of the tyre and the rain and the accident on the A road and all that bit, but the fact that Robin had conducted a private, impromptu interview with one of the witnesses made him raise his eyebrows. Especially as it had emerged that this was the third interview running at Adam's house. Anderson seemed to accept the face value that it had all been in the interest of the case, but his thoughts were unreadable.

They'd justified heading out of the station for lunch by saying they needed to get their minds clear and plan the next steps. Sunday lunchtime, rural pub garden, and enough sunshine to sit out in. If that didn't focus their minds, nothing would.

Robin leaned back in his seat, grateful for small mercies and determined to make the most of the unseasonal warmth now that he had a moment—if a horribly guilt-laden moment—to enjoy it. According to the forecast, a chill blast from the east was just around the corner; however, the chill blast from the detective superintendant, demanding progress reports so he could fend off the local media, still rang in his ears.

While Robin sat in the sunshine, torn between fond reminiscence and guilt at having run off the rails somehow, the warmth of Adam's body still an almost-tangible presence, Anderson went off to get the sandwiches ordered in. He soon returned with a couple of mineral waters, a wooden spoon with a number—proof of their order, presumably—written on it, and his phone clamped to his ear.

"Any news?" Robin asked when he was done.

"Yes," Anderson said, grinning as he added, "and no."

Robin groaned. "I'll take the 'no' first."

"Davis has been working her magic again. Ian Youngs didn't currently have a girlfriend, not according to his mother. Another potential avenue turned into a dead end."

Surprise, surprise. "So what's the 'yes'?"

"Ah, you'll like this." Anderson, infuriatingly, stopped to take a drink. "He had a girlfriend—pretty serious relationship by all accounts—but they split up a year ago. He took it badly."

That counted as maybe a quarter of a lead. "Did this girlfriend have a name?"

Anderson looked horribly smug. "Oh yes, that's the best bit."

Robin took a beer mat and fanned himself with it, for want of being allowed to get his hands around his sergeant's neck and wring it. "Are you going to share it or make me suffer even more? This heat's getting ridiculous for the time of year."

"Claire Waites."

Robin nearly spilled his drink. "Blimey. The same Claire Waites that knows some scandal about Narraway? Isn't this getting a bit incestuous?"

"Maybe more than just a coincidence, sir. Mrs. Youngs, who Davis reckons couldn't stand the woman, seemed to think that part of the reason her son was applying for the St. Crispin's job was to get back at her." Anderson looked up as the waitress came across with their order. "Thanks, love."

"So he wanted to succeed where she hadn't?"

"Yeah. One in the eye or something like that. Davis seems to think Mrs. Youngs found slagging off the ex cathartic."

More scratching at the itch, the one that kept telling Robin that the path to Youngs's murder started that first time round. "I wonder if that's worth me paying for your lunch?"

"Decide when you've heard the next bit. Apparently . . ."

Robin felt the vibration in his pocket but couldn't fish his phone out before the piercing ringtone started, although at least it wasn't some embarrassing, dated pop song. Please God it wasn't Adam. Not now, not here, with Anderson within earshot.

"Robin Bright. Hello?" He mouthed, *desk sergeant* to Anderson, who grimaced. "Yes? Bloody hell."

Anderson looked up, face full of questions. Robin turned away, in no mood to mime.

"Right. We'll get over there straightaway. Thank you." Robin ended the call, put the phone back in his pocket slowly, then looked wistfully at his uneaten food and thought of his rumbling stomach. Another minute or two wouldn't make a huge difference, would it?

"Sounds serious. What's up?"

"It *is* serious. Marjorie Bookham just went round to see Oliver Narraway. She found him dead. Lying in his lounge."

"And not from natural causes, I assume?" Anderson was already up, getting his car keys ready.

"Seems not." Robin swigged back the last of his drink—who knew when he'd get another—and grabbed the sandwich off his plate to eat en route. "All the wheels are already in motion." Dr. Brew, Grace, the same crew who'd been at the school. Would they find evidence of a connection between the two deaths? Because there surely had to be one.

The effect of a police car, an ambulance, and a small posse of rubberneckers outside Oliver Narraway's cottage took away its old-world charm. Stopping only to suggest that the constables by the door get rid of the onlookers and to slip on his protective suit, Robin made his way round the building to where Marjorie Bookham was sitting on a wooden bench by a rustic table, the sort of seat in the sort of setting that should have been a delight on such a mild day. She was pale, rubbing her hands together, clearly distraught.

"Why the hell is nobody looking after her?" Robin hissed at his sergeant. "I don't want her carted off to hospital with shock.

Mrs. Bookham," he added, loud enough for her to hear. "I'm sorry you've had to wait."

"No need to apologise. I told the constable I'd stay because I was sure you'd need to see me." She produced a wan smile.

"Did nobody offer to sit with you?" Anderson looked troubled. "They'll get a rollicking from me."

"Oh, no, don't make a palaver. That young constable was fussing over me, but I told him he'd be better employed keeping the ghouls from the door. Or the garden gate." The little woman fought bravely and kept her upper lip stiff. "Please sit down if you want to talk. I feel so awkward while you're standing." The slight catch in her voice indicated tears weren't far away; the policemen obeyed the orders.

Robin wondered if he had a clean handkerchief in any of his pockets, in case the handbag on the table didn't contain any. Unlikely, given how little time he'd spent at home recently. "When did you get here?"

"I suppose it must have been about half past one. I'm afraid it all seems a bit unreal, as if it's happened to someone else and not me." The stiff upper lip was wobbling now. "I didn't look at my watch. I should have done, shouldn't I? What time did I ring the police?"

"They said the call came through at one forty." Robin kept his voice low and gentle. He hated having to cope with tears.

"That would be about right, I guess. I looked in my handbag, but my mobile wasn't there." Mrs. Bookham got her bag, fished out a handkerchief, then began rummaging as though the missing item might suddenly appear. "I had to go next door—thank goodness Victor lives there. Victor Reed. He let me use his landline to call 999. Oh. Here it is, the stupid thing. Down where I usually keep my lipstick. Who put it there?"

"Take a deep breath," Robin said, taking a pretty deep breath himself and lining his thoughts up. If Victor lived next door, that meant he might have seen something. It also begged the question of why Adam, not Reed, delivered the governor post to Narraway. That could wait, though, because he needed to calm Mrs. Bookham down and get some answers from *her*. "Sergeant, could you make sure the doctor knows we're here?"

"Yes, sir," Anderson replied with the slightest hint of a nod. He evidently knew his boss wanted to give her some space.

"Was he expecting you? Oliver Narraway, I mean." Robin kept his voice calm and comforting. Best bedside manner to be used on fragile witnesses. *Or illicit lovers*, he remembered with a frisson of remorse.

"No. I was playing hooky away from home again." Mrs. Bookham managed another smile. "Derek was watching the lunchtime kickoff on television, and I just had to get out of the house. I couldn't face him shouting at Manchester United. I had a book Oliver had lent me, so I thought I'd bring it back." She leaned forward, picking up the slightly dog-eared paperback that had been lying, forlorn, on the table. "He won't be needing it now." She was in full flow, flicking the pages of the book as though she'd find the answers she needed there. "I was hoping he'd offer me a cup of tea and we could talk governor business. Anything to get away from Derek's endless moaning about Wayne Rooney. I wish to God I'd stayed at home and put up with it."

"What happened when you got here?"

She kept worrying at the book. "I rang and rang the bell, and there was no reply. I wondered if Oliver had gone out. I'm afraid I got a bit cross, as I didn't want to have to go straight home. Then I wondered if he was just having a nap or something—you know, typical man, after lunch. So, like a stupid bloody nosy old cow, I went round the back and looked in at the French windows, and there he was, on the floor . . ." She pressed her handkerchief to her mouth.

"I'm so sorry. I know it's painful, but I have to ask these things while it's all still fresh in your mind." He waited for her to compose herself. "How could you be sure he was dead and hadn't just fainted?"

She looked confused. "Well, I couldn't be. I mean, I couldn't get into the house and find out, could I? I banged on the window and shouted, just in case he'd had a fall or something, but he didn't respond. And his face—I could see it because he was lying turned towards the windows—his face was all . . . peculiar. That's when I had to go round to Victor's to ring for the ambulance and the police. Both of them. Just in case."

"Quite right too. Did you happen to see anyone hanging around here when you arrived? Or anything at all to make you suspicious?"

"I . . . I don't know. Nothing I could put my finger on. Although I did get a distinct impression of something. It was when I was banging on the window trying to wake Oliver up . . ." She seemed to be struggling to find the right words, out of her depth. "I felt as if I was being watched."

"Watched? From where?"

"I don't know, maybe from the bushes at the side of the garden. I didn't dare look around, just in case I saw somebody." She suddenly smiled, a dimpled smile that transformed her face, lighting up the beauty that the years hadn't erased. "You'll think me very silly, Inspector, but I couldn't have looked behind me for all the tea in China. There might have been a murderer lurking in the shrubbery and . . ." The smile disappeared, and the hands on the paperback shook like leaves in an autumn wind.

"Now, don't upset yourself further. Shall I call my sergeant and get him to rustle you up a cup of tea?"

"That's kind, but I don't think even tea has enough miraculous properties." The hands were deliberately stilled. "I'm not sure anything's ever going to take that image of Oliver from my memory."

"Give it time," Robin said, not sure he believed in time's miraculous healing properties any more than tea's.

"Here." Mrs. Bookham passed across the mobile phone, hands trembling. "Would you mind ringing Derek and asking him to come and get me? I'm not sure I could even enter the number properly at the moment, let alone walk to my house."

"Of course." Robin found the contacts folder easily enough. "Is it stored in here?"

"Yes, it's under Home. I—"

"I'll take Marjorie back, Mr. Bright." Victor Reed's voice came through the hedge, although they could barely see the man himself. "I saw you'd arrived. If there's anything I can do to help, please say."

"That's very kind of you." Robin smiled, not entirely convinced the motive was altruistic. Reed had no apparent motive for either crime, but his proximity to the scene of the second murder gave Robin pause for thought. "Just stay that side of the hedge for the moment—this is a crime scene—and I'll get the constable to go with you."

"I'll make sure I behave myself." Reed seemed genuine enough.

"Are you sure?" Mrs. Bookham looked at her phone, still nestled in Robin's hand. "Derek could miss ten minutes of his precious football..."

The hedge rustled where Reed was evidently getting agitated. "I insist. And I'm going to insist that *he* makes you a cup of tea and cossets you for the rest of the day."

"Really?" She managed a faint smile. "They say every cloud has a silver lining."

Robin waited until Reed's car was under way before going in search of his sergeant, who turned out to be coming in search of him.

"Nasty business, sir." Anderson ran his hands through his hair. "Looks like a similar MO to Youngs's death."

"Likely to be the same killer then, unless we've got a clever copycat. Thank you, constable," Robin said, brushing past the young officer with a nod. "Keep up the good work with the ghouls."

"They've almost all gone away, Inspector. Apart from the ones pretending to consult the timetable at the bus stop," the policeman added, rolling his eyes.

Anderson guided his boss through into the lounge. "Getting complicated, isn't it?"

"You've a great way of understating things." Robin smiled, although that was wiped off his face at the sight of the body, a body that seemed to have been strangled.

Narraway looked less belligerent in death, and there appeared to be little evidence of a fight, although maybe more of a struggle than Youngs had put up. A quick survey of the scene persuaded Robin they'd be better off leaving Grace, who was on CSI duty again, to see what she could rummage out. No obvious clues, so he'd let the experts run with that part of the job.

"Okay to go through here?" Robin pointed to the French windows.

"Yes, sir. I've processed them. Nothing there. They were locked."

"And not been opened for a while," Anderson said as he stiffly turned the key and forced the doors open.

It was good to get back out into the garden, into sweet fresh air, away from the stale nicotine smell that permeated the cottage.

"Do you think we could have saved him?" Anderson kicked at the gravel path. "If he'd come clean about whoever it was he saw on the path at the back of the school?"

Or if Robin hadn't been sniffing around Adam Matthews and had kept his mind on the case? "I doubt it. Don't beat yourself up."

Anderson's glance was a bit too knowing again. "Makes that phone call your mate heard yesterday highly suspicious. I'll get Davis onto accessing Narraway's phone records."

"She'll love you," Robin said sarcastically. And since when had Adam been his *mate*? "When we were at the pub, you started to tell me something. This business with Narraway put it out of my mind."

Anderson looked puzzled, before light dawned. "Oh, yeah. It was about Duncan. I think you'll appreciate this titbit a lot more now than you'd have done back at the pub. Possible motive."

"For him to have killed Ian Youngs?"

"Not quite, which is the irony of it, given the timing. If I'd told you over lunch, it would have just been a bit of gossip. Now it's half a reason why he might have wanted to kill Oliver Narraway."

"Bloody hell." Robin tipped his head towards the front door. "Tell me the details when we're back inside. I'm not convinced the Lindenshaw mafia aren't hiding in the hedge."

Anderson rolled his eyes, but he kept silent until they were in the house. "Can I carry on?"

"Please do."

"Brian Duncan applied for a job two months ago, as an accountant with Chilcombe Holdings. He was short-listed and made it through to the interview stage. Any idea who was on the panel?"

Robin wasn't in the mood to play games, especially when it concerned the labyrinthine goings-on of village life. "From your bloody inane grin, it has to be Narraway. What the hell was he doing there?"

The sergeant continued to smile. "Old Pals Act. It's his cousin's company, and he often uses—used—Narraway to sit in on interviews. Whatever else the man was or did, he'd apparently had something to offer when it came to recruiting people."

"How did you find that out?"

"Pal of Helen's works for Chilcombe Holdings. On reception, so she knows who's in and out of the company and what they're doing. She heard about Youngs on the radio, knew Narraway was at St. Crispin's . . ." The gossip network was a mixed blessing, but maybe this time it had come up trumps.

"Back to the interview. Duncan didn't get the job?"

"Spot on. Narraway was sounding off later about how he'd given all the candidates a hard time during the interview, but if Duncan thinks he was singled out for the treatment, I suppose he might think the bloke stopped him getting the job." Anderson shrugged.

"Neither Duncan nor Narraway saw fit to mention that interview."

"Too right. And if Narraway knew Duncan, why didn't he tell us straightaway that he was the bloke he'd seen with the dog?"

"Maybe he didn't want the personal connection to come out so easily because it might tip us off to something? Maybe he just enjoyed being awkward." Witnesses did. Robin had come across more than one who wouldn't tell the police anything, on principle. Even the innocent, or presumed innocent, like Adam, habitually withheld evidence for one reason or another. The job would be a fucking sight easier if people just spilled the beans in the first place.

Robin thought for a moment. "Right. Try this: Narraway's dead, so now he can't name or identify Brian Duncan as being the man in the lane with the dog."

"Makes sense to me."

Robin rubbed his knuckles together. "Okay. When we're done here, we're going straight back to see Brian Duncan, and his wife, as well, even if we have to drag her off her sickbed." He stopped. "Assuming he's at home, of course."

"Any chance of asking the gods of coincidence to get Marjorie Bookham to tell you she saw a man with a Labrador lurking around here?"

"She saw somebody. No," Robin corrected himself, "what she actually said was she felt she was being watched." He pointed at the garden. "Come on, time for a shufti."

They went back outside, giving a couple of teenagers who were slowly sauntering past the cottage a dirty look. Did the citizens of Lindenshaw have nothing better to do on a lovely Sunday afternoon?

"She must have been about here." Robin trod gingerly as they reached the French windows, although Grace would already have had her own shufti round the garden first. "She felt uncomfortable. Said she was too scared to turn around and look at whose eye was on her. If there was anyone here at all."

"Plenty of places to hide, though. Like the shrubbery at the school."

Robin shivered at the association. "Let's start with looking in the bushes. Grace can process anything we spot."

"Good idea. She wouldn't necessarily have known she had to concentrate on this area. No sign of forced entry to the house or anything to suggest that Narraway hadn't just let his killer in through the front door."

"Maybe we'll strike lucky and find some dog hairs. Labrador." Robin went down on his haunches, fingering the bushes with care; if there was something to be found, they didn't want to spoil things for Grace.

But there wasn't. Robin straightened up, rubbing the small of his back.

"Nothing?"

"Not a sausage."

"We couldn't be so lucky." Anderson shrugged. "Earlier, when you gave me the subtle heave-ho so you could talk to Mrs. Bookham, I nipped upstairs and had a look around. I wasn't just checking the house; I saw you both out of the window."

"And?" Robin knew from the edge to the sergeant's voice that he had an important point to make.

"I don't know what you think, sir, but her attack of the vapours struck me as being slightly over the top. I know she'd found Narraway dead, but it wasn't like there was tons of blood and gore everywhere."

"I can see you've been on the empathy course." Robin remembered the shaking hands, the haunted look in Marjorie Bookham's eyes. It had seemed genuine enough, unless she was an actress to rival Helen Mirren. "You know, I've known police constables to lose their dinners over corpses. It can be a hell of a shock."

Anderson didn't look sure. "I'll take your word for it, sir, but she strikes me as a bit of a drama queen. I wouldn't be surprised if she's milking this for all it's worth."

"I'm not sure I blame her. Maybe it's the only way to get any sympathy out of her husband." His great-uncle had been the same—not interested in much else than a hot meal on the table at the right time, football always on the telly, and getting cross if it didn't happen. Unimaginative and programmed into a 1950s mind-set. No wonder Robin's great-aunt had left the bloke for the man who came and tuned the piano. "We should talk to Victor Reed as soon as he's back."

"Sounds like his car's just pulled up." Anderson jerked a thumb over his shoulder.

"Let's nab him before he's had a chance to settle." Robin led the way back through the garden and next door, giving the people of Lindenshaw a chance to have a gawp at their protective suits.

Victor Reed's cottage matched Narraway's, although the garden wasn't as tidy as the one next door and the paintwork was showing its age. The speed with which the door was opened at their knock suggested Reed had been watching them walk up the path.

Robin avoided small talk, apart from thanking Reed again for taking Mrs. Bookham home, getting straight into the practicalities even as they stood on the doorstep. "We need to be absolutely clear on what happened and whether you might have seen anything. Were you in the garden earlier today?"

"I'm afraid not." Reed waved his hand in the direction of the village centre. "I was at church earlier, and then we went for a walk. I'd not been back long when Marjorie came over in a flap."

"She was upset?"

"Inspector, she was beside herself. You saw her, trying to be brave, but she's a sensitive woman, really."

Anderson kept his head over his notebook, but Robin could have sworn he was trying not to smirk. Maybe Mrs. Bookham *was* sensitive, under that brisk, efficient exterior.

Reed, who hadn't seemed to notice the smirk, ploughed on. "I couldn't have seen anything, anyway; the laurel hedge is so thick."

That was a valid point. He'd certainly have needed a ladder to see over it, and seeing through it was well nigh impossible. "I've racked my brain, but I can't think of anything or anyone I saw that was in any way suspicious." Reed picked a broken twig from the winter jasmine by the door. "Poor Marjorie. She was in a terrible pickle by the time I dropped her off home. Come on in." Reed stood back to let them into the hall. "She was remarkably stoic on Thursday, although I don't suppose she actually saw Youngs's body then. This was different."

"Is her husband looking after her? He does realise how much of a shock she's had?" From what he'd heard of the man, Robin didn't have any confidence in Derek Bookham's levels of empathy.

"Oh yes. He must have been worried about the state she was in because he volunteered to make her a cup of tea before I could force him to do it. Unprecedented, I suspect."

"It isn't easy for anyone to find a dead body," Anderson chipped in.

"I know, Sergeant. I found Youngs, remember?"

"Sorry."

"Marjorie came straight over to use the phone, didn't she? Once she'd found Narraway dead." Robin couldn't keep the feelings of guilt at bay. If only he'd come back here last night and probed Narraway about that overheard phone call, then he might have forced the man into saying who he'd been talking to. Then he could have spoken to *them*, perhaps staving off this act of violence. Surely the murderer—if it was indeed the person on the phone—wouldn't have acted if the police were looking over his or her shoulder?

"I believe so. Poor girl was in an awful state. Kept saying she was sure there was someone in the bushes. I went upstairs to look, but if there had been someone there, he'd scarpered. And then I went out into the lane and double-checked nobody was hanging about, because Marjorie was so persistent."

"She wasn't frightened of being left in here on her own?" Robin eyed the door, the large windows. How easy would it be for someone to get into this house? Or the similar one next door?

"She said she felt safe indoors. I told her where the rolling pin was, just in case." Reed took one last look at the impenetrable hedge and blew air out through his nose.

"She'd have used it?" Anderson asked.

"No doubt about it, if she'd been in a crisis. I'm just amazed she hasn't taken one to Derek before now. Oh. No, I didn't mean . . . She's not violent or anything, it's just that Derek would try the patience of a saint."

"Yes, we got that impression." Robin made a mental note of it, though. Little throwaway line or something more significant?

"I bet you have. Derek Bookham would like to have lived in the era when women were expected to be tied to the kitchen sink and men spent their time working or at the pub or the golf club."

It was a possible motive to take a rolling pin to him, but there seemed to be no reason for her to want to kill Narraway. Or Youngs.

"Why does she put up with it?" Great-Aunt Jenny and the piano tuner hadn't. "I take it *Mrs.* Bookham doesn't agree with that point of view?"

"I'm sure she doesn't, although she hides it well." Reed sighed. "Or maybe she's just infinitely patient. Ignore what I said about the rolling pin, eh?"

"I won't tell anyone," Robin said. Why didn't anything seem to be moving forward in this bloody investigation? "Just clarify me one thing, though. Why don't—didn't—you bring Narraway his governor post if he lives just next door?"

"Why should I? I'm not an office boy."

And Adam is? Robin got angry at the idea. "I'd have thought it was just common decency. Helping Mrs. Shepherd out."

Reed sighed. "I used to do it. But Oliver always wants—wanted— to nab me for a chat. I think he used to get lonely. I tried just putting it through the door, but he always seemed to catch me."

The story might be true, but it still stuck in Robin's craw. They finished the interview there, with the usual caveat about contacting them if Reed remembered anything important, then went in search of Grace, who was scouring Narraway's front garden.

"Please tell me you've got something we can get our teeth into," Robin implored.

"Only in the negative. No signs of a struggle inside, no sign of forced entry. No sign of much, really." Grace got up, wiping the soil from her knees. "I blame the forensic police shows on television.

Now everyone's an expert on the best way to avoid leaving fibres or whatever. Latex gloves and God knows what else."

"Gloves." Robin drew in a deep breath, clearing the mind that was getting increasingly muzzy under the combined effects of the case and the lingering memories of the night before. He took a swift look round, but nobody was lurking to overhear them. "I can't help thinking about those surgical gloves I saw in Brian Duncan's case."

"You're too suspicious, Chief Inspector. Plenty of first-aiders have those. It all dates back to the AIDS scare, when nobody was willing to touch a drop of blood. Pick their noses and eat it happily but don't want any of the red stuff." She grinned gleefully.

"Do you mind?" Anderson had turned a touch green. "I've just had my lunch."

"Murderer let himself, or herself, out?" Robin asked, secretly pleased to see his sergeant's discomfort.

"Yeah. The front door's on a Yale, so it would have locked behind him. The only open windows are too small to squeeze through, so the victim must have let him—or her—in."

Robin nodded. "Isn't that usually the way? Most people get done in by one of their nearest and dearest."

Grace jerked her thumb towards the house. "I think he was sitting in that chair and the killer came up behind him. Doctor agrees. He'd have fought a bit, but in the end, he was overcome and just slid to the floor. I found a few fibres, but whether they'll be of any use . . ." She shrugged.

Robin pulled at his ear, thoughtfully. "Any dog hairs?"

"Are you expecting any?"

"Black Labrador, maybe. Not Narraway's, as I don't think he kept one."

"No sign of a dog, anyway."

"We've got a witness who says there might have been someone lurking in the shrubbery. Any chance you could give it another once-over?" Robin asked, smiling.

"I'll see what I can do, Inspector."

"Thanks." Robin gestured for Anderson to give him the car keys. "There's nothing else to be seen here. Brian Duncan?"

Anderson nodded. "I think so."

Before he started the car, Robin took one more long look at Narraway's house. "That hedge is tall, but it's straggly right at the back. Reed's wiry enough to nip through it. He could have done the deed, nipped back again, and nobody would be the wiser."

"Convenient, but what's his motive? And isn't he pretty well eliminated from killing Youngs?"

"I suppose so." Robin sighed. "I'm clutching at straws."

"I can give you another straw to clutch at, if you want."

"Really?"

"The constable at the door said he saw that teacher from the school—Matthews—come past here just before we arrived. He knows him from the gym."

Robin slowly pulled across his seat belt, asking—in as casual a tone as he could manage—"What's significant about that?"

"He said he stopped and asked what was going on. Sounded a bit shifty. Couldn't get away quick enough afterwards."

"But he's as much use to us as a suspect as Reed is," Robin replied, making a show of concentrating on pulling out into the road. "Got an alibi for Youngs's death. And no motive for Narraway's."

"Okay, sir. Don't get eggy. I just thought you'd like to know."

Robin wasn't aware he'd been "eggy." He'd need to watch that. "Thank you."

But no thanks for making him doubt Adam's motives. Robin kept his eyes on the road, his usual careful style of driving becoming more and more ragged, until a particularly unpleasant crunching of gears made Anderson draw his breath in sharply.

"All right, sir?"

"Fine," Robin replied, lying through his teeth. Adam near the scene of the crime today. Adam overhearing—or at least saying he'd overheard—the murdered man the day before. Adam taking post to Narraway when Reed lived so close. The further he got through the list, the sicker Robin felt. There was one possibility he'd not considered, or not let himself consider: Adam in cahoots with the real killer, ensnaring the rozzer while the second murder was being set up.

Could he have fallen for the oldest trick in the book?

Chapter Eighteen

After the incident with the gears, Robin put on the radio. Football commentary would amuse Anderson and let *him* clear his brain.

He was being oversuspicious, surely. Adam had probably just been out on a run, and hearing of Narraway's death had unsettled him, especially after the nightmare he'd had last night and Robin's warning to take care still ringing in his ears.

"Do you think anyone in this case has told us the whole truth and nothing but, sir?" Anderson's words made him jump.

"Buggered if I know." Not even Adam had been entirely forthcoming. *Oh God, more niggling doubts.* He suddenly slowed and pulled the car to the side of the road, having spotted someone to take his frustrations out on. Neil Musgrave hadn't done much to deserve it, but he was close at hand. Not even *that bloke* had told them the truth.

The vicar was sauntering along the street, maybe enjoying the parochial equivalent of a tea break on the busiest working day of the week, although the expression on the vicar's face suggested anything but relaxation.

"Want me to join you, sir?" Anderson asked.

"No, don't want to spook him. You keep an eye out in case he whacks me with his thurible," Robin said, getting out of the car before the sergeant could ask him what a thurible was.

"Reverend, have you a moment?"

"Of course, Inspector, so long as it doesn't take too long. I'm on my way to see Marjorie." Musgrave's face was etched with concern. "Derek rang up in quite a tizzy over her. Poor girl—such a shock."

It must have been, for Mr. Bookham to be in such a state.

"I won't delay you, but you'll appreciate the nature of our job. We find out new bits of information, and then it's back to square one, checking everything again. You said you took a walk out on the school field on Thursday, down in the far corner by the footpath?"

"Ye-es," the vicar replied, with a note of uncertainty. "I wanted a bit of peace."

"Peace? Weren't the children all out on the field playing?" If lunchtimes were anything like they'd been in Robin's day, the place would have resembled a battleground.

"They were, but that doesn't bother me." Musgrave managed a smile. "There are worse things to listen to."

Robin wasn't sure he agreed. Some of the games he remembered didn't even bear thinking about. "Did you see anyone come along the path?"

"Not that I remember."

"What about at the back of the field, the far side from the school?"

Musgrave furrowed his brow, then nodded, slowly. "Yes, there was somebody. A man, walking a black dog. I couldn't make out the breed."

Robin beat the palm of his hand with his notebook. "Why didn't you tell us that before? Didn't you think it could be important?"

"I'd forgotten." Musgrave studied the pavement. "It was a difficult day. We were all in a bit of shock."

"And you hadn't remembered before now?" Anderson, who'd come to join them, seemed as sceptical as Robin about this temporary amnesia.

"I'm afraid not. As you can imagine, I've been rather busy. Many of my parishioners are upset and anxious." The vicar looked up, facing Robin. "It's been a hard few days for all of us."

It was a reasonable explanation, but this case had been full of reasonable explanations.

"Had you ever seen that man or his dog before?" Robin asked.

"No, I don't think so. You should ask Oliver." The vicar's hand shot to his mouth. "Oh, I'm so sorry. I didn't think."

Robin smiled. "That's all right. These things always take a while to sink in, especially when they're such a bolt out of the blue. Why should we have asked Mr. Narraway?"

Musgrave spoke slowly, clearly shaken. "I think he might have known the chap with the dog. They appeared to be talking."

Still not proof that it was Duncan, but an indication that Oliver had been lying about what had happened when he'd been having his cigar. Why the hell hadn't Robin got hold of a picture of the bloke to show around? "You didn't hear what they said, did you?"

"I'm sorry. I was too far away."

"Did it look like they were passing the time of day or were they—" not putting words into witnesses' mouths wasn't as easy as it appeared "—looking agitated?"

"Now I think about it, they did. I'd forgotten all about it. Just thought it was Oliver getting on his high horse because the man had his dog too near the school field or something." Musgrave stopped, horrified. "Lord. You think they knew each other, don't you? That Oliver's death might be related to that young man's?"

"We have to consider every possibility. Although," Robin added, not unkindly, "I'd ask you to keep that opinion to yourself. Not just for the sake of the investigation. We don't want a third murder on our hands." He immediately regretted being so frank, worried that he'd have a fainting vicar to deal with—and Musgrave wasn't a small man.

"Sorry." The vicar steadied himself on a garden wall. "Out of my comfort zone with all this stuff."

"I suspect we all are. I'd better let you get away."

"Yes, thank you. Sorry." Musgrave continued along the pavement, less confidence in his step now.

Robin watched him go, both of them clearly disheartened. Not just the victim and his family suffered the repercussions of murder—grief, betrayal, loss of innocence—but the ripples spread out, touching and tainting everything. Even his relationship with Adam. And, on the back of that, his career.

It'd been three days since that first murder. Three days since he'd opened the door to the classroom and spotted Adam sitting at a desk, looking pale. Three days in which he'd acted less ethically than ever before. Three days in which he'd hurtled headlong into a place he wasn't sure he wanted to be.

"Sir?" Anderson's voice made him jump again. "You were miles away."

"Sorry. Just thinking what a bloody mess murder is." Robin got back in the car, started it up again, and eased into gear and onto the road.

"I think you put the wind up the vicar."

"I know." Robin checked his rearview mirror, watching Musgrave turn around a corner. "I think he just realised that careless talk still costs lives. Maybe whatever Narraway said to the man with the Labrador cost him his."

"You really think that?"

"God knows." Robin sighed. "Maybe the Almighty will tell Musgrave the truth over evensong."

Five o'clock on a Sunday afternoon, when normal people were snoozing on the sofa in front of a black-and-white film or getting their minds around what they were having for their evening meal, all the poor bloody rozzers could look forward to was more legwork, more questions. And precious few answers.

Robin wondered if he should go and see Adam again, once they'd finished with the Duncans. He could always approach it by asking whether Adam had seen anything suspicious when he'd been out on his run and gradually move round to why he'd been near Narraway's house at all and what he'd been upset about. But the thought of the temptation Adam represented kept blurring Robin's thinking. Last night had been about two tired and worried souls finding comfort together at the expense of probity. That excuse couldn't be allowed to apply again.

"Narraway's death will be bad news for the school, sir," Anderson said, out of the blue, just as they pulled up at the Duncans' drive. "Mud sticks."

"I don't envy Mrs. Shepherd her job tomorrow." Maybe fate was exacting justice for all the crap the school had allowed to be dumped on Robin.

Brian Duncan was out in his garden, giving his hedge what might have been the first clip of the year.

"Hello . . . Inspector?" Duncan seemed to recall who Robin was just as he got out his warrant card.

"We've some more questions." Robin fished out his notebook. "You probably don't want to answer them out here."

"Ah, yes. Come this way." He led them round the house and into the conservatory, offering the policemen chairs that basked in what remained of the day's sunlight. The furniture was good quality but had seen better days.

"Are you happy to talk in here?" Duncan kept his voice low. "I don't want to disturb Lizzie. She needs her sleep."

Robin shrugged. "I don't care where we talk, so long as I get told the truth. Both of us, separately, have been told that you walked your dog over at Tythebarn on Thursday lunchtime."

"That's right." Duncan shifted uncomfortably in his seat. "What's the obsession with dog walking all of a sudden?"

"Less the activity than the time concerned, sir," Anderson chipped in—politely, but without smiling.

"For the third time"—Duncan, fingers drumming, either nervously or in anger, on the arm of the chair, kept his eyes fixed on the floor—"I took Branston—that's his name—down to the site of the old chicken place. Oak Lane Farm. The area's very popular with dog walkers, it's the sm—"

"The smells. Yes, so we were told." Those bloody details again; they should have smelt the rat the first time. "Only we don't believe you actually took your dog there on the day Ian Youngs was killed. We have eyewitnesses who said they saw you with your Labrador in the lane at the back of St. Crispin's, Thursday lunchtime."

"Thursday?" Duncan looked up, jaw working like he was going to argue, but no sound was emerging.

"Thursday." Robin waited for a response.

"Ah, yes. Yes, that's right. I'm sorry. It was such a worrying time, I got confused." Duncan smiled weakly. The belligerent edge to his voice had disappeared. "I'd taken Branston to Tythebarn on *Wednesday*—Thursday's all a bit of a blur to me."

"You didn't seem that tired or flustered when I asked you about it yesterday." Anderson clearly didn't believe him. "Are you sure you weren't just lying?"

"Why should I lie about something so . . . so trivial?"

"Murder isn't trivial, Mr. Duncan, and when someone consistently feeds us misinformation, we want to know why."

Duncan drooped back in his chair. "Look, I didn't want Lizzie to know what I was up to. We're so desperate for her to get a better job. I really was tired on Thursday and not thinking very clearly. I'd decided to go over to St. Crispin's and plead with the governors to defer recruitment on compassionate grounds so that she could have a second chance."

"And you just happened to take your dog with you?" Anderson rolled his eyes. "They'd never have allowed him on-site, surely?"

"What?" Duncan, bewildered, looked from Robin to his sergeant then back again. "I'd have tied him at the gate, of course. Anyway, he was part of my cover."

Robin leaned forward. "What?"

"My cover story with Lizzie. So she thought I really was walking the dog, not throwing myself on my knees."

"What stopped you? I mean, you obviously didn't talk to the governors or they'd have mentioned it." Unless the police had been kept in the dark about that episode too.

Duncan slumped forwards, head in hands. "I wimped out. I walked up the lane by the school, but by the time I got to the gate, my courage had deserted me."

Robin exchanged a glance with his sergeant—clearly neither of them were convinced. Anderson carried on with the questions. "Funny how you got the result you wanted, though. Are you sure you didn't change your plans? It would have been simple just to slip around the school building and make sure the process *had* to be halted for the day."

Duncan moved his hands off his face. "Are you honestly suggesting I strangled that poor chap at the school?"

"I don't think Sergeant Anderson mentioned strangulation," Robin said quietly.

Duncan took a deep breath. "He didn't need to. It's been all over the local news. You can't try to catch me out like that. I know I said we're getting desperate for money, but do you really think I'd have resorted to murder to further Lizzie's chances?"

"Where were you at lunchtime today?" Robin's sudden change of direction caught Duncan off balance. "Between one and half past?"

"What? Today?" Duncan was flustered. "I nipped into the village to get some groceries while Lizzie had a nap. She's been dead on her feet, poor girl."

"She seemed rather chipper on Friday." Although maybe the tiredness had been exaggerated, to get her husband out of her hair.

"She *was* chipper when you saw her. It all seemed to hit her last evening. Delayed shock maybe, or all the adrenaline being used up." It was possible, although not even a doctor's note would have persuaded Robin.

Anderson kept up the pressure. "Can anybody verify that you were in the village today?"

"As a matter of fact, they can." Duncan seemed pleased with himself. "Or at least my credit card record should be able to. I was in the 'open all hours' store. I didn't see any of the regulars, not even the usual weekend girl, but I paid by card. Lucky for me, I guess."

"Very," Anderson muttered, although Duncan hadn't seemed to hear, concentrating on getting out his wallet and fumbling around in it until he'd found his Visa card.

"Here." He waved it, as though it would have incontrovertible proof of his whereabouts printed on it. "You should be able to verify I was *where* I said *when* I said. And what's all this about, anyway?"

Time for Robin to take over. "Oliver Narraway was killed this afternoon, sometime just before two o'clock."

This time Duncan's shock seemed real enough. That illusion shattered as he opened his mouth. "Who? Am I supposed to know this man?"

"Oh yes." Robin had heard enough lies. "You were seen talking to him at the back of the school field on Thursday lunchtime. And now *he's* dead, as well."

"Oh, *that* chap." Duncan sounded a bit too airy. "You're surely not suggesting I killed him? I was just asking him about St. Crispin's school. Getting some inside information from one of the locals."

"Really?" Robin leaned forward, cramping the witness, a witness who now had beads of sweat breaking out on his brow. "You just happened to start talking about St. Crispin's, purely by coincidence, with someone who's on the school's governing body?"

If Robin had been able to paint and had wanted to make a sketch called "Really Rattled But Trying Like Hell to Hide It," then Duncan would have been the ideal model. "His picture's on their website. I have an exceptionally good facility with faces, and I remembered—"

"I bet you remembered him." Robin was sick of all the arsing about too. "You thought he stopped you getting that job with Chilcombe Holdings."

Duncan looked from one policeman to the other again, like a rabbit in the headlights. "How the fuck did you know about that?"

"A reliable source. A more reliable source than you," Anderson turned the screw. "Why have you given us such a catalogue of lies about knowing him?"

Duncan's mouth worked, silently. If he was buying thinking time he was making himself seem an idiot while doing it. Was he finally cracking?

"Because you'd have suspected me of something," he said at last. "Even when you were here bothering Lizzie, even though she couldn't have had anything to do with what happened at St. Crispin's, you had us in your sights. Then you came and hounded me at the bookshop."

"I'd hardly call it hounding," Robin sneered. "Did your wife warn you I was coming beforehand, so you could get your story straight?"

"I resent that." Duncan sat up, the flickering embers of fight igniting again.

"And *I* resent you not giving us the truth if you've nothing to hide." Robin waited for an answer, but Duncan didn't seem to have one. "Maybe you'd like to think about whether you got confused about the shop or whether you were in Lindenshaw, murdering Narraway."

"Brian? What's going on?" Mrs. Duncan. At just the wrong moment.

"Don't worry, Lizzie . . ." Duncan's voice faded away as his wife, in a blue dressing gown over what seemed to be a nightdress, appeared at the conservatory doorway.

Robin got up. "Mrs. Duncan. Have my seat. Please."

"Thank you. I won't refuse the offer." She looked pale, anxious, and dead on her feet; her husband had been right about how much she'd gone downhill since Friday.

"We were asking your husband where he was this lunchtime." Anderson's voice was softer now, full of charm.

Mrs. Duncan cast a sharp sideways glance at her husband before she replied. "He'd gone down to the local Co-op, I think. I'm afraid I was asleep. It's all caught up with me."

"So you can't verify his story?" The sergeant smiled, not unkindly.

"I didn't see him with my own eyes, if that's what you mean, but groceries don't buy themselves." She returned the smile.

"I'll get the receipt before you go, gentlemen." Duncan made to get up, fortified by his wife's presence and clearly keen to be rid of his visitors.

Robin hesitated, unsure whether to tighten the screw further. Lizzie Duncan really didn't give the impression she could undergo any degree of cross-examination, and nobody wanted an accusation of the police obtaining evidence while being overly heavy-handed. He caught Anderson on the brink of another question and raised his eyebrows to warn him off.

"Just one final thing." Robin turned his attention back to Duncan, aware of the superiority that standing while the interviewee sat gave him. "When we met in the bookshop, you had a pair of latex gloves in your briefcase. That struck me as rather unusual. How would you explain them? And I'd appreciate nothing but the truth this time. If we have to return because you've lied again . . ."

"I'm a trained first-aider, aren't I, Lizzie?" Duncan looked at his wife, who nodded. "I always carry a couple of sets of gloves in case I have to attend to a casualty, either in the shop or when I'm out and about."

"We'd better take them then, along with that receipt. The ones out of your briefcase and any other used ones." Not that Duncan would be so dumb, surely, as not to have got rid of them if he'd used them on Youngs. But maybe forensics could match up the material or that elusive fragrance. "And one last thing. When Narraway rang you yesterday, what did he say?"

Lizzie Duncan gave a sharp intake of breath. "Narraway rang you?"

"No, he didn't. I don't know what you're playing at, Inspector, but you can't catch me out like that. I haven't spoken to Oliver Narraway since Thursday." Duncan sprang onto his feet, looking like he was spoiling for a fight.

"Brian!" Lizzie Duncan threw up her hands, as though she might strike her husband. "You said you wouldn't tell them about that."

"It's too late. They know." Duncan jabbed his finger at Robin. "Only they think they know more than they do. Narraway didn't ring here yesterday. Or any time I can remember."

Much as he hated to admit it, Robin had the feeling Duncan might just be telling the truth at last.

Once they got back to the station, they could check if the receipt was a forgery, if they wanted to, although that seemed far-fetched. Who would go to all that trouble when there must be easier ways of forging an alibi?

Frustrated, Robin put the keys in the car's ignition but didn't feel like firing it up. "If Duncan really was out doing the shopping when this receipt says he was, he couldn't have been killing Narraway."

"Maybe he's got a time machine," Anderson said from the passenger seat. "Joke."

"It's not a funny one." Robin looked in the side mirror at the Duncans' house. "You know, just because his card was at the shop, it doesn't mean *he* was. Mrs. Duncan—or any obliging friend—could have come down and used it, giving him a neat little alibi."

"Too true."

Robin started the car. "Right. Let's see if we can sort that. Now. The shop address is on here—I'll bung it in the satnav."

They got to the Co-op without the satnav sending them down any dead ends and unexpectedly found a parking space on the road outside. The Closed sign on the shop door explained why.

"'Open all hours' shop, my arse." Robin felt like banging the door down. Why the hell did they have to shut at half past four, even if it was Sunday? Especially when the sign in the window said they were open until eight *every* night.

"Be fair. It does say, 'Due to staff sickness.'" Anderson gave his boss a sly, sideways look. "I don't think they did it deliberately to annoy you."

"I'm not so sure about that. If I get all the way back here tomorrow and it's still shut, I'll go mad." Robin clenched and unclenched his fists. Why was there never a Ryan Atherley–shaped punchbag when he needed one?

"I'd leave it to the local bobby, sir. They can ask whether it was Duncan using the card. Chances are it was a weekend girl or boy and they won't remember."

Anderson was right. Chasing up this sort of thing wasn't the best use of their time. And the nagging question remained: where was any real evidence that Duncan had killed either of the victims?

"I can understand just about anyone taking a pop at Narraway, but I can't get my head around Duncan killing Youngs, sir. Surely no one would commit murder just to make sure his wife got another crack at a job interview?"

"Didn't you watch him, though? He looked desperate when he spoke about her job." *Right, time to make a sensible plan of campaign.* "We'll leave this place to the local bobby like you said. You and Davis get a look into the Duncans' finances and see how much strain they're under. Pressure makes people behave peculiarly."

"Enough to commit murder? Come on."

"I know." Robin groaned. They had to be missing something. Either there was a whole aspect to Youngs's life that they'd failed to unearth or they were missing the bleeding obvious, something right under their noses. "Claire Waites should be back from her weekend of shopping, drinking, and molesting young men in clubs. I'm going to see if I can pin her down tomorrow."

"Not literally, I hope."

"Ha fucking ha."

Now he had to persuade himself not to have fantasies about pinning Adam down. He couldn't get the guy out of his head—personally or professionally, given that the bloke had been running past Narraway's house.

After dropping Anderson back at the station, Robin stopped his car in the lay-by just before the Lindenshaw turn. He should get back on the road, carry straight on home, and leave a note thanking his cleaner for doing the washing and the other things she'd no doubt done to hold the fort. Check if any post had come the day before.

Have a bath. Have a drink and crash out in front of the box. Forget about the case for an hour. Forget about Adam's green eyes.

But he still had to find out what Adam had been doing near Narraway's cottage. *Had* to know, and not just with his rozzer hat on. His phone went off, somebody texting him.

You got a minute? Heard something you might want to know. Can ring tomorrow if not convenient now. Understand that it's awkward. Adam.

He swung out into the road and flicked his indicator on, getting ready to turn towards the village.

Chapter Nineteen

The doorbell ringing sent Campbell into paroxysms of joy, his tail wagging like a demented metronome. Adam wondered whether the dog knew who was on the doorstep, either from sound or smell, and whether it would turn out to be their favourite policeman.

"Hello, again!" Adam said, fighting Campbell back as he opened the door. "You might as well pack a suitcase and move in. Oh God," he added, feeling a flush rush up his face. "That was out of order. Sorry, I—"

"Shut up and let me in. I don't have time to arse about."

Oh hell. Tetchy again. Just when he thought they'd got a truce in place. "Come in. Have you eaten?"

Robin looked puzzled, as though he couldn't grasp the answer. "Not since lunchtime. And not properly then."

"Narraway? I know. Come in, and I'll rustle something up."

"Thanks. Hello, boy." Robin stroked Campbell's back.

Adam resisted making a joke about Campbell being Robin's devoted slave. Things were moving too fast for both of them, and in all directions but the right one. "Soup all right for you?"

"I'd eat anything at the moment. Even your dog food." He rubbed Campbell's ears.

"He'd fight you for it." Adam rummaged in the kitchen cupboard while Robin and the dog continued their mutual love fest by the breakfast bar. "This is becoming habitual. You, me, my house, cooking food. I feel like a Stepford wife."

"Ha-ha." Robin lifted his hand off Campbell's head, eyes full of concern. "Am I becoming a pest? It's just easier to talk here, rather than drag you to the station. I—"

"Oh hush. This is the nearest we'll get to going on a date at the moment. Can't be seen tête-à-tête over a jacket potato at the café. Got a briefing tonight?"

"Already had one, earlier." Robin tipped his head from side to side, rolling his shoulders, easing muscles that must have been knotted tight. "Nothing's shown up yet from the house-to-house search. We'll start again tomorrow, but we've done everyone in Narraway's road. I didn't realise your chair of governors lived next door," Robin said casually.

"Oh, yes. Very cosy. Oliver was the one who got Victor onto the governing body, apparently. I think he expected he'd found someone who shared his point of view." Adam shrugged. "He got that wrong."

"No love lost between them?" Robin, alert now, had stopped the shoulder rolling.

"No, but . . . You're not thinking Victor could have been involved? Why would he do that?"

"We'll be checking where he was, anyway. Strikes me as odd, though, if he lived next door, why you had to take Narraway his post," Robin said, in just too offhand a tone.

"Because Victor thought it was beneath him." Adam stopped halfway through spooning soup from tin to pan. "If you ask him, he'll say it's because he's an executive, not an office boy, which is what he told Jennifer. Told her to put it in the mail, but she feels that's a waste of money. Is that important?"

"I have no idea." Robin blew out his cheeks.

Adam got the soup heating up. "Bloody mess, isn't it?"

"Tell me about it. You didn't happen to see anything when you were out running earlier today?"

"Trevor reported back, did he? The copper at the cottage," Adam added when Robin appeared confused. "We used to play football together. Not a sausage, I'm afraid. I'd been the other side of the village. When he told me what happened to Oliver, I thought I was going to lose my stomach contents again. Hell of a shock."

"I bet it was." There was an uncomfortable edge to the inspector's voice. "I'm sorry. The constable said you'd acted shiftily."

"Oh, for fuck's sake." Adam grabbed the nearest thing—a wooden spoon, in lieu of Robin's head—and slammed it on the worktop. "Of course I was shifty. I'd deliberately come that way. I was wondering whether to drop in on Oliver to see if I could find out who he'd been on the phone with. So I could help *you*."

"Really?" Robin's eyes held a peculiar mixture of hope and suspicion.

"Of course, you idiot. Look, I didn't kill Oliver Narraway. I couldn't have. I'd spent the previous two hours at the gym. And I can find plenty of people to back me up."

"Okay. I had to ask. You know that."

"Yeah, I know." Adam sighed. "The job. The murders. I know we'd not have met, if not for them, but it sometimes feels like they'll always come between us, even when you've caught whoever did it."

"I hope to God not. Not the job, anyway." Robin left his seat, edging past a reluctant Campbell, and put his hand on Adam's shoulder. "Are you trying to tell me you couldn't ever go out with a rozzer?"

"No. No, honestly." Adam tilted his head briefly onto Robin's hand but he kept stirring the soup. "I didn't suppose that I'd be under suspicion. Not like one of those TV shows where the detective's family keeps being connected to the murders."

"You're not under suspicion now," Robin said, almost sounding like he meant it. Maybe he couldn't give one hundred per cent reassurance until they had somebody else banged up for it. "What did you want to tell me?"

Apart from the fact that I'm falling for you hook, line, and sinker?

"Some dirt on Ian Youngs. I'll tell you while you eat."

Soup, cheese, the last of the nice rolls from Waitrose. Robin at the breakfast bar again and a hint of solid, comfortable domestic bliss.

Robin broke the bread, layering on some butter. "You have my undivided attention."

"Alistair, the bloke I suffer torture alongside at the gym, was at teacher-training college with me." Adam saw—with glee—what might have been a flicker of jealousy, quickly suppressed, in Robin's eye. "He was telling me one of the teachers at his present school knew Youngs when *he* was training. Following all this?"

Robin looked up from his soup. "Like a bloodhound."

"Youngs apparently made dirty films when he was a poor impoverished student. To pay his way through uni." Adam grabbed for a cloth as Robin choked on his soup, sending a shower of droplets over the breakfast bar. "Steady!"

"Sorry," Robin said, when he'd finished coughing. "Dirty films? You mean porn?"

"I wouldn't know, as I don't watch that sort of thing." Adam didn't need to watch dirty films, anyway; he could get excited enough thinking about what Robin might look like spread-eagled over a bed.

"Had Alistair's mate seen the films?"

"The mate may have, although Alistair was a bit cagey about whether *he* had. Wouldn't surprise me. Always used to be talking about big tits, until he discovered they did nothing for me." Adam mopped up a stray bit of soup. "The way he tells it, this mate of his was out on the lash one night with Youngs, back in teacher-training college days. Both got a bit plastered and your man confessed how he was supplementing his income. Swore the other bloke to secrecy the next day, made some threats."

"And they kept it secret until now?"

"I guess so."

"But now Youngs has been murdered, they're not so fussy. No respect for the dead, eh?"

"Does it help?" Adam didn't dare think that he'd provided the key clue to solving the mystery, but he couldn't help wanting Robin to be grateful. "Any school would think twice about taking on a headteacher who'd been dangling his piece of meat on the small screen."

"Maybe. Although it feels arse over tip. Let's say somebody knew about these films and decided to cause trouble. Wouldn't it be more likely that Youngs would have killed *them* than the other way around?"

"I guess so." No brownie points, then. "Although . . . remember that odd remark he made in the school office? About people at St. Crispin's liking discipline—no, 'being strict.' That was it. Could that have been a reference to the films?"

"Sort of 'Spank me, teacher' stuff? Maybe. Who do you think he had in mind?" Robin had fished out his notebook and was jotting furiously, so maybe there *were* brownie points to be earned.

"God alone knows."

"You said that everybody has the hots for your yummy mummy. Couldn't be her he was referring to, could it? Right age."

"Christine Probert? She'd flay you alive if she heard you call her a yummy mummy. Shouldn't PCs be PC?" Adam was chuffed with his joke, although even Campbell seemed to yawn at it.

"Oh, ha-ha." Robin wasn't amused. "Mrs. Probert. She met Youngs when he visited. Could he have been involved with her?"

"Only in his dreams. That's the thing with Christine: she's absolutely true to her hubby. Nearest thing to a perfect couple I've ever known," Adam said, wistfully. "I sometimes envy her. She found her Mr. Right."

"So you believe in Mr. Right?" Robin laid down his cutlery neatly. He avoided Adam's eye.

"Yeah. Don't you?"

"It's like yetis. They say these things exist, but I've never seen one." Robin looked up. "Maybe one day . . ."

"Maybe," Adam said, trying not to appear too stupidly happy. They'd have time enough to talk about addressing their inadequate love lives when this case was sealed.

"And are you one hundred percent sure Mrs. Probert's not the sort of woman who'd be in one of these dirty films?"

"I'd put fifty quid on her not being. That's like saying Marjorie could have been in them." Adam grinned at the notion. That was *real* abominable snowman territory. "Poor Christine. I don't think she has the least idea the effect she has on blokes. She'd probably be horrified if she knew the sort of thoughts she arouses."

Robin moved in his seat, clearly uncomfortable. "We should change the subject before we get onto what sorts of thoughts you arouse in me."

"I know." Adam watched Robin finish the soup. "I should get an early night. So should you. You're looking a bit ragged."

"Ragged? Bleeding knackered." Robin laid down his spoon and rubbed Campbell's ear, as though that helped him focus his thoughts. "It's a shame we need to have our early nights in two separate beds but don't go suggesting anything different. I'm spending tonight at home, get it? And all future nights, until this is sorted."

Time for pragmatism. "Yeah, I get it. I'm promising you a proper 'early night' then, though. Assuming you'll still be interested." *Maybe Robin will bring his handcuffs.*

"You're thinking smut."

"You're reading minds?" Adam felt himself blushing.

"Yeah. And that means I need to go." Campbell's yelp showed he was less than impressed at being trodden on in Robin's haste to leave. "Oh hell! Didn't see your paw there, boy."

"He'll be upset if you don't say sorry," Adam remarked, for want of anything better to say.

Robin made a theatrical bow. "Sorry, Campbell." He smiled at Adam, despite the awkwardness between them. "See, boyfriends can be biddable."

Boyfriend? What did that mean? "I'll remember that when we have our early night."

"That should be at my place, then. When we get there. I've imposed too much on your hospitality." Robin was halfway out of the door, clearly wanting to get away before they said—or did—anything they'd regret. A farewell shake of hands in the hallway, then it really was time for good-bye.

"Sleep well." Robin rubbed Adam's arm. "And don't dream about what might have been going on in those dirty films. You wouldn't like it."

Adam grinned. "How can you be sure? You don't live in my head." Even if the policeman had been a permanent fixture in his thoughts since Thursday.

Robin laughed, opened the front door, then stopped. The laughter disappeared. "Don't mention what you told me about those films. Not to anyone."

"I won't." Robin didn't have to add to the warning. Youngs had been a stranger; Narraway was too close to home—literally—for comfort.

Chapter Twenty

Robin sat in his office, scandalously early on Monday morning, going through his notes for what seemed like the umpteenth time. Four days since Ian Youngs had died, and they were no further forward in the investigation, unless you could call a second murder an advance.

A knock on the door, followed by Anderson's cheery grin appearing around the corner of it, rescued him.

"Claire Waites is here, sir. Want me to stay?"

"It's not a formal interview, so I'll take my own notes. Aren't you supposed to be trawling through Ian Youngs's accounts to find an audit trail on that dirty-film money?"

"Davis says the statements don't go back that far, and I can't find a human to talk to at the bank at this unearthly hour."

"You'd better stay, then." Always useful to have somebody else present; two sets of ears often heard two slightly different versions of what had been said. "It's probably a wild-goose chase with that money—all done in brown envelopes."

"You have inside knowledge about that, sir?" Anderson said, ducking back round the door before Robin could shout at him. He'd have to get his own back for that one. In the meantime, he could get a small degree of revenge by getting down to the interview room and choosing the comfiest chair.

Robin found that one of the friendlier—if such a word could be used for it—interview rooms was free. Here, it wouldn't feel so much like they were giving Claire Waites the third degree. He chose the best seat but had to get out of it straightaway as she entered, Anderson on her heels and trying to hide a grin. She was a classy-looking brunette, calm and confident.

"Thank you for coming over here."

"So long as I can get into school on time." Ms. Waites took a seat. "And I'd rather this than see you at home. I had enough explaining to do about your phone call last evening."

"Is your partner always so suspicious?" Anderson perched on the edge of a table, evidently trying to look relaxed.

Ms. Waites rolled her eyes. "He is where Ian Youngs is concerned. I'm afraid Ian has—sorry *had*—never really accepted the fact that we'd broken up for good."

"You didn't seem that upset about his death. I mean, you didn't even call off your shopping trip." Anderson smiled, but he was straight in for the kill, as usual.

She flushed. "You probably think I'm a heartless cow, but it's not like that. It was my sister's treat, celebrating her finishing chemo. It would have taken a lot more than an ex-boyfriend's death to make me cancel it. It's the living who matter, Sergeant."

Anderson mumbled an apology, leaving Robin to cut in. "Did she have a good time?"

"She did. I've not seen Sarah so happy in ages." Ms. Waites smiled. "Not even what happened yesterday can take the edge off it."

"Yesterday?" Anderson slid off the desk. "Oliver Narraway, you mean?"

"Who? No, I mean my car breaking down on the way home and my having to hang around for hours to get it fixed." She looked from Robin to the sergeant and back again. "Is that the same Narraway who was head over at Tythebarn?"

"That's him. He was killed, yesterday lunchtime." Robin watched her reaction, but the surprise seemed genuine enough.

"Poor bloke. Is it connected to Ian's murder?"

"We have to assume so. One of the things we wanted to ask is what you'd heard about him. When he was at Tythebarn."

"Not the obvious."

"Sorry?"

"He was a bit of a touchy-feely old bugger, always hugging the dinner ladies, but he never touched the kids. I'd swear to that."

"You know that for an absolute fact?" Anderson asked, looking up from his notes.

"Well, nobody can know absolutely," Ms. Waites said, tossing her head. "But that's not what people were saying in Tythebarn. They said he had his fingers in the school till. Never proven, although I suspect they didn't go probing too deep. It was about the time his wife died, so they just eased him out. The school was closing, anyway."

"Why the hell couldn't somebody have told us this before?" Robin rubbed the back of his head in frustration. "Everybody's been so bloody cagey."

"They would be. Narraway's got friends in high places. Nobody would have dared sully his name without concrete evidence. Now he's dead, they'll be going for the jugular, poor old sod."

Like Youngs and those dirty films. Talking of which . . . "Did you know that Ian Youngs had made porn films when he was still a student?"

"Of course I did." She snorted, the calm of earlier giving way to fire flaring from her nostrils. "That's why we split up. Do you know, I'd never have found out if it hadn't been for a hen party I went to last year? We were out in Dublin, and one of the girls had brought her laptop so we could look at some 'pictures' over a bottle of bubbly before we hit the town."

"Dirty pictures?" Anderson, inevitably, had pricked up his ears.

"More art than pornography, although I suppose that depends on your point of view. Nothing worse than you'd find on a Dieux du Stade calendar."

Robin hoped that he wasn't flushing at the thought of the DDS calendar he had pinned up in his study at home. "You were certain it was him?"

"Of course, even though while we were looking at the pictures I didn't actually see a lot of his *face*. Oh, *do* grow up." Ms. Waites gave Anderson a withering look, wiping the inane grin off his face. "How could I have missed those ears?"

The sergeant fought back. "If they were just pictures, how did you find out about the films?"

"Google fu, or whatever it's called. By the time I got home, I had plenty of suspicions. And he couldn't deny it."

"I hope your pupils don't know what you get up to," Anderson said.

Ms. Waites jabbed her finger at him. "Don't start on that. This was hardly more than looking at a few bums and abs. I've never done anything outside school I'd be ashamed about. Unlike *some people*."

Robin shot Anderson a quick glance, but it didn't seem like either of them were being fingered. "Who are the *some people* you have in mind?"

"Ian, of course," she replied, a bit too quickly.

"Anyone else?"

"No." Her burning cheeks gave the lie to her words, but repeating the question didn't change the answer.

"Yesterday, when your car broke down, it must have been boring for you, hanging around. Were you on your own?"

If Ms. Waites was put off by Anderson's sudden change of tack, she quickly recovered her composure. "I'm afraid I was. Although I managed to find a coffee shop, stocked up on my caffeine, then went back and worked through a ton of marking and planning."

"Can anybody verify that?"

"Not unless they remember walking past my car and noticing someone with their head over a pile of books." She paused. "Why this sudden interest in what I was doing? What do my whereabouts yesterday have to do with Ian's murder?"

"We're investigating two deaths, now. And you knew both of the victims." Anderson leaned forward, but a warning nudge from Robin stopped him from asking anything further. If the sergeant's thoughts had gone down the same track as his, they'd have to handle the rest of this "informal" interview carefully.

"I wasn't even near Lindenshaw on Thursday. I took some children to the music festival over at the secondary school. The teacher I went with can verify it," she added, contemptuously.

"And her name is? Just so my notes are complete." Robin smiled sweetly, but he made sure he'd written everything down before he let their witness go. Anderson could see her out and then it would be caffeine time.

"Should we get her back in? Under caution?" Anderson asked, as they made their way to the canteen. "She'd have motive to kill Youngs, if he was pestering her. And he'd have let her get good and close."

"I suppose she used a TARDIS to get away from this music festival?" Robin grimaced. "If the alibi doesn't check out, then we'll call her back. It's your turn to buy the coffee."

"It always seems to be my turn, sir."

"It'll continue being your turn if you can't come up with a reason why Claire Waites might have wanted to kill Narraway. I'll see you in my office. Need a pee." And time to gather his increasingly muddled thoughts.

The face Robin saw staring back from the toilet mirror reminded him—with a jolt—of his father. He could have sworn half those wrinkles hadn't been there a week ago, or was it just the harsh police station lights showing every blemish in a way the kinder ambience of his bathroom avoided? He splashed some water on his face, trying to force his body and mind into perking up. He'd never known a case to be so obtuse, so full of loose ends that led nowhere or seemed to knot round themselves again.

And with a key witness who Robin couldn't get out of his mind, no matter how much he tried to keep his thoughts on the case.

His boss wanted answers, the media wanted answers, the citizens of Lindenshaw had probably put on prayer vigils, and the national press had set up camp in the café on the high street. The fabric of his bit of middle England was coming apart by slow degrees, and he had to stop it. With an arrest. An arrest that seemed as far off as when the case had opened.

What a fucking mess. He could see this becoming one of the great unsolved British crimes, hanging over his career like a black cloud and being featured on television reconstruction programmes until kingdom come.

When he got back to his office, Anderson was at his desk, talking on the phone. Something about the set of his jaw suggested this was more bad news.

"Yes, thank you." Anderson put the phone down. "That was the credit card company. Confirming that Duncan's card was used when and where he said it was."

Robin didn't expect anything different in this nightmare of a case. Even though he was convinced the bloke was lying. "That's about par for the bloody course. Heard anything about what the people at the shop said?"

Anderson shrugged. "Not yet."

"And what about Narraway's phone calls?"

"Still waiting." The sergeant tidied some papers into a neat pile. "Wouldn't like to be the kids in Claire Waites's class today. She's in a stinker of a mood."

"You had your ear bent?"

"Almost to breaking point. About everything. Us, for asking about how we could verify her whereabouts. At Youngs, for being in dirty pictures. At the pictures themselves. Seems they weren't just the usual heavy-breathing smut. Touch of BDSM. Him and a dominatrix."

"Oh great." Robin closed his eyes. Maybe he'd open them and find it had all been a dream, that this was Thursday morning again and he had nothing worse than a robbery to deal with. Then he could just saunter over to St. Crispin's, volunteer to do some community liaison, just happen to run across Adam and . . .

"Are you asleep, sir?"

"Eh?" Perhaps he had been, literally, caught napping. "No, just thinking."

"About BDSM?"

"Not my scene, Sergeant." Then why did the reference make him uncomfortable, like there was something he'd missed? *Of course!* "Youngs made some remark at the school though, didn't he? Hang on." He made a point of searching through the statements, although he knew exactly what he was looking for. "Here. 'Bet they like being strict about all sorts of things.'"

"You don't think your Mrs. Shepherd is the woman with the whip? Or Matthews himself? Perhaps the films weren't just straight." Anderson looked away hurriedly.

Robin bit his lip. If Anderson had guessed that Adam was gay, so be it, but until there was any evidence it had a bearing on the case, it wasn't a point for discussion. "God knows what he meant. We should get them all back in and ask about those films. And Narraway's financial irregularities."

"You wanted a theory about why Claire Waites killed Narraway?" Anderson grinned. "He was behind the blue movies—you know, touchy-feely dirty old man—and she struck him down like an avenging angel."

"If I thought you were being even half-serious I'd send you to get your head examined. I hope the assistant chief constable doesn't say anything like that when he makes his press statement today. Maybe—"

The shrill sound of the phone interrupted them.

"Sergeant Anderson. Yes. Right. Inspector Bright was hoping you'd get back to us this morning. He's here." The sergeant passed the phone across, deferring to seniority.

"Thanks. Hello? Ah, yes." The local bobby from Kinebridge reporting in. "Oh, really? They're positive, are they? Right." Robin cast a quick glance at his sergeant, who was almost jumping up and down with impatience. "Thank you. I'll ring back if I need anything else."

"Out with it." Anderson had only waited a microsecond, if that, after Robin put the phone down.

"We were right about the shop having Sunday staff. Just as well they did. One of them was Lizzie Duncan's pupil back in the days she taught the infants. This lad wasn't serving, just stocking the shelves, but he got a good view of everything." Robin swung back in his chair, grinning happily. "It wasn't Brian Duncan who came in at lunchtime to get those groceries. It was his wife."

"Back to Kinebridge?" Anderson already had his car keys ready in his hand.

"Via Lindenshaw. I want to show Victor Reed that picture of Duncan." The one the ever-resourceful Davis had run off Facebook. "See if he was at Narra—" A sharp rap on the door made Robin slam his chair back down again, nearly propelling him out of it. "Bloody hell! Come in."

Davis stuck her head round the door, smiling nervously and waving a piece of paper.

Just to complicate this Gordian knot of a case, the phone records had arrived. Saturday, Oliver Narraway had rung—within a few minutes of each other—the Duncans, Victor Reed, the Bookhams, and the Lindenshaw newsagents.

Robin thought he'd better laugh, or else he'd cry.

Victor Reed didn't appear surprised at the policemen's reappearance on his doorstep, nor at the picture they thrust into his hand. He put on his glasses, studying it carefully.

"No, I don't think I've seen him here. Or anywhere. Not a memorable face, though."

"Maybe successful murderers are prone to slipping through people's memories. Secret of their success." Whoever was behind this pair of murders had managed to keep their motivation under the radar, too. No accusations, no snide little comments, apart from Narraway's about Lizzie Duncan and that had led them . . . where, exactly? Narraway to his death, maybe. "You're absolutely sure?"

"I'd have told you if I'd remembered him. I wouldn't obstruct you, Inspector."

"No. Sorry." Robin changed tack. "I believe Narraway rang you, on Saturday?"

"Oh yes. He wanted to talk about the implications of continuing with an interim head on the school budget. Hardly earth-shattering stuff."

"Odd that he rang you when he only lives next door." Anderson, notebook in hand, was jotting down Reed's answers with an intensity that suggested every word was vital.

"Who knows—sorry, knew—the workings of Oliver's mind?" Reed shrugged. "He's done it before, rather than trot the fifty yards over here."

"Back to unlikely visitors." Robin wasn't sure he believed Reed's answer—like the fact that Adam had to take the governor post over, it made no sense—but they'd no way of proving he was lying. "Did you see anybody visiting Narraway during the last few weeks who made you think twice?"

"Like one of the applicants, you mean?"

"That's just what I mean. Claire Waites, for example." Robin watched for a reaction, but Reed just seemed puzzled, rolling the name around on his tongue.

"Claire Waites? Oh, yes. *Her*. I wouldn't have thought she'd dare show her face around here."

"By which you mean . . .?"

"Don't you know? Then perhaps I shouldn't tell you." Reed looked down at Duncan's picture again, avoiding eye contact.

Robin thought there might just be a third murder—there, then. "I'm sick and tired of people arsing me about, pleading protocol, or throwing their toys out of the pram. We're past the point of anything but a straight answer. We know about the spat with Marjorie when you interviewed before. We need the details."

"Oh." Reed lowered his voice. "Don't want the wife to hear. Confidential and all that."

"We could do this at the station, if you prefer?"

"Good God, no. Hang on." Reed shut the door connecting the lounge and hallway. "She, Claire Waites, had launched into accountability—the old 'Caesar's wife must be above suspicion' thing. After which, Neil mentioned some cases in the newspaper about teachers drinking and being rowdy on holiday. He wanted her opinion on whether they should be setting an example off-site."

"Did he get it? Her opinion?" Anderson asked, no doubt thinking of ex-boyfriends and porn films.

"Not before Oliver chipped in with some comment about the interference of the nanny state in everything." Reed looked guiltily towards his neighbour's house. "Shouldn't speak ill of the dead, but you said I wasn't to pussyfoot. Actually, Ms. Waites handled him quite well, only she never got to give us all of her argument because Marjorie came in with the metaphorical fists flying."

Robin hadn't thought she'd have so much gumption in her. "Saying what?"

"That the governors could expect people who worked for them to be as pure as the driven snow when they were on school premises or out somewhere on school business, but apart from that, people should be allowed to live the sort of life they pleased, so long as they weren't breaking the law."

"I bet that raised a few eyebrows." Anderson rolled his eyes.

"Raised them? Neil's nearly skidded round to the back of his head. I'm not sure anyone could believe this was our mild-mannered, 'got to go and get Derek's tea ready' Marjorie. *He'd* never have expressed such an opinion."

"Did the vicar argue with her?" Anderson continued, although Robin was only half paying attention. Something jarred in what had just been said. Hadn't somebody told him the exact opposite? Yes, Adam had referred to rumours about Marjorie insisting teachers uphold high standards outside of school. Had those rumours got it the wrong way round?

"Of course not," Reed replied. "He always turns the other cheek. Ms. Waites reacted ferociously, saying Marjorie was completely wrong."

Robin recalled the story about the dirty films. No wonder Claire Waites had been on the defensive. "Go on," he said.

"She and Marjorie went at it hammer, tongs, and the poker thrown in, before Jeremy Tunstall blew the whistle and ended round one." Victor started to grin then checked himself, as though it had been a shame to interrupt such a promising fight. "We'd seen enough to send Ms. Waites packing, but on the way out, she really blotted her copybook." He stopped, clearly weighing whether to say any more.

"Ye-es?" Robin asked. When was all this pussyfooting around going to end?

"I overheard—not intentionally." Reed squirmed, standing on one foot and then the other, like a naughty schoolboy reporting to the teacher. "She and Marjorie must have thought they were alone, but I was round the corner. She called her a painted whore."

"Bloody hell," Anderson said.

Robin clarified. "Marjorie Bookham called Claire Waites a whore?"

"No." Reed rubbed his chin. "That's the tricky bit. It was the other way round."

Robin appreciated the drive to Kinebridge. Never the world's best passenger—except when he'd been with Adam, who at least seemed to be a safe pair of hands at the wheel—he used the journey for thinking.

The sight of the road down to the school did nothing for his mood. The place seemed to be taunting him, reminding him how useless he'd felt when he'd been a pupil there and how useless he was now. Reminding him that the one thing he wanted from the place—Adam—was the one thing he couldn't have. Maybe it was the tiredness talking, maybe it was all the old hurts, hidden in the depths of his mind, coming to the surface again. Whatever it was, it could go to hell.

He switched his attention back to the case. "Do you think Reed was lying about why Narraway was ringing him?"

"No idea, sir." Anderson kept his eyes on the road; he'd had a bollocking before for not paying enough attention while driving.

"I wondered if his ringing, rather than going round, meant he might not have wanted *Mrs.* Reed to hear what he had to say."

"Could be."

Robin took to staring out of the window again, brooding over whatever jarring note there'd been in what Reed had said, until the sharp insistence of the phone made him jump. Davis, with the results of her enquiries with the other recipients of Narraway's calls. Marjorie Bookham said the man had rung to discuss the next round of recruitment, the newsagent said Narraway had wanted to complain about the wrong paper being delivered, and Duncan said he had no idea what the call was about. He'd been so fed up, he'd put the phone down on the table and let Narraway talk into thin air. Somebody had to be telling porky-pies, but which of them?

"Lying."

Anderson glanced at his boss, then back at the road. "Sorry, sir?"

Robin hadn't realised he'd spoken his thoughts. "Somebody's lying, and not just about the phone calls. Reed said Marjorie Bookham insisted people could behave how they wanted out of school. Matthews told me that Claire Waites had said that. Mrs. Bookham told me something similar."

"Maybe they're all lying," Anderson said, with a gleeful grin.

Maybe, and if so, how could they sort out the truth?

Back at the Duncans' house, they ended up in the same seats out in the conservatory, but this time both husband and wife—the latter looking in remarkably good health—were present from the start. Neither looked comfortable, which was what Robin wanted.

"I'm sure we've told you all we can, Inspector." Mrs. Duncan was straight on the offensive, not even waiting for the first volley of questions to be fired off.

"That's funny, because we're equally sure you haven't. In fact, you've both been leading us up the garden path. Every time." Robin drummed his fingers on the arm of his wicker chair.

"Now steady on." Mr. Duncan sat up angrily.

"We know you lied about where you'd been walking your dog. We have reason to believe you lied about your conversation with Oliver Narraway when you ran across him on Thursday. And now it turns out you've lied about being in the shop yesterday."

Mrs. Duncan's sharp intake of breath was stifled as her hands covered her mouth.

"It's all right, Lizzie." Duncan's spirits seemed to rally. "It's not as if they can charge you with fraud, just because you used my card. You had my permission."

"You fool." Mrs. Duncan spat the words out. "Why the hell couldn't you have just kept your trap shut and said you were at home with me?"

"You must be very devoted to your husband, to drag yourself down to the shop just to try to give him an alibi for murder." Anderson turned the screw.

"Alibi for *what*?" She looked at her husband, at the police, then back at her husband in what seemed an overelaborate mime.

"Oh, cut the nonsense." Robin couldn't face another barrage of lies. "You tried to construct a cover for the time Oliver Narraway was killed."

"Narraway? What's he got to do with it?" Mrs. Duncan looked genuinely bewildered.

"Your husband met him last Thursday lunchtime. Didn't you, Mr. Duncan? Was he being his usual charming self and you decided to get your own back on him for robbing you of that job?"

Mr. Duncan, wild-eyed, ran his hands through his hair. "Of course not. I didn't even realise it *was* him until later. It was out of context, Mr. Bright, like seeing your dentist in the street. I didn't recognise him, and I doubt he recognised me. And I wasn't murdering him yesterday, I swear to God."

Why did Mr. Duncan change his story like his shirt? The "out of context" excuse seemed no more convincing than had the one about seeing Oliver's picture on the website. Add to that the rubbish about where he'd been walking the dog and the stuff in the shop. Why should Robin believe the seemingly heartfelt plea that Mr. Duncan hadn't committed the murder?

Robin leaned forward, angrily gripping the arms of his chair. "Are you honestly expecting us to believe that? Any of it?"

"Believe what you want, but it's the truth."

"So what on earth *were* you doing?" Robin, aware of an insistent drumming, realised it was his own fingers hammering on the chair arm once more.

"A spot of burglary."

"What?" This crazy case. Where the fuck was it going now?

"I was over at the Business Park, on the Stanebridge ring road. It's where I used to work, at Dunbridge's. You can verify all of that." Mr. Duncan, voice cracking under the strain, sounded tired and defeated.

"We will," Anderson said, tapping the notebook where he'd jotted everything down.

"I still had an office key, so I didn't have to break in. I took some old papers. To do with me losing my job there. Oh, *don't*, Lizzie," he snapped at his wife's sneer.

"Such a clever idea. Such a mess. I knew it was pointless leaving things to you." Mrs. Duncan looked contemptuously down her nose at her husband.

Robin, stunned at the unexpected venom in Mrs. Duncan's voice, wished Adam and the rest of his barmy band of governors could have been there. They'd have thought twice about putting their charges in this woman's hands.

"Didn't they take the keys back when they gave you the boot?" Anderson said.

"Of course they did. It was easy enough to make a copy of them beforehand. Just in case." Mr. Duncan looked suitably ashamed of himself.

"Why did you need to go to all that trouble?" Robin asked. They'd need to check the story out, naturally, but for once it seemed like this couple was telling them—however reluctantly—the truth.

"Because he didn't lose his job due to the economic recession. They accused him of financial misconduct but couldn't prove it. He was allowed to leave of his own accord, with a bland reference. The sort that makes it impossible to get a job elsewhere."

"I said I didn't do it, Lizzie. You know that. And these papers I got should demonstrate that."

"Is that what the gloves in your briefcase were for? Making sure you didn't leave any fingerprints at the scene of the crime?" Robin asked.

"Sort of. I *did* used to be the first-aider at Dunbridge's, so it seemed poetic justice."

"And why the hell didn't you tell us this before? No. Don't give a stream of self-justification." Robin leaned forwards in his chair. "Tell me the absolute truth about what you've done the last few days. Especially where it concerns Narraway."

The story tumbled out. Yes, he'd recognised Narraway at the back of the school. Yes, the bloke had given him some stick about missing out on the job. Mr. Duncan had become defensive; they'd had words. He'd told the truth, he insisted, about intending to visit St. Crispin's and then chickening out.

"And when Narraway rang you?"

"It was to gloat. He'd kept some of my interview paperwork and had been doing some digging. He said he knew why I'd been given the boot and that it wouldn't look well for Lizzie with St. Crispin's." Mr. Duncan slumped in his chair, broken. "It's God's honest truth, Inspector. And I know it gives me even more reason to kill the man, but I didn't."

Robin wasn't sure Mr. Duncan would recognise God's truth even if it poked him in the eye, but at least this seemed to be the closest he'd come. With a shudder, he remembered all the lies *he'd* taken refuge in down the years, both at school and before coming out. Diversionary tactics, pointing blame elsewhere—he'd been an expert.

No surprise that Narraway had turned out to be every bit as nasty as they'd expected. Acting holier than thou over financial irregularities when he'd had his fingers in the till? Just like Ryan Atherley beating Robin up for being a pansy when he was deep in the closet himself. And if Narraway had made Duncan want to kill him, with his "digging," who else had he dug about?

Please God it wasn't Adam.

Chapter Twenty-one

The quiet of the Lindenshaw churchyard, the pleasant scent of flowers and hum of insects seemed tainted now. Robin sat on a wooden bench in the sunshine with Anderson perched on a headstone—one of the not-wobbly ones—close by, infecting the idyllic scene with talk of murder while waiting for the vicar. And still neither of them were any closer to a solution.

One more name in the frame, though, and maybe the first one to have half a motive to kill Youngs. Davis had been busy again, going all around the houses to get the phone number of the teacher who went to the music festival with Claire Waites. Following it up to find Ms. Waites had been late coming back from lunch that day, late enough to have had time to go to Lindenshaw.

"She kept quiet about that." Just when they seemed to have sorted out the Duncans' version of the truth from the real thing, here was yet another person mucking them about. And he still had to get to the truth of why the story Adam had told him about Marjorie and teachers' personal lives hadn't got the facts right.

"She would keep quiet, wouldn't she?" Anderson, on cue, rolled his eyes. At least *he* was consistent. "Doesn't have a lot of luck with her car, does she? Do you really think she had problems with the locking wheel nuts?"

"God knows." Tricky thing, changing a tyre at the best of times, as he knew to his cost. The other teacher had apparently said Ms. Waites's hands were filthy when she got back, so maybe she'd been wrestling with the jack, although it would be easy enough to fake a bit of dirt. As he'd kept his own hands dirty in case he needed to explain his night at Adam's.

He continued. "Think about it: Youngs showed no sign of struggle. He'd have trusted Claire Waites to get up close and personal, maybe more than he'd have trusted anybody else. So would Narraway, if he's as much of a ladies' man as your dinner la—supervisory whatsits made out."

"Sir, do you remember that strange smell hanging about Youngs?" Anderson scratched his head with a Biro.

"The floral stuff? I chased forensics about it again this morning. It seemed too fake floral to be eau de cologne."

"That's what I wondered too. Hairspray?"

"No idea. I'm not the expert on women's toiletries. Mr. Musgrave!" Robin rose to greet the vicar. "Thank you for seeing us."

"I won't say it's my pleasure. Not given the circumstances." Musgrave looked tired and suddenly much older. When tragedy struck in such a small community, it scattered people like ninepins. "I just can't get my head around what's been happening. Such wickedness. Did you know the media have set up camp outside the tea shop?"

"Do you include that in the wickedness?" Most of the locals probably would.

"I wouldn't if they didn't keep telling a pack of lies."

"They'd say it was their interpretation of the truth," Anderson said, kicking at the gravel.

Memories of an earlier conversation suddenly flashed into Robin's mind. "Last Thursday, when there was some discussion about whether one of you had met Ian Youngs before, Marjorie Bookham seemed convinced you'd crossed swords with him, rather than just met at a concert. Have you any idea why she should have said that, if it wasn't true?"

"Funny you should say that because I've been thinking about it. Quite out of character for Marjorie to cause mischief." The vicar closed his eyes, as though seeking divine inspiration. "You know, it's odd. When Youngs came for interview, she kept looking at him as if she was—I'm trying to find absolutely the right words here—feeling unsettled in his presence."

"She said she hadn't met him before." Back to thoughts of deflecting attention elsewhere.

"So I believe." Musgrave's eyes flew open. "There's something more, though. I'd forgotten about it, with all the hoo-ha over Ian Youngs and then you coming along and taking our statements."

"Forgotten about what?" Robin snapped.

"Marjorie was observing the pupil-panel session when they were interrogating Youngs. When she came out, she was rather upset. I had to get her a cup of tea."

"Did she say what the matter was?" Anderson leaned forwards, keen as Campbell on the trail of a biscuit.

"Oh, not really. She implied it was women's trouble, so I didn't enquire further."

"No, quite." That would have been far too daring in Lindenshaw.

"But she was white as a sheet." Musgrave was pretty ashen himself. "Like she'd seen a ghost."

"A ghost?" Anderson said, with obvious incredulity.

"Forget the spectral stuff for the moment," Robin said, trying to keep his temper at bay. "Think back to when you interviewed before. Claire Waites had an argument with the governors."

"Ye-es." Musgrave nodded.

"Who was the person who said that teachers could live how they liked outside of school?" Robin waited, watching as Musgrave clearly debated how to answer.

"Marjorie," the vicar said at last, wincing. "I'm not sure she really thought before speaking. She'd been under a lot of pressure at the time, with her husband . . ."

"Thank you." Robin ended things there. Quite out of character for Marjorie Bookham to cause mischief? Maybe it was time to reassess her.

Adam sat at his desk after the children had gone home, with a pile of marking to do and no inclination to pick up his pen and get started. The previous night he'd had another dream about finding Youngs dead in his kitchen, only Oliver was lying next to Youngs this time. He'd woken, sweat dripping from him, gone and fetched Campbell, and let him sleep on the end of the bed, which had always been a canine no-go area. Shame he couldn't have fetched Robin to do the comfort duty.

"Adam?" Jennifer peered round the classroom door.

Adam shook himself out of morbid thoughts. "Something you want me to help with? Not that wire again?"

"Not this time. Just some business with sorting out the children's permission slips for the trip to the museum. I appear to have two for some and none for others."

"That's not my class, though."

"I know." Jennifer pulled the door to behind her. "It's Gillian's class, but she's hopeless. I need someone I can trust."

"Okay."

Nice to be thought trustworthy. Adam hoped Robin had the same trust in him as Jennifer did. Rising to follow Jennifer into the school office, he caught sight of his reflection. Did he always wear that inane grin when he thought of Robin? And would he ever stop feeling guilty about being the only person who seemed to have benefited by these murders, apart, of course, from the murderer?

Marjorie was in the school office, cradling a cup of tea. "Hello, Adam. To the rescue again?"

"That's me. I've left my white charger and the shining armour at home, so I'll just have to rely on my brains." He picked up a pile of pink slips and a class list and tried to make sense of them.

"I can't ever remember not looking forward to going into school, but I've been dreading today. Especially after poor Oliver . . ." Jennifer blew her nose.

Adam kept his head down—literally. He wasn't good with weeping women. Weeping policemen might be a whole other matter, but chance would be a fine thing.

"Do you think the police will be back here again? They must have made your life a misery," Marjorie cooed, soothingly.

"Oh, I'm not worried about them. That young Robin Bright's turned into quite a charmer."

Don't I know it? Adam bit his lip, in case he let out some telltale noise to show just what a charmer the guy was. And what was Marjorie's game, acting dim like that? Of course the police would be back—again and again until this thing was solved.

"I didn't realise you knew him," Marjorie said.

"Oh, he went here. I never forget the old pupils. It's the thought of the children that's kept me going these last few days, when I've felt like crawling under a stone."

"Then what's the matter?" Marjorie's sympathy was starting to sound perfunctory. "The media?"

"No, they've decamped into the village. It's the parents."

"Oh, them." Marjorie sounded relieved. "All the gossip. Ignore it."

"It's not just that. It was bad enough on Thursday, but what with Oliver . . . the reputation of St. Crispin's will be shot to pieces. I wish we could have kept it out of the papers. They'll be taking their children away as soon as they can find a place elsewhere."

Adam, with a vice suddenly gripping his stomach, realised this could have an impact on him too. Why the hell had it taken until now to realise that if the school leached children, then they might reorganise the staff and he could be out on his ear?

"Jennifer!" Marjorie's voice had such a piercing quality that Adam almost dropped his handful of paper. "There have been two murders and all you can think about is bad publicity?"

"Actually, Marjorie, I was thinking about the *children*. They're so proud of their school, and now it's sullied for them. People will always say, 'You were at the place they found the dead body.' They'll be having nightmares."

Adam carried on checking the list, but his enthusiasm for the job had waned. The pupils weren't the only ones having nightmares, were they? Maybe Robin had been prone to bad dreams when he'd been bullied. Maybe they could talk about them, help each other out . . .

Marjorie's voice sounded soothing again. "Yes, I know. Sorry. I don't know why I'm so tetchy."

"It's been a strain for everyone. We're not ourselves." Jennifer sighed. "Tell you what, there's a picture of that policeman in the rogues' gallery. You can amuse yourself with it while I top your tea up."

"I've had enough tea, thank you. And enough of policemen. Even charming ones."

Before Adam could find any sort of a sensible response, Jennifer saved him by ploughing on.

"He's a lot more charming than he used to be. Nervous little thing. Never seemed happy."

"I'll go talk to Gillian about these." Adam gathered all the slips of paper and tried to edge towards the door before he was tempted to leap to Robin's defence. Maybe if somebody had asked him *why* he was unhappy back then, they could have done something about it.

"That sergeant's a charmer too," Jennifer said, dreamily. "He asked if I'd been out frolicking on the greensward on Thursday."

"Blimey. Had he swallowed your dictionary?" Adam hadn't imagined policemen being quite so erudite.

"He meant had I been joining in the children's picnic. He seemed surprised when I said I'd worked through lunch."

"No wonder," Marjorie said, coming over and perching on Jennifer's desk.

"What do you mean?"

Marjorie grinned. "You'd have had no alibi, stuck here, with just about everyone else out and about. Number one suspect, I'd have said."

"Oh, Marjorie, you are silly." Jennifer giggled. "Actually, I have a cast-iron alibi. I was on the phone to the county IT department, trying to sort out the SAP system."

"Now *we'll* have to get out the dictionary," Adam said. "Or my buzzword bingo sheet."

"Actually—" Jennifer lowered her voice "—I keep panicking over whether I let somebody into the school by mistake during that time. I was terribly flustered over some glitches in the system, and it's possible I might have opened the door without thinking."

"I can't believe you'd ever have done that. Even with only ten percent of your brain on the job, you'd ward off any intruders." Adam was rewarded by a smile from the secretary and a mouthed *thank you* from Marjorie, who he'd rightly guessed had been trying to raise Jennifer's spirits.

"Right. Work to do. See you later, girls." Adam had almost made it out the door and was prepared to leg it off to the safety of the staffroom when the buzzer sounded.

"Hello?"

"Inspector Bright. Can I come in?"

"Of course." Jennifer operated the door release.

Adam was stuck. He couldn't scuttle off now, not without raising suspicion. "If it's the police, maybe I should go. Need to see Gillian about these. Don't want to be in the way."

"You won't be," Robin said, coming through the main door at the tag end of the conversation. "Afternoon," he added, nodding at Adam and then nonchalantly signing in the visitors' book.

Adam couldn't help but admire the professional manner and the standard of acting. Was Robin's heart dancing as much as his was, or did he have that under control, as well?

"You don't need a badge. The children have all gone home." Jennifer gave dispensation with a wave of her hand.

"There aren't any badges, anyway." Robin picked up a sad-looking sheet from which all the stickers had been removed.

"I'd better replace that." Jennifer reached for a file, made a puzzled face, reached for a different one, then slowly drew out another sheet of badges. "Someone's been moving my files about."

"A slap on the hand for whoever's done that," Adam said, immediately regretting it when Robin gave him *that* look. The "don't be such an idiot" one.

"It's as well you're here, Inspector," Jennifer continued, "because I've just this minute thought of something. I'd forgotten all about it."

Adam looked at Marjorie, who rolled her eyes.

"Confessing to the crime, are we?" Marjorie said, with a hint of impatience.

Jennifer flushed. "Only to having a poor memory." She explained about the telephone call, how there was a possibility that she may have let somebody in by mistake while distracted.

"Think carefully," Robin said, face hardened at Jennifer's revelation. "You've been ultracautious with all of us coming and going. Do you honestly think you'd have just let anyone in, automatically?"

"No, I don't." Jennifer looked from Robin to Adam to Marjorie, then back again to the policeman. "But I can't swear that it didn't happen. And there's more."

"What now?" Robin spoke slowly, coldly. Adam thought the bloke must be formidable during a formal interview.

"When Youngs was here, one of my files got moved. I've just remembered that he must have been the one who did it."

"You think he copied something from it?"

Jennifer had everyone's rapt attention. "He might have done. I'd had the file out while he was looking at the pictures, and then I had to go and get Adam to mend the wire, and when I came back, it was put away in the wrong place. Then I was so tied up with the phone call to the county and then the . . . the murder, I didn't think of it again. It didn't seem important."

"What file was it?"

"My school governors file."

"Very odd," Robin said, in a voice that had lost its hard edge and was perhaps too deliberately casual. "Actually, I came here to catch Mrs. Bookham. Your husband said I'd find you here."

"And find me you have," Marjorie said brightly.

"Don't you go upsetting her." Jennifer waggled her finger, just as she must have waggled it at the young Robin.

"I won't." The policeman smiled sweetly. "Can we use the library?"

"Of course."

"I'll just go make sure it's empty." Adam gave Robin a smile and scuttled off. A couple of teachers were lingering in the library, and Adam politely shooed them away. He resisted the temptation to hide behind the bookrack and listen in, then went off to find Gillian, but not before dropping back to the office and saying he'd cleared the scene, earning himself a smile from Robin in the process.

Maybe luck would be on his side and he'd find a vital clue among the permission slips, and then he'd have an excuse to get the inspector—and that smile—all to himself for another evening.

Robin led the way to the library, forcing himself not to look through the glass panel on Adam's door as he passed. He knew the bloke wasn't in his class, but seeing his working environment would be a comfort. Certainly something more pleasant to consider than the upcoming interview.

He made the usual polite conversation with Marjorie, hoping she was bearing up under the strain of the last few days, trying to lull her before he asked the vital questions.

Tell me about that first set of interviews. Why did one of the candidates call you a whore? No, maybe that would be too blunt. Wait till they were settled, mention Claire Waites and . . .

"What is it you wanted to ask me, Inspector?" Marjorie sat herself primly on one of the little chairs. "I can't remember anything else about Sunday."

"It wasn't that." Robin fiddled with his notebook. "I just wanted to clarify about the ruckus. With Claire Waites."

"Oh. Her." Marjorie coloured.

"You said you got into a bit of a fight?"

"We did. She was an obnoxious cow. Supercilious and self-righteous, talking about expected standards of behaviour. Well, she's living with a man, and they're not married. How hypocritical can you get?"

Ah, self-righteousness. Alive and well in Lindenshaw, and as prevalent as lying.

"I've heard that she called you a name."

"A whore, Inspector. She called me a whore." Marjorie's hand began to shake; she stilled it on the edge of the table where Robin had perched.

"But . . . why?"

"I gave her a hard time, and she didn't like it. Lost her rag, lost her chance of the job. The . . . the 'whore' comment was just a parting shot. Nothing more than that."

"I've heard two different versions of that argument. Initially I was told she was adamant that teachers didn't have to behave out of school as they did inside."

"Ye-es." Marjorie's grip on the table tightened, knuckles white with tension.

"I have two people who'll swear *you* were the one who held that view, not her."

Marjorie opened her mouth, shut it again, then forced a smile. "You've got me—what's the expression?—bang to rights. I did say that. I'm not very proud of it, either. I don't think I was myself at the time. Forgive me for leading you astray, but I'm extremely ashamed of expressing such an opinion."

She seemed plausible, but people kept seeming to be plausible. He waited to see if anything else was forthcoming, but Marjorie appeared to feel she'd given answer enough.

"Is there anything else? I need to get home soon and sort Derek's tea."

"Just one more thing." Robin lowered his voice. "About Thursday. We were told that you acted like you'd seen a ghost after you'd been in with the pupil panel and Ian Youngs. What about him upset you so much?"

Marjorie blanched. "I hoped nobody would notice."

"I'm afraid they did." Robin waited.

"Can I rely on your confidentiality, Inspector?" She fumbled in her pocket for a handkerchief. "He . . . he made me think of my son. I've got a secret, one I'd never like to come to Derek's ears." She wrung the little scrap of material in her hands. "Maybe it'll help you understand why I said what I did to Claire Waites."

Robin still waited, trying to look sympathetic and not interrupting the flow of words. Maybe they were getting to the truth at last, but whether it was truth relevant to this case, who knew.

"Before I met my husband, I had a baby. I was just a teenaged girl so you can imagine the disgrace. My family hushed it all up and were going to have the child adopted."

Not the revelation Robin had expected, but—if true—no great surprise given what he knew of Derek and his ilk. "And did they? Have it adopted, I mean?"

"No, they couldn't." The hanky wringing became more intense. "He was stillborn. I'd rather not talk about it anymore."

"I understand that. I just don't see the connection to Youngs."

"I'm sorry. I didn't make myself clear. I'd been looking through the applications again, during the pupil-panel session. I shouldn't have been, I know, but Youngs mentioned something I wanted to double-check against what he'd written." She studied her hands as the first tears began to trickle down her cheeks. "I hadn't noticed his date of birth, before. It was the same as my little Tom."

"I'm sorry." He was. Sorry at the woman's loss and sorry at another potential line of enquiry gone begging.

Robin sat in the library wondering whether he could find a reason to talk to Adam before he left the school. Not that he needed to justify it to himself, but he didn't want the bloke to come under suspicion—one way or another—from his colleagues. He'd feel a bastard for having sneaked out of the school without talking to him, but surely Adam would understand that the case took precedence?

"Want a cuppa?"

Robin looked up to see Adam peering round the door, just as he'd done the previous Thursday. "I'd love one, but I can't."

"You keep saying that," Adam replied, sotto voce before saying loudly, "I understand. Case to solve." He smiled, winked, and mouthed, *Keep in touch*, before disappearing again.

Robin, stupidly happy given that he'd have to ring Anderson as soon as he found a signal, to impart bad news, gathered his things together and left the school whistling. He got back to his car, got out his phone, unloaded his tale of woe then asked Anderson if he'd had any luck with Claire Waites.

"She said she'd got a headache from all those bloody recorders blaring out—her words, not mine—and had gone out to get some paracetamol and codeine tablets. Her car had a puncture on the way back, and she'd had to fix it. She got shirty when I challenged her to back it up."

"I bet she did." Robin eased himself into his car. "Nothing to back it up, I guess?"

"Plenty of bluster. Demanded I go round to her school right now and look in her car boot. She said she hadn't had a chance to get the flat one changed. I've got the local bobby on it—couldn't have her driving around too long without a spare."

"Easy enough to fake a puncture, though." Drastic, but murderers did drastic things.

"There's something else. I asked her about Narraway. If she'd told Youngs about what he'd been up to back at Tythebarn. She had." Anderson sounded too pleased with himself.

"And is that all you've got to gloat over?"

"Give me a break, sir. Of course not. She let slip that Youngs had rung her."

"Had he?"

"Yep. She said it was just his weekly 'please take me back, Claire' call and that she gave him a mouthful. He'd rung her right in the middle of the music festival."

"Bloody hell." Then he must have rung her while he was at St. Crispin's. To bend her ear or to talk about Narraway? Robin remembered the piece of paper and Jennifer's file with the school governors' details in. Had Youngs been getting Narraway's contact details?

"Sir?" Anderson must have been getting concerned at the silence down the line.

"Just thinking, Sergeant." But not getting very far. Youngs wanting to put pressure on Narraway to help him get through the interviews? Why should that lead to either of them being killed?

"Here's something to think about, then, sir. What if Ian Youngs shared that baby's birthday because he *was* the baby?" Anderson sounded doubly smug. "Taken away by nurses and the mother told that it had died. Things like that used to happen."

They did. And if he'd found out . . . "Do you think he might have let something slip, accidentally on purpose? That would explain why she looked so white."

"But why? With the intention of blackmailing her into helping him get the job? I'm not sure that horse runs, sir. Why would she kill her own child?"

Anderson was right. They were clutching at straws, again. "Get Davis to check it out, anyway. Get hold of a copy of his birth certificate or something."

"Will do, sir. You're coming back here?"

"Yes. If only to let the chief flay me for lack of progress."

"We'll get a break soon, sir, you'll see. Maybe it'll turn out that Claire Waites is calling our bluff and that tyre's right as rain."

"Yeah, maybe." And maybe the name of the culprit would be wafted down from Heaven to the sound of trumpets.

Chapter Twenty-two

The flogging at the grating had been endured.

Robin couldn't blame his boss for wanting results—he had *his* boss on his back and she took no prisoners. And the media wanted answers, as did the residents of Lindenshaw, who alleged they were too scared to leave their homes, although there were plenty of them milling about—probably on the way to the pub to discuss the murders—as Robin drove through. He drew the car up outside Adam's house, wondered whether to give him a call first to say he was just there to discuss business, then decided to chance it. The "just business" bit wasn't entirely true.

Adam answered the door wearing as welcoming a smile as Robin had seen in ages. "Back again? Want that cup of tea now?"

"Daft bugger. I don't come here just to be fed and watered." A pang of guilt at always imposing on the teacher's hospitality, both in terms of food and being an understanding ear, hit him square in the gut. He *was* hungry, but it could wait.

"You can send me a Harrods hamper to make up for emptying my cupboards." Adam ushered Robin into the kitchen, where Campbell greeted him like a long-lost friend. "Reckon there'll be a lot of evening up to be done when this case is finished with. What's the latest, or can't you tell me?"

"The latest? Lies, lies, and more lies. God, I'm tired." Robin rested his elbows on the breakfast bar and his head in his hands. Campbell, who'd clearly decided their guest needed some TLC, nuzzled his leg.

"You look awful." Adam's voice, full of sympathy, held the same potentially devastating tone it had when they'd stood at the top of the stairs on Saturday night. Robin pushed that from his mind.

"I feel awful. No solution in sight, that bloody school is wrecking my life again."

"Isn't that a bit overdramatic?" Adam sat down opposite, close enough to touch Robin but signally not doing so. "Sorry, that sounds harsh. I just don't want you letting that place get to you anymore. You're more important than any school, any murderer."

"Am I?" Why did the bloke have to be so damned soothing? If Adam hung around, Robin would find himself getting over this whole bloody bullying thing, and then what would he have to fire up his sense of justice, the need to defend the innocent victim that made him such a good copper?

"Penny for your thoughts."

Damn it. "Not now. Too complex. Psychoanalyse me after I get this case finished with."

"Psychoanalyse? You've got the wrong bloke, mate. Tea and sympathy, that's me." Adam smiled, green eyes flashing.

"And there was me thinking you were bed and board. Oh God, sorry." Robin grabbed Adam's hand. "Bad joke. Didn't mean it. Maybe I should just go before I put my foot in it again."

"Have a rest, first." Adam took Robin's arm and guided him into the lounge. "Shoes off, now. Get on the settee. Shut your eyes."

"Oh, teacher. You are awful." Robin put on a silly voice, easing himself through an awkward moment. "You still get six weeks holiday in the summer?"

"Yeah, although much of it's taken up with planning and the like." Adam fussed over pulling the curtains. "Why?"

"Oh, just thinking I could do with a break. Assuming this is sorted. Assuming I can get some days off at the same time as you. Assuming you'd want to spend a weekend away or something. Maybe we could just start with a date." Robin, nestled into a corner of the settee, wasn't sure he was making much sense. He felt his eyes closing.

Adam's voice was soothing, again. "Yes, that sounds like a great idea. Just shut up and get some rest."

Robin had never taken a nap that felt so good.

By the time he'd woken—refreshed, mind finally clearing—he could hear the sounds of activity, comforting domestic activity, in the kitchen along with Campbell whining.

"Poor lad. He sounds like he's bursting," Robin said, coming into the kitchen.

"He is. The door squeaks, and I didn't want to wake you. I'd better let him relieve himself at last." Adam opened the door. He was right; it was like treading on a giant mouse. Robin eyed the pile of washing-up in the sink—breakfast, dinner, and something looking like it was soaking from the day before. Maybe some of that stuff was *his*. He rolled up his sleeves and started to run the hot tap, creating a frothy tide of sweet-smelling bubbles.

"You don't need to do that. It'll keep." Adam, back from supervising Campbell's activities, sneaked his arms around Robin's waist. "Feeling better now?"

"I do, it won't, much, and hands off. I'm sorting these, then going home." He leaned back briefly into Adam's embrace, then shook it off. "Sorry, but not yet, remember?"

"Yeah, I know." Adam admitted defeat and turned his attention to finding a clean tea towel. "I'll dry, though."

"Done." Domestic duties—dull, mundane, just the thing to soothe the mind when done alongside somebody you'd fallen for.

"And make sure you get a decent night's sleep. I'm not parading you round Lindenshaw while you look like crap. Spoil my reputation as a puller."

"You have one to preserve?" Robin carried on doing his dishes. "I'll try, but it's not like turning off a light switch. And when I do get off, the dreams don't help. Sorry." He remembered Adam's nightmare. "Foot in mouth again."

"I've had *that* dream every time I've gone to sleep since Youngs died, sometimes two or three times a night. Apart from when—you know—you were with me." Adam kept drying the same plate, although there couldn't have been even a drop of water on it anymore. "Only now I find two dead bodies in here."

"I'm such an idiot. I didn't think." Robin wished the plughole would open and swallow him along with the dirty water.

Adam smiled, wanly. "Tell me what you've been dreaming of, then."

"So long as you promise not to laugh." Robin concentrated on a particularly ghastly plate. "Me as a schoolboy again, usually. Sometimes we're having a picnic on the field, when regiments of murderers turn up wielding stockings with gobstoppers knotted in them."

"You're winding me up." Adam flicked at him with the tea towel.

"Not a word of a lie. That was last night's treat. Tonight I'm expecting dirty films and illegitimate children. Maybe with a side order of coincidental dates of birth on application forms. Don't ask."

"I have no idea what you're talking about, but you can scrub the last bit. They don't have them anymore."

"Don't have what?" Robin asked, vaguely, as he wiped the last fork and emptied out the suds.

"Don't have ages on application forms. Not in the local schools, anyway. Equalities and all that, so you don't discard somebody just because you think they're a bit long in the tooth. Still, you normally just look at when they did their A levels and work back to get their year of birth."

"Bloody hell." Robin looked down at his still-soapy hands, then lifted one to his nose. "What a fucking idiot." He grabbed the tea towel and dried his hands.

"Is anything wrong?" Adam looked puzzled and more than a bit worried. "Sometimes you can get a reaction to the detergent. Maybe you should have worn gloves."

"Gloves?" Robin looked at the yellow Marigold washing-up gloves draped on the windowsill. "Of course. Right. Got to dash."

"Something I said?"

"Oh yes, sunshine." He landed Adam a smacking kiss, then grabbed his car keys off the breakfast bar. "You're a genius. I think you might just have got all the jigsaw bits lined up and ready to be put into place." And with that, Robin got out his phone and rang Anderson.

He went back to the police station, but this time with no feeling of dread or reluctance, to find Anderson was already there, his boss's phone call having found him knocking back a pint with one of the uniform lads at the pub just down the road. The inspector insisted he leave the beer and get back to the office.

He'd promised a full explanation when they met, and when he'd had time to get his own thoughts in order, which he'd done by the time he'd parked and dashed up the stairs.

"What a bloody fool," Robin said, flinging open his office door and slinging his briefcase on the desk.

"Sorry, sir?"

"I've been a bloody fool. Taken in by the soft stuff, tears on the shoulder and the rest of the crap." Made maudlin by falling for Adam, maybe, seeing the world in an overly affectionate light. Still, he had Adam to thank for this break.

"Nope. Still not getting it."

"Okay. Marjorie Bookham said she'd seen Ian Youngs's date of birth on his application form. She couldn't have. It wouldn't have been on there. They don't list them anymore."

"Don't they? We could look. Davis got copies of the paperwork from Mrs. Shepherd. She wouldn't have twigged about the date being important. Hold on." Anderson rummaged out a file. "Yep. You're right."

"Of course I am." Robin grinned, smugly.

Anderson swung his chair back against the radiator. "So Marjorie Bookham lied. Which means she possibly made up the story about the illegitimate child?"

"That's how I see it. Like she's lied about other things, and pretty convincingly each time. Something else about Youngs must have spooked her. And I have an idea what it was." Robin settled himself in his chair, leaning back as he might lean into Adam's comforting embrace. "All that hand-wringing in Narraway's garden. Good actress."

"Ye-es." Anderson still seemed puzzled.

"Think about it. I know it seems mad, but she's an attractive woman, you know. In a sort of Margaret Thatcher way."

"But I . . . Oh!" The sergeant brought his chair crashing back onto all four legs. "You're not serious?"

"I am. And if Narraway knew about it, he might not have been able to resist a dig." Robin drummed his fingers on the desk at unconsidered trifles not snapped up. "He made some snarky remarks about her, didn't he?"

"And he rang her the day before he died." Anderson reached for paper and pen. "Okay, slow down. We can't run before we walk. Let's list what you think happened and see how we can back any of it up."

"Right. She killed both of them. And you don't need to worry about how she could have got close enough to do it. Who was going to worry about meek and mild Mrs. Bookham?"

"Horse falls at the first fence, sir." Anderson narrowed his eyes. "If Narraway knew she'd killed Youngs, wouldn't he have been on his guard?"

"I bet he didn't know that, though. I'm sure he thought it was Duncan. Otherwise—" Robin's chain of logic was interrupted by a rap on the door. "Come in!"

Grace, the CSI, put her head around the door. "I thought I saw your car in the car park. Glad I caught you."

"I hope *I'm* glad you caught me." *Please don't let it be a spanner in the works. Not now.*

"Do you remember that strange smell on Youngs's neck?"

Anderson groaned. "I'm not likely to forget. I nearly got my face slapped by Mrs. Probert when I was trying to see if she wore the same fragrance."

"You kept that quiet," Robin said, automatically. Not a spanner, then. He'd already got an inkling of what was to come. "The results have come back?"

"Yes. The official report is en route, but my mate at the lab told me. It was something like Lenor."

"Lenor?" Anderson looked puzzled again.

"Oh, bloody hell, Sergeant. It's a brand of fabric conditioner. For the washing machine."

"I knew that," Anderson clearly lied. "I was just wondering how it got on him. Doesn't it get rinsed off your clothes?"

"Yep." Grace nodded. "They checked Youngs's stuff, and it was clear. They think it either came from whatever was used to strangle him or the murderer's gloves. And that's not all, sir." Now she looked triumphant, about to pull an elephant out of her hat, not just a rabbit. "The fibres under his nails were nylon. The sorts of stuff stockings are made from."

Robin resisted punching the air. "Or tights?"

"Exactly. Is that significant?"

"Oh yes. It could be game, set, and match."

Chapter Twenty-three

"We should have rung." Anderson looked out of the passenger window, although there was little to see now that they were off the main road. Lindenshaw Parish Council vehemently opposed street lighting, for which Robin was grateful, considering how much time he'd spent here the last few evenings.

"And give her the chance to realise she's been rumbled?"

"At least it would avoid a wild-goose chase. What if she's out?" Anderson rubbed some condensation from the window.

"At this time on a Monday evening? It'll be a miracle if they're still awake." But better to do it now than to give her any more time in which to get her story straight. "And if it turns out that bloody doctor was right with all his crap about gobstoppers knotted up in tights, I'll seriously consider handing in my warrant card. I should have considered that right at the start."

"It was too far-fetched an idea for anyone to consider, sir." Anderson shook his head. "Things are still bugging me. Loose ends, like how Youngs got back into the school."

"Maybe we'll never know that. My money's on that outside door not being properly shut. Or on the entry system malfunctioning, Adam says he's had to mend the buzzer no end of times—maybe the rest of it's on the blink too."

"Adam?" Anderson asked, amused.

"Shut your racket," Robin replied, furious with himself at having maybe said the name with less objectivity than he should have done. "Anyway, I'm not convinced St. Crispin's is as impenetrable as it likes to think it is. How hard would it be to watch someone entering the code and just remember it?"

"Someone who happens to be giving you a tour of the school? Or one of the teachers like your Adam?" Anderson smirked over the word *your*.

"Any more and you'll be back on the beat," Robin joked. The truth was going to come out sometime, if he and Adam became an item, but *they* should be in charge of letting it escape, not Anderson. And especially not at this stage of things.

"Noted, sir," Anderson replied, clearly meaning it. He'd watch his boss's back. "Safe to discuss Claire Waites?"

"Depends what you want to say about her. And better make it snappy." They'd reached the Bookhams' road.

"She must have known the connection with Marjorie, which is presumably why she let rip with the 'whore' remark. So why not tell us?"

"God knows. Unless . . ." Robin brought the car to a halt about thirty yards from the Bookhams' front door. "Remember the remark about 'some people'?"

"No. Enlighten me."

"She said she'd done nothing she was ashamed of, 'unlike some people.' She said she meant Youngs. I thought she was lying at the time; I'm convinced of it now. What if it was Marjorie she was digging at? The dirty films?"

"Stupid cow. Look what happened to Narraway because he tried to play his cards too close to his chest."

"Marjorie could have Claire's name and address, wouldn't she, off the application form?" A hard knot started to form in Robin's stomach. "I hope to God she doesn't use them." They didn't want a third corpse on their hands.

The Bookhams' cottage seemed to be occupied, given the lights shining inside, but no response was coming to Anderson ringing the doorbell. "She's taking her time answering. I reckon you were right when you said they'd gone to bed, sir."

"Not unless they've left the telly on. I bet they're dozing on the sofa. *Gardeners' Question Time* or something equally enthralling."

"Do they still show that, sir?" Anderson rang the bell a third time.

"All right, all right!" A grumpy, male voice sounded from the hallway. "If you're selling something, you can hop it right now."

"Sorry to disturb you, Mr. Bookham," Robin said, smiling and showing his warrant card. "I know it's late, but this is urgent. Can we talk to your wife, please?"

"Marjorie? Why?" Light suddenly seemed to dawn. "Oh. About those murders, I suppose."

"That's it." Robin smiled again.

"Well, she isn't here. I suppose she's out on governors' business or something, although ten thirty seems late for one of those bloody meetings, even if they do seem to be interminable. Damned inconvenient too. I've had to get my own coffee." Mr. Bookham shut the door.

"Bloody hell!" Anderson went to ring the doorbell again, but Robin stopped him.

"Leave it. For all we know, she's done a runner."

"Wouldn't he have noticed her taking a bag or something?" Anderson waved his hand. "No, stupid question. Of course he wouldn't. Have you got her mobile number?"

"Not on me. You'd better ring the station and get it." Robin jangled his car keys in his hand. "Come on. There's nothing we can do here."

"But, sir"—Anderson seemed rooted to the doorstep—"couldn't the husband give us her number?"

"He could, but he's the sort of stroppy bugger who'd probably say he couldn't find it." Robin stopped by the gate, weighing his options as well as his keys.

"If we ring her, we risk spooking her, and if we don't, it's a long, cold wait in the car to see if she turns up here." Anderson shivered, as though to emphasise his words.

"What if he rings his wife first?"

"I'd put money on his not bothering." Anderson shivered again. "Adam would have her number."

Robin bit his tongue on the Adam part. "He might. So would Jennifer Shepherd or Victor Reed."

"Your choice then, sir."

"Reed." Less potential for embarrassment.

"Where do you think she's gone?" Anderson asked as Robin started the car. "My money's on paying a visit to Claire Waites."

"Is it? You could be right." Although *she* wasn't likely to be as free and easy with Mrs. Bookham as the men had been. "Ring her anyway, even if it's just to warn her not to let Marjorie Bookham in."

Anderson rang Claire Waites, but he got a gobful for his troubles, having woken her up. *She* wasn't frightened by any half-baked old cow. Was her partner with her? No, he was away on business, but that didn't matter. *She* could look after herself.

"You can make the next call," Anderson said, grimacing.

"Thank you," Robin said, returning the scowl. "And you can persuade my boss to get the search teams out tomorrow, scouring the ground between Marjorie's house and the school."

"Looking under bushes for washing-up gloves? She's too clever for that, sir. I'd be looking in the dustbins. Easy enough to drop them in someone's rubbish. I wonder what day they get emptied around here?"

"Sometime next week. I know that because I put Mum's out last Monday. Fortnightly rota." Robin turned left, drawing up outside Narraway's house, with the police tape still forlornly festooning its hedge. "And if she's too clever for the bushes, she's too clever for the dustbin. If she used a pair of tights, they'd have been washed and put away by now. Do you fancy rummaging through her underwear drawer?"

"Shame it isn't Mrs. Probert's. No, sorry." Anderson held up his hands. "Uncalled for. I'd be inclined to go through Reed's bin, though. I bet that's why she made him go look for the mysterious stranger. Gave her time to get rid of the evidence."

"Mysterious and nonexistent?" Robin groaned. "Too dark to do it now. We'll get a team on it tomorrow."

"I'm getting Reed's answerphone," Anderson said, making a face at his mobile.

"He's probably gone to bed. Come on, let's get round there." Time to burn some rubber on the quiet Lindenshaw roads. That would give the neighbours something to look at.

They got Marjorie's number, a clearly shaken, rather tired and slightly confused Victor Reed producing one of his files and soon flicking through to the right page. Maybe a similar document to the one Youngs had copied down a number from, if Mrs. Bookham's number had been what was on his piece of paper.

"What's this for, Inspector?" Reed asked, blearily.

"We're concerned about Marjorie Bookham." No need to elaborate further at present. "She's not at home and we need to find her."

"She's not here. And I don't think there's anything official going on, governor-wise." Reed checked his file again. "No. No training at county, even. Maybe she and Christine—Mrs. Probert—are somewhere having a glass of wine? Girls' night out and all that."

"We'll ring her now and ask." Go round too, if they didn't get an answer. "Can we have her contact details?"

"You can have the whole list." Reed thrust it into their hands and ushered them out the door.

Mrs. Probert, too, was less than pleased to be rung at this time of night—mainly because it might unsettle the children—although she seemed sympathetic to Robin's plight once he'd had the chance to say his piece. If he'd given the impression that they were concerned for Marjorie Bookham's safety, it was only a minor lie. But Mrs. Probert hadn't seen her, nor had any idea where she might be.

And wherever Mrs. Bookham was, she wasn't answering her phone.

"Where next? Mrs. Shepherd?" Anderson ran his name down the list of names. "If Mrs. Bookham heard her talking about Youngs and that file . . ."

"Ring her," Robin said, getting back into the car. The wild-goose chase continued; it was no surprise when the secretary confessed to having no idea where her friend was and laughed at the police's concern for her safety. Would nobody involved with this case take the risks seriously?

"Anybody else we should try?" Anderson asked.

"You could work through that list and ask them all if they've seen Mrs. Bookham. Warn them all, while you're at it." Or just go through the Lindenshaw phone book? It might be just as productive.

"Do you want to ring Adam or should I?" Anderson stared at his mobile, as if it might have the answer.

"You can do the honours. I'll ring the vicar." No risk then of the sergeant hearing any panic in his boss's voice. A cold, hard knot of fear hit the pit of Robin's stomach. Surely Adam wasn't really in danger? He had Campbell to protect him, although what use the big lump would prove . . .

"No answer, sir. All I'm getting is that the call can't be taken." Anderson shrugged.

Robin had the engine switched on before his sergeant had finished speaking.

"Steady on." Anderson, fumbling with his seat belt, bounced against the car door as they did a screeching U-turn.

"He always answers his phone." Robin took a deep, steadying breath. "And he was in the office, as well, when Jennifer was talking about her file. Hell, he was in the office when Youngs wrote that note to himself."

"Hardly enough to make him a target." The sergeant's voice of reason cut no ice with his boss.

"You wouldn't have thought Narraway was a target, either."

"But it seems like Narraway knew about what she'd been up to. Surely Adam doesn't?"

No, or else he'd have said, wouldn't he? Robin eased off the accelerator. He was being ridiculous, seeing a threat where there was none. He'd look even more of a failure if he crashed the car en route and Adam was in no more danger than having to fight Campbell for a share of the duvet.

Robin tried not to be alarmed as they parked outside Adam's house and saw lights still burning. It may have been late for Derek, but not necessarily for the younger members of the Lindenshaw community. Maybe Adam was catching up on the inevitable marking. Robin took a deep breath, turning to see Anderson giving him a funny look and realising he'd left the bloke's question unanswered, wrapped in his own silent thoughts the rest of the journey here.

"Right," he said, opening the car door. "Let's see if we've found her."

"Hello!" Adam said with a big grin, opening the door to Robin's insistent doorbell ringing. "Didn't expect to see you again so soon." The sight of Anderson put the dampers on the grin.

"It's business," Robin said, trying not to sound too curt. Nor too relieved that Adam wasn't already lying on the floor, blue in the face. "Is Marjorie Bookham here?"

"Yes. Are you telepathic?" Adam, looking a bit bewildered, ushered them in. "She said she hadn't told Derek she was coming here."

"She hadn't. Call it a lucky guess."

"But why...?" Adam said, as he opened the kitchen door. Robin's quiet "Shh!" silenced him.

"Mrs. Bookham. Glad we caught you." The deliberately chosen words made her start.

"Oh, Inspector! You startled me."

Campbell abandoned Mrs. Bookham's side and made a beeline for Robin, nuzzling his hand.

"Not tonight. There's a good boy." He gently disentangled himself from the dog's attention, giving his sergeant a dirty look that effectively wiped the smirk off his face. Just as well he hadn't relied on Campbell for bodyguard duty; the dog was dotted with biscuit crumbs, and he'd looked comfortably settled at her feet. "We've been ringing round trying to find you, Mrs. Bookham. You had us worried."

"You daft things. And call me Marjorie." She gave the impression that she might have been strengthened with Dutch courage. Maybe the coffee Adam had been serving was Irish. "I was just talking to Adam about headteachers. And what we're going to do now that we won't have poor Oliver to help us select a new one."

"Marjorie was trying to persuade me to get more involved, but you can't choose your own boss, can you?" Adam, who seemed even more bewildered now, appealed directly to Anderson.

"Don't answer that," Robin said, before his sergeant could make one of his trademark sarcastic remarks.

"Can I get you coffee or tea or something?" Adam asked, evidently immediately regretting it. "No. Stupid question. I'll make myself scarce while you... do whatever you have to. Come on, Campbell."

"Thanks. We won't be long," Robin said, trying to convey in five words and a long glance that he was sorry for invading his house yet again and on such unpleasant business.

"Mrs. Bookham," he said, once the three of them were alone, "why did you lie to me about Ian Youngs?"

She laid down her coffee cup with only a slight tremble. "Lie to you?"

"You said you'd seen his date of birth on his application form. They're not asked to give them, anymore."

She shot a glance at the kitchen door, which Adam had just gone through. "Oh, yes. Silly me. I must have read it somewhere else. Or did Jeremy Tunstall tell us? He was always saying things he shouldn't. Leaky vessel."

More deflecting attention, done with aplomb.

"No, Mrs. Bookham, we think that's a lie. Like all the others." Robin took the seat Adam had just vacated, at the other side of the breakfast bar from their witness. "You knew him already, didn't you?"

"No, of course I didn't. I'd have said. It was Neil—the vicar—who reckoned he'd met him somewhere. I think you're getting mixed up."

Yes, very good actress. Missed her calling, stuck here in Lindenshaw with Derek. Or could they have got all this horribly wrong? Was she just as innocent as she portrayed herself to be and the real murderer still roaming free? Luckily, Anderson stepped in, just as the doubts surfaced.

"And I think you're being less than candid," the sergeant said, still leaning against the cupboard as he'd been since they'd entered the room, making notes and keeping his own counsel. "Of course, you're bound to be. Not the sort of connection you'd want anyone to know about."

"Better to continue this at the station." Robin got to his feet. "Sergeant, could you caution Mrs. Bookham?"

"Certainly, sir." Anderson straightened himself and began, with relish, "I am arresting you for—"

"We don't need any of that. I'm not going anywhere." Mrs. Bookham sat, defiantly clasping her handbag. "And there's nothing I have to say that can't be said here."

"Really? You want to risk Adam being able to hear everything we say?"

"He's far too well bred to listen in," she replied, sniffing loudly. "And if he did, he wouldn't hear anything to surprise him."

"Are you sure you want him to hear about why you got such a shock when Ian Youngs turned up at the school?"

"Oh." She fiddled with her handbag clasp, maybe about to rummage out her handkerchief. "He wouldn't tell Derek about the child. Adam's gay, you know. He's used to keeping secrets."

Robin let the remark ride. "I don't think there *was* a child. And if there was, I don't think your bearing it had anything to do with last Thursday. You'd met Youngs before. When you made those films."

"Films? What films?" Her cheeks, suddenly white as a ghost's, gave the lie to her words.

They had to press on; now she was beginning to be rattled.

"Read the caution, please, Anderson." This time there was no interruption. "We should continue this at the station."

"No. We can discuss this here. I won't go."

Resisting arrest? They could cuff her and manhandle her into the car, but something gave Robin pause about doing that. Mrs. Bookham appeared to be calm, but there was a cold glint in her eyes and a hard edge, well hidden, to her voice. It added to an unexpected atmosphere of danger that hung in the kitchen, a place where he'd always felt so calm and at ease.

"It must have been the shock of your life, seeing him turn up at the school," Robin continued. "Your murky past coming back to haunt you."

"You have no idea what it was like that morning when I saw those ears. You know, it's funny, but I recognised them first, even though he'd had longer hair back . . . back then." Mrs. Bookham continued to fiddle with her handbag while Anderson scribbled down notes as fast as he could, although this sudden burst of candour seemed too easily come by. "I think they made him cover them over. Not the sort of feature you want in a leading man."

This was becoming surreal. Robin cracked on with the questions before Anderson could ask what physical features had made Youngs such a natural leading man for smutty films.

"Wasn't he equally embarrassed to see you?"

"Oh no. He's always been quite shameless. That's what was so exciting, at one time." Mrs. Bookham sighed, wistfully. "When the filming business finished, everyone involved said they'd keep it under wraps. Our secret. It was so long ago, and nothing had happened, even after Claire Waites had her outburst. I thought I was safe now."

"Not in the days of Google search. Nobody's safe anymore." Robin wished, in retrospect, he'd taken up the offer of a cup of tea. He had a feeling they were in for the long haul.

"Thank God my Derek can't use anything more complicated than the remote control." She took a deep breath. "Still, I don't regret it."

"Regret what? Killing Youngs?" Robin's voice was icily calm, voicing what they'd all been skirting around.

"No. I didn't *kill* him, Inspector. I was talking about making those films. I was bored."

"Getting into porn seems a bit excessive. Couldn't you have taken up a hobby or something?" Anderson asked.

Robin imagined, with a shudder, his mother giving up bridge in favour of donning a basque and suspenders. Better to shift that mental image and concentrate on why this woman was suddenly being so candid. And why she exuded, in those steely eyes and voice, an air of danger.

"You mean joining the Women's Institute or taking up crown green bowling?" Mrs. Bookham snorted. "I was in my prime, Sergeant. Forty was on my horizon, but Derek had already gone from thirty-nine to past it overnight. He's never been much inclined towards bed, except when he's three sheets to the wind. And that's not an appetising thought."

"But how did you get into it? They don't advertise in *Country Life*."

Robin bridled at the remark. Something wasn't right here, and Anderson's sarcastic tongue wasn't helping things.

"I met Ian at a volunteer-recruitment event, of all things. He could be utterly charming when he put his mind to it. We started meeting up, and he told me all about the little sideline he had. You can guess the rest. Do I have to spell it out?"

"We can imagine," Robin said, before Anderson could chip in.

"I thought the films were fun at first. A real thrill compared to festering in Lindenshaw. When Ian got bored with me, I missed them more than I missed him." She looked dreamy, as though miles and years away, wrapped in lost hopes. "When I was a girl, I wanted to be in films, but my parents wouldn't let me try for drama school. And of course, Derek wouldn't want his wife to have anything to do with the stage, so even the Lindenshaw Amateur Dramatic Society wouldn't have been suitable."

Not even if they'd been putting on *Macbeth*? She'd have been a shoo-in for the leading lady on this showing. All that talent and enthusiasm gone to waste. Robin could sympathise, having nearly had all the spirit crushed out of him at school. There but for the grace of God?

No, he'd never have turned to murder. Not even murdering Ryan Atherley.

"Can I go now? I've washed all my dirty linen for you."

"Talking of that," Anderson said, "do you always use gloves when you do the washing, Mrs. Bookham?"

Mrs. Bookham appeared momentarily flustered at the altered line of attack. "Of course. Detergent brings my hands out in a terrible rash. Is there a law against it?"

"No, but there's a law against murder. They found traces of washing conditioner on Ian Youngs's body. No fingerprints, though. I guess gloves are doubly handy."

"What *are* you talking about?" She clutched her handbag even closer, fiddling with the clasp again.

"For covering your traces," the sergeant pressed on, relentless. "Interesting thing is they didn't just find softener on his neck. There were traces of nylon. Like he'd been strangled with a pair of tights. Newly washed, maybe?"

Robin held his breath, waiting for Mrs. Bookham's faultless performance to falter.

"Sergeant, you're a very sweet boy, but what on earth are you talking about?" She flashed a stunning, flirtatious smile at the young policeman.

Oh, she was good. Either they'd gone on the biggest chase in the history of wild geese or this woman had Meryl Streep–level talent. It was time to find out which.

"You missed your calling, didn't you?" Robin said, with what he hoped was just as stunning a smile. "If I had a hat, I'd doff it to you now. But the act has to end, Mrs. Bookham. You have to tell us why you killed Ian Youngs."

"Do I? Do I really?" She reached into her handbag. Remembering the scene in Narraway's garden and all the handkerchief palaver, Robin pulled a tissue from the box by the sink.

Unfortunately, she didn't want her handkerchief. From her sensible and staid brown leather handbag, she produced a small pistol that she pointed first at Anderson and then at Robin, whose initial bizarre thought was relief that Adam had left the room.

"Where the hell did that come from?" Anderson blurted out.

"It's Derek's. His father acquired it during the war. He's kept it in very good condition. Just in case we had burglars or anything," she said brightly, as though explaining to five-year-olds how to stick glitter on a Christmas card. No wonder she'd been so happy to be candid, with her own armed backup.

"Wouldn't it have been easier to use that to kill Youngs?" Anderson no longer slumped against the cupboard; he stood to attention now, as ramrod straight as Robin was on his stool.

"Easier, yes, but far stupider. Tights you can put back in the drawer or stick in a dustbin, and nobody would notice. This"—she waggled the weapon—"is far too obvious. Murderers need to keep it simple, you know. I've read books about it."

"So have we." Robin kept his voice low and pleasant. "You're far too levelheaded to do this, Mrs. Bookham. Marjorie. Put it down."

The strategy didn't work; the gun got waved around. "Maybe I'm tired of being rational and respectable Marjorie Bookham. I've had to put up with it too long. It's much more fun playing this role."

"Murderess?" Robin asked.

"I didn't enjoy *that*. But the feeling of power, of doing *something* is so liberating. That's why I liked it when I heard we were getting a new headteacher. Being able to say yea or nay, making a big, important decision rather than just choosing what we have for tea." Her eyes shone. "And then *he* comes along, bringing the past dragging along behind him."

"Youngs tried to blackmail you? Threatened to tell Derek?" Robin kept half his mind on the interview and half on weighing their options. Would Mrs. Bookham pull the trigger? If she thought she was acting out the part of a modern-day Lady Macbeth, then they might all be in trouble.

"Of course he did. I'd been expecting it from the moment I set eyes on him that Thursday. He got hold of my number—from that bloody file of Jennifer's in her office—and rang my mobile over lunch. When I was in the ladies' loo, for God's sake. Almost the only place in the school the bloody thing works."

Maybe if it hadn't been for that, Youngs would have still been alive. On such small things the course of a life—or death—could hinge.

"Did he want money?" Anderson asked.

"Oh, Sergeant. You're so funny." Despite her carefully pointed gun, its position adjusted every time either of the policemen moved. Her voice had a flirtatious edge as she continued. "Of course not. Although, it might have been better if he had. He wanted me to rig the process. Give him some inside information so he'd cruise through the interview. Influence the others so that he got the job. If I didn't, he'd have told Derek everything. Every little detail."

"What a charmer," Robin said, trying to sound sympathetic.

"You have no idea what he was like. He enjoyed seeing me squirm and knowing I couldn't blow the whistle on him. I had to take decisive action."

"How did you have time to get home and back and . . .?" Robin made a small, vicious wringing gesture.

"I didn't go home at all. I'd done some hand-washing that morning, and Derek wouldn't have noticed if I'd put it out back then, long before he went to the pub. He never notices anything like that—only if his food's on the table or the football's on the TV. He probably hasn't noticed I'm gone now."

"Oh, he has. He seemed quite put out."

"Oh." She looked perturbed, then shook her head. "That's only because I wasn't there to make his supper, I suppose."

Even though they'd been rumbled, Robin kept his own counsel—better not to fuel her irritation at the male of the species.

"If you hadn't been home, then where did the washing-up gloves come from?"

"I brought them with me, in a plastic bag. The staffroom dishwasher is on the blink—again—and it wouldn't have been fair to leave Jennifer to do all the washing-up. Victor and his cronies would have been no use, and you can't expect the teachers to clear up after us."

"Were they the same gloves you'd used to do the washing?"

"They were. My spares. I'd put a hole in the others and not had the chance to get new ones. I stuffed them in a plastic bag as they were still wet." The little domestic details, so freely offered, contrasted with the steely look in her eye and the ominous pointing of the gun.

"Did you have the tights in your bag, as well?"

"Not with the intention of using them to kill somebody!" Mrs. Bookham looked aggrieved at the suggestion. "I always carry a spare pair. Just as well, seeing as I put a hole in mine about ten o'clock that morning, snagging them on a bucket when I was soaking an old jumper in conditioner. It makes woollens regain their shape, you know."

"I'm sure it does," Robin said, feeling this was all getting a bit surreal "And then?"

"And then I changed my tights, put the old ones in the bag with the gloves, and forgot all about them until I was in the loo and saw them in there. I took it as an omen. There'd been this film, you see, where we were playing about with . . ." She put one hand to her throat while the other gripped the gun. "It seemed like poetic justice. I'd had the sense to arrange to meet him, to talk things through. All I had to do was keep my nerve."

"You met him in the kitchen?"

"Yes. He'd memorised the code for the door at some point, so he sneaked into the school and was waiting there for me."

"And you got in through the kitchen door?"

"Of course. You know St. Crispin's, Inspector, from experience. It's easy not to be seen if you don't want to be."

Of course. Robin could remember every one of the bolt-holes he'd used, all the sneaking around.

"I came round the far side of the building. He was expecting me, so I played sweet and cooperative. I said I'd do my best for him, for old times' sake. I came on to him, I suppose. I'm quite a good actress, really."

Yes, they'd all had plenty of evidence of that. Robin let her carry on—she was clearly enjoying having centre stage, and it would give him time to work out what to do about that gun. Maybe Adam would be listening in, or was he too much of a gentleman to do that? If he had heard what was going on, surely he'd ring for backup?

Mrs. Bookham continued. "I had those tights, but I didn't think they'd be enough, so I picked up one of the decorative stones from the plant pots in the corridor and tied it up in them. It's odd, you know."

"What is?" asked Anderson, at whom the remark seemed to be aimed at.

"It was like watching a television murder mystery. I was conscious of doing it, stepping into the role as a murderess like it wasn't me, just a character I was playing."

Robin wasn't convinced about the psychological side being played up; she'd proved how credible she could be.

"He didn't fight back?" He kept his voice even. The gun was wavering now as Mrs. Bookham clearly relived that fateful lunchtime.

"Not until it was too late. He was always terribly trusting, especially when it came to sex. At first, he thought I might be replaying something from one of our films, so I egged him on, saying I'd meet him after school and carry on the scene. I'd just give him a little reminder of benefits still to come. I was surprised how quickly it was over."

"As easy as that?"

"Of course. Men are fools, you know, where women are concerned. Except Adam, of course, but maybe he's as daft for a pretty face and a pert backside."

Robin thought he heard his sergeant snigger. He briefly considered grabbing the gun and winging the bloke himself.

"That took a lot of guts," Anderson said. "How could you be sure you wouldn't be interrupted?"

"I had Victor to thank for that. He'd put down a three-line whip that nobody was allowed to go near that kitchen, not even up to the window. Candidates not to be gawped at. Ironic, isn't it?" Mrs. Bookham smiled. And tightened her grip on the gun.

"Was Oliver Narraway just as easily fooled?" Robin asked, trying to keep the renewed nervousness out of his voice.

"Oh yes. Always a sucker for a woman with a sob story. He'd heard Claire Waites call me a whore, and I'd got so upset afterwards he took me for a stiff drink so I could get ready to face Derek. Everything came out, of course, about the films. He was remarkably understanding."

Or maybe he seemed to be, Robin guessed. Saving up nuggets of information until they could be converted into gold?

"So why kill him?" Had she simply developed a taste for killing? That gun looked horribly menacing, and she seemed terribly calm and composed.

"Because he got panicky." Mrs. Bookham rolled her eyes. "After you'd been to visit him on Saturday, he was scared stiff. He thought that because you'd been to see Tunstall, all the stuff he'd kept hidden about fiddling the books would come out. Don't look so surprised, Inspector. I knew all about that. When his wife died, he confided in me. We got used to keeping each other's secrets."

"Very cosy," Anderson said, earning himself a dirty look from his boss. They mustn't put her back up.

"You'll have to find someone new to confide in," Robin said, smiling. "You'll miss him, I bet."

"I know I will, but I had little choice, don't you see?"

If Robin thought that easing Mrs. Bookham into the role of injured party rather than murderess would make her lay down the gun, he was wrong. Her grip on it tightened.

"He rang me, to come over and talk things through. The silly sod wanted to tell me he'd meant to tell *you* he'd seen me on Thursday, going away from the school and doubling back on myself. But he'd forgotten." She rolled her eyes. "He didn't even twig that I might have killed Ian, he just thought I might have seen the murderer and could have some valuable information to share. I couldn't have him telling you that, could I? Or anybody else."

"So he didn't actually suspect you?"

"Of course not. He was convinced it was Brian Duncan. I said he was probably right and that I might have seen somebody. I suggested we talk about it over a cup of tea and that I'd go and make it. I went behind him, putting my arms round his neck, like I'd done before, to give him a hug while he sat there like the king of the castle." She didn't say any more, and Robin didn't ask. It would all come out in court—and in the forensics, now that they had a clearer idea of what to look for. Especially in Victor's dustbin.

"Then you played the part of the distressed witness. I have to say, Mrs. Bookham, you had me completely fooled. Brilliant performance."

"I had a sympathetic audience, Inspector." The hint of flirtation bubbled up again.

"We're still sympathetic." Robin glanced at the gun. "What does the next act hold in store?"

"You tell me. I don't want to have to use this, but I will, if need be. Preferably you'll just let me walk out of the back door."

"And then what?" As an idea, it appealed, if it reduced the chance of none of them—not even Campbell—ending up as the third victim. She wouldn't get far, surely?

"Nothing. From you, that is. I've been building myself up a running-away fund, and now all I need to do is access it. I have plans. You just need to let me put them into operation."

"And if we don't?"

"Then I use this." Mrs. Bookham waggled the gun. "Here now, or somewhere else later. What do they say in those films? 'I won't go down without a fight' or something like that."

Robin had never before noticed the ticking of Adam's kitchen clock. Now it sounded loud and clear, slowly marking off the stalemate.

A sharp knock on the door made them all start.

"Sorry about this," Adam said, half-poking his head around the door, "but Campbell needs to *go* and he'll only do it—" He stopped, clearly noting the panic on Robin's face.

Mrs. Bookham smiled, sweetly. "Adam, you'd better come in."

"No, it's all right, I'll take him round the front." He tried to retreat but couldn't avoid seeing the gun and the way it was pointed at Robin.

"I insist you stay, dear. Maybe you can persuade our friends here to sort out our impasse?" Mrs. Bookham was no longer playing a part. The literal femme fatale was playing this for real.

From the corner of his eye, Robin saw Adam flinch and edge Campbell, who'd followed his master, behind him. The gallant gesture was noted with a spurt of loving pride.

"What's the choice between?" Adam said, voice surprisingly steady.

"Letting me go on my way or using this." Mrs. Bookham kept the gun aimed at Robin.

"You don't want to shoot any of us, Marjorie. Especially not the inspector. He's far too handsome."

"I know he is, Adam, which is the pity of it." She waved her gunless left hand expressively. "Talk some sense into him, won't you? Tell him to just let me walk out of the door."

"Maybe she has a point, Robin. It's not worth the heroics. Too much at stake."

The use of his Christian name had more effect than the logic. Adam was right: far better to let her go than risk any of their lives. Especially Adam's.

"Sir . . ." Anderson sounded like he was ready to argue.

Robin raised his hand. "No. He's right. Mrs. Bookham, I—"

Whatever concession he was about to make got cut off in its prime. Somebody else in the room, other than Anderson, didn't agree with the strategy, or maybe he was just so desperate to be let out that he felt decisive action was needed.

Campbell, who Robin had always thought of as a ponderous lump, proved to have a surprising turn of speed. He whipped out from behind Adam's legs, skirted the breakfast bar, and lunged at Mrs. Bookham arm, knocking her slightly off-balance. While she'd seemed absolutely serious about her intention of shooting the policemen, should the circumstances warrant it, she appeared less certain about shooting the dog. Her aim wavered, the grip on the gun lessened, and Robin simply reached over and grabbed it.

The relief in the room was palpable, as was the chaos. Anderson fought past Adam to grab Mrs. Bookham, while Adam pulled a snarling Campbell off her and bundled him out the back door as Robin struggled to get the ammunition safely out of the gun and put the thing in his pocket. The bullets he handed to Adam, who turned three shades whiter as they were tipped into his hand.

"What am I to do with these?" he asked, hands shaking so much he almost spilled them.

"Keep them safe, of course." Robin managed a smile, before turning his attention to Mrs. Bookham, but Anderson had her arms pinned and was deftly putting cuffs on her. Who knew what other surprises she might have up her sleeve, although she seemed to have opted for playing a different role.

"Poor Derek. He'll have to get his own breakfast in the morning. Whatever will he do?" she said, meekly turning her hands in the cuffs.

"I'd better ring Derek and let him know what's going on," Adam said, fumbling in his pocket, then rummaging with a shaking hand in a glass dish where his car keys, a kitchen timer, and some other stuff was stored. "Where's my phone got to? I could have sworn I left it here."

"We wondered why you weren't answering." Robin caught his sergeant's eye and shrugged. Anderson just tightened his grip on her arm again, but the fight had gone from their prisoner. He edged her towards the front door.

"You rang? I had no idea." Adam moved aside a storage jar and fished out the missing mobile. "What the hell's it doing here?" He fiddled with the buttons. "And turned off. I never turn it off."

"I wouldn't be surprised if your guest did that while you made her coffee."

The cold, hard knot that had hit Robin's stomach earlier returned with a vengeance. He'd been too absorbed with the matter in hand to realise that Marjorie had gone there—to Adam's house—with the gun already in her handbag and ready to use. It struck home now.

"Tea," Adam said, bitterly. "She had tea. And sympathy. Remember I said that was what I did?"

Robin patted his arm, not trusting himself to do—or say— anything else. "I have to go. I'll ring."

"You do that." Adam smiled. "Plenty of time."

Robin left the house and immediately lost what little he had in his stomach in the nearest flower bed.

Chapter Twenty-four

Days passed before Robin turned up on Adam's doorstep, bottle of wine in his hand and a weary smile on his face. He'd rung to say that Derek Bookham had come to the station the night of the gun alarm, blustering as usual, berating his wife for having taken it from his desk and a catalogue of other misdemeanours. It had been enough to lead Mrs. Bookham into a full, recorded confession—changing her chosen role once again, maybe? Robin had said he needed to call round in an official capacity. Victim support, he'd called it, although Adam was pretty sure inspectors didn't discharge that sort of duty. Still, he hadn't said no.

Now Friday had come, with no school or murders to worry about the next day, takeaway already ordered in and the whole night to kick off their shoes and relax. As if relaxing was going to be top of Adam's agenda. His priority had to be establishing whether some strenuous physical exertion would be allowed.

"Go and make yourself comfortable in the lounge while I open this," Adam said, taking the bottle from Robin. "Your biggest fan will be in to keep you company."

"*My* biggest fan?" Robin said, patting Adam's cheek. "The feeling's mutual. I should have brought *him* a present."

"Your undying devotion—or at least ten minutes of it—will be enough." Adam opened the kitchen door to let Campbell escape and make a beeline for his favourite rozzer. By the time he returned with two glasses of red, policeman and dog were ensconced on the sofa like the pair had been together all their lives.

"Shall I go? I don't want to play third wheel."

"Idiot." Robin took his drink. "I need this. Come on, boy, let me drink it in peace." He eased the dog onto the floor, where he settled contentedly at Robin's feet.

"You've earned it."

"Don't I know it." Robin fiddled with his already-loosened tie.

"Here. Let me or you'll spill your wine." Adam eased the tie off, folded it, and placed it on the table.

"Thank you." Robin leaned in for a kiss.

"That had better be all for the moment," Adam said, as he—eventually—broke free. "The takeaway will be here soon, and you don't want to shock the delivery boy. There'll be plenty of time for all that later."

"*All* that?" Robin said, grinning.

"So long as it's allowed. Do we have to wait for Marjorie to go to trial?"

"I'm not sure I could wait that long." Robin took another sip of wine, then stared into his glass. "She'll be charged with two counts of murder, with a side order of what happened in there." He jerked his thumb towards the kitchen. "I doubt you'd even be called as a witness, unless she changes her plea."

"I would never have guessed she could do it. Although, now I look back and keep thinking of times she was probably acting. Telling little lies and stirring things." Adam took a long draught of wine. "And then I think that's probably just hindsight and I'm making it all up."

"Perhaps it's just as well you won't end up in the witness box." Robin smiled mischievously, easing off his shoes and making himself comfortable.

"Why?"

"You'd be unreliable. Too sympathetic all round. A good defence brief would eat you for breakfast." Robin stroked Adam's cheek. "I'm glad it's all over. I never realised a headship was worth blackmailing for."

"Neither did I." Eye-opener on every score, the last few weeks. "I suspect it was the only way Youngs would have got one."

"And how have you come to that conclusion?"

"Oh, tongues have been a wagging. Bad news and gossip spread like wildfire. I wish they'd done earlier. Maybe it would have helped." Adam hoped they could shake this case off once and for all, but it seemed to want to cling.

Robin shrugged. "Yeah. And then again maybe it wouldn't. Why does real life always seem farther fetched than fiction?"

"Beats me." Adam sipped his wine appreciatively. Robin seemed to have good taste in lots of things. "Do you always manage to tie up all the loose ends in your cases?"

"Not usually. Life's too messy." He ran his finger round his glass. "Like now. It bugs me why she didn't twig earlier that her past was coming back to haunt her. She must have seen Youngs's name when you short-listed, surely?"

"She might not have known his real name. If he called himself Hugh Jampton or whatever back in those days."

"Hugh Jampton? Really?"

"I don't know. I don't watch the bloody things. Still, you got a result."

"Yes, but . . ." Robin sighed. "There are bits of the story that don't add up. Her happening to get a hole in her tights and having to change them. And why was there so much conditioner around?"

"Is that what's bugging you? You don't think you've got the wrong person?" Adam couldn't contemplate returning to square one.

"Not unless the confession's worthless and the forensics are all to pot. Don't worry." Robin rubbed Adam's leg. "It's just that I'm starting to wonder whether she didn't have this all planned in advance. The niggling voice in my head says she brought those tights in deliberately. Fresh from the washing bowl so she could get a better tension or something."

"How does she explain it?"

"Says she popped an old jumper in to soak in conditioner to regain its softness, just before she came out. That could be true, but what with the name business . . ." He shrugged again.

"Maybe we'll never know. Not unless she sees the light and writes a book. *Confessions of Lady Macbeth, Reformed*." Campbell, who'd finally achieved his aim of getting on the settee between them, had planted his unpleasantly wet nose on Adam's hand and made him jump. "Hey! Go away. You're not wanted." Adam manoeuvred a reluctant dog back off the settee.

"He knows he's a hero. There'll be no living with him now." Robin slipped his arm around Adam's waist. "I'm glad life's back to normal. That nothing else is likely to come between us apart from *him*."

"So am I." Adam leaned into the embrace, turning to share a kiss. Then there was nothing said for a while, just a bit of hands-on police investigation. "Safe to be seen with me in public, now? I could put an article in the Lindenshaw parish magazine, outing us."

"I wouldn't bother. Anderson's already guessed, and my mother gets back from holiday soon. Between them, they'll have it all over the county in a matter of days, although I'm going to ask them to restrain themselves until the trial's done." Robin stopped, suddenly serious. "Will it affect *your* chances? Of getting a promotion, to deputy head somewhere, I mean?"

"It shouldn't. I know gay deputies. Gay headteachers. Their governors don't bat an eyelid." *Time for another kiss.* "Mind you, if I'm setting my sights on promotion, I suppose I'd better start learning all the jargon and the tricks of the trade. Maybe I can practice on you?"

"Meaning?"

"Well, they always say you should demonstrate the impact you've had. How you've pursued excellence." Adam nudged his head in the direction of the ceiling—and the bathroom. He hadn't forgotten the promise of a shower. "I've got some ideas we could put into place."

Robin laughed. "So long as you're not expecting me to write a reference."

Dear Reader,

Thank you for reading Charlie Cochrane's *The Best Corpse for the Job*!

We know your time is precious and you have many, many entertainment options, so it means a lot that you've chosen to spend your time reading. We really hope you enjoyed it.

We'd be honored if you'd consider posting a review—good or bad—on sites like **Amazon, Barnes & Noble, Kobo, Goodreads, Twitter, Facebook, Tumblr,** and your blog or website. We'd also be honored if you told your friends and family about this book. Word of mouth is a book's lifeblood!

For more information on upcoming releases, author interviews, blog tours, contests, giveaways, and more, please sign up for our weekly, spam-free newsletter and visit us around the web:

Newsletter: tinyurl.com/RiptideSignup
Twitter: twitter.com/RiptideBooks
Facebook: facebook.com/RiptidePublishing
Goodreads: tinyurl.com/RiptideOnGoodreads
Tumblr: riptidepublishing.tumblr.com

Thank you so much for Reading the Rainbow!

RiptidePublishing.com

Acknowledgements

Thanks to everyone who made this possible, particularly my infinitely patient family and the spiffing team at Riptide.

Also by
Charlie Cochrane

Cambridge Fellows Mysteries
Lessons in Love
Lessons in Desire
Lessons in Discovery
Lessons in Power
Lessons in Temptation
Lessons in Seduction
Lessons in Trust
All Lessons Learned
Lessons for Survivors (coming soon)
Lessons for Suspicious Minds (coming soon)

Second Helpings
Sand
Tumble Turn
Awfully Glad
Promises Made Under Fire
The Shade on a Fine Day
Music in the Midst of Desolation
All That Jazz
Dreams of a Hero
The Angel in the Window
Wolves of the West
What You Will
Horns and Haloes

About the Author

As Charlie Cochrane couldn't be trusted to do any of her jobs of choice—like managing a rugby team—she writes. Her favourite genre is gay fiction, predominantly historical romances/mysteries.

Charlie's Cambridge Fellows series, set in Edwardian England, was instrumental in her being named Author of the Year 2009 by the review site Speak Its Name. She's a member of the Romantic Novelists' Association, Mystery People, and International Thriller Writers, with titles published by Carina, Samhain, Bold Strokes Books, MLR, and Riptide.

To sign up for her newsletter, email her at:
cochrane.charlie2@googlemail.com

Or catch her at:
Facebook: facebook.com/charlie.cochrane.18
Twitter: twitter.com/charliecochrane
Goodreads: tinyurl.com/GoodreadsCC
Blog: charliecochrane.livejournal.com
Website: www.charliecochrane.co.uk

Enjoy this book?
Find more mysteries at
RiptidePublishing.com!

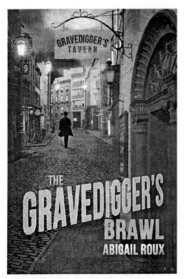 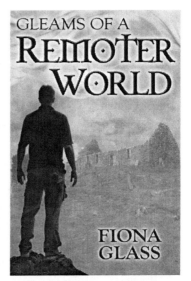

The Gravedigger's Brawl
ISBN: 978-1-937551-53-7

Gleams of a Remoter World
ISBN: 978-1-937551-76-6

Earn Bonus Bucks!
Earn 1 Bonus Buck for each dollar you spend. Find out how at RiptidePublishing.com/news/bonus-bucks.

Win Free Ebooks for a Year!
Pre-order coming soon titles directly through our site and you'll receive one entry into a drawing to win free books for a year! Get the details at RiptidePublishing.com/contests.

CPSIA information can be obtained at www.ICGtesting.com
Printed in the USA
LVOW12s2303130115

422741LV00005B/334/P